The Wallpaper Chase
A Doxie Detective Adventure

LUCIE WILLIAMS

To Glyka: the best, the most wonderful doxie there ever was.

You will be forever in our hearts.

CHAPTER I

After the third break-in I decided I needed a dog or an alarm system. Or both. Since the alarm system was just a question of walking down to the hardware store on Lexington Avenue, I decided to begin with that. But there was one unpleasant task to be completed before this: I had to call Denise Kübler, the Swiss artist, to inform her that her artworks had been stolen. Edouard, her long suffering husband, answered the phone on the third ring. It surprised me, since Denise usually grabbed the phone before him. He recognized me immediately and exclaimed: "Alexandra! Oh my dear, I haven't been able to call you to tell you the news yet, I'm so sorry. Denise is dead."

I was so shocked that I was silent for a full minute. I couldn't believe, Denise, the frail, cotton-candy haired artist, whom I had nicknamed Attila, was dead. There was a small cough at the other end of the line and Edouard added: "She was killed during a break-in at our house, two weeks ago. I'm sorry to have to announce it to you so…brutally…Alexandra."

Still in shock, I said a few words of condolence and promised to call him again very soon.

***

I walked distractedly out of the gallery and locked the door. While I strolled down Lexington Avenue, I thought about Denise. A mutual friend had shown me her work and I had liked it and offered to organize an exhibition at the gallery. I still liked the work, but in the few months

I'd known Denise, I'd come to think of her as "Attila". What had looked at first like a sweet-faced, frail old lady, with cotton candy hair and tortoise-rimmed spectacles, was, in fact, a terror. When we organized her show, she had managed to antagonize everyone: the photographer, the framer, the poster designer, the printer...She had made everybody so furious, it was a miracle we had managed to organize the exhibition. The printer's wife had definitely been heard to mutter dark threats. So I could very well imagine Denise confronting a burglar and making him so angry that he bashed in her head. Still, it was sad news, and I wondered how Edouard would cope. He was a charming man and a brilliant scholar, but he was in the first stages of Parkinson's disease and Denise, albeit roughly and without much consideration for his feelings, had been taking care of him. Still, I seemed to remember they had two adult children, who would hopefully deal with the problem.

I tried to dismiss Denise's tragic death from my mind and to concentrate on more mundane things, such as the alarm system, which was sorely needed. I still found it difficult to understand why anyone would want to burglarize my small art gallery, and what's more, two days in a row. Most of the artworks I sell at "Tate" have price tags below the thousand dollar mark. But then, New York is New York, and they'll steal anything that's not nailed down...

The hardware store was pretty full when I arrived. I managed to get one of the salesmen to advise me on what to buy and went to the cash register. I was waiting to pay for my purchase, when there was a small scuffle in front of me. There had been two people before me; a man who had finished paying and was getting his stuff bagged, and a young man who'd been waiting patiently in line and politely stepped back to let the man go by in the cramped space. Suddenly a woman came up from behind us, pushed ahead of the young man, slapped her purchases down on the counter and took out her wallet. The young man was so surprised his jaw dropped. He then took a step forward and told the woman, in a conciliatory tone: "Excuse me, madam, but I was before you?" She took one quick look at him, and said scathingly: "There was no one here, so why don't you wait like everyone else and leave a pregnant woman alone!"

Now, I have –like most people, I guess- a few pet peeves. Injustice is the major one, which very often gets me in trouble. Pregnant women who think the world owes them something happen to be another one. Especially pregnant women who are as flat as a flounder. The young man was speechless: my blood boiled.

I took two steps forward and taking the rolls of masking tape from the young man's hand, put them on the counter in front of the cashier, saying: "Please ring these up: this young man has waited long enough."

There was a howl of rage beside me, as the woman yelled: "Just who do you think you are? How dare you butt in? No one asked for your opinion, lady! What do you think you're doing, passing in front of a pregnant woman!"

I was getting a bit fed up of her antics, so I turned around to face her and said, in a quiet voice: "First of all, I don't see what your pregnancy has to do with the issue, unless you think either this young man or I are responsible for your state…" She gasped and the cashier and two clients who had been standing nearby giggled, "Secondly, unless you plaster a sign on your forehead no-one can guess you're pregnant, thirdly your state is no excuse for rudeness and bad education, and fourthly, this young man was first, I was after him, so you will get your turn after me."

I turned my back on her, as she sputtered and threatened and hurled a string of insults at me, which I studiously ignored. The young man had paid and was leaving and I put my alarm system on the counter. There was a movement next to me as the woman tried to push her purchases in front. The cashier took one look at me and rang up my alarm box, grabbed the cash and hurriedly finished bagging my box.

I left the shop mumbling to myself: why did I always get myself into unpleasant situations?

On my way back to the gallery, carrying my purchase in a bag, I saw a patrol car parked in front of the building. My heart missed a beat: had there been another break-in at the gallery? In broad daylight?

I checked the gallery door, which was mercifully intact. Still, they probably wanted to talk to me, so, seeing the two policemen going into the lobby of the building, I followed them. They went up the stairs leading to the second floor: obviously they had the address wrong. I went after them calling out: "Excuse me, sir?"

The police officer closest to me turned around: "Yes?" I walked up a few more steps until I was on the landing. I had dragged my (pleasantly) plump frame down to the hardware store and back through a warm June afternoon. Going up one floor had taken the last of my breath and I gasped: "Are you looking for me?" He asked politely:

"And you are?"

"I'm Alexandra Tate: I own "Tate", the gallery downstairs. Aren't you here about yesterday's break-in?"

The police officer shook his head: "No, miss, I'm sorry: we're here about today's break-in." He indicated one of the two doors on the landing, which stood open, its lock obviously broken.

There was some furious barking inside the apartment. I saw Mrs. Herz, from 2B, in Mrs. Dettwiler's flat, talking to the other officer. I asked anxiously: "Is Mrs. Dettwiler alright?" The cop looked at me compassionately: "I'm afraid not, miss. She was attacked and has a pretty bad concussion: the ambulance just left." I bit my lip: "Oh no, poor lady! Is she going to be ok?" The policeman just shrugged and started to go back inside the apartment.

There was a clatter of heels up the stairs from the lobby and the police officer and I both turned to look at the new arrival. A tall, thin woman with an angry expression on her face appeared. She called the cop: "Are you the officer in charge? I'm Nadine Dettwiler, Sophie Dettwiler's daughter. I came as soon as I could. Where's my mother?"

The officer tried to tell her as gently as possible that her mother had been taken to the hospital. She was slightly taken aback but showed no sign of grief.

The other officer came out of the apartment, followed by Mrs. Herz, who seemed very distressed (certainly more than the daughter, I thought!). She was holding in her arms Mrs. Dettwiler's longhaired dachshund Dulce.

Phew! I need to stop barking, or I'll get a sore throat! Gosh these people are slow! Took me ever so long to get Ma Herz's attention! Oh, hi Alex! What are you doing here? Did you see how high I am?

The little dog let out a small woof when she saw me, and then she was quiet. But as soon as she saw Nadine Dettwiler, she started barking again. It seemed quite obvious to me that the small creature was trying to communicate with her mistress' daughter.

Here's Nadine... Nadine! Nadine! Your mum was attacked! Sorry, I wasn't able to defend her, but I did call for help!"

Nadine just wrinkled her nose and looked at the dog with dismay and annoyance: "Oh no, that dog! What am I going to do with it while my mother's in the hospital?"

We exchanged looks with Mrs. Herz and she clutched Dulce closer to her, in a protective gesture. An idea was taking root into my head as I watched Nadine charging into the apartment to see what had been stolen.

I stayed on the landing with Mrs. Herz, all the while scratching Dulce's chin. The dog knew me quite well, as Mrs. Dettwiler dropped by from time to time at "Tate" and was a good customer: we also met in the building sometimes when I picked up my mail or took out the garbage. Mrs. Herz explained that it was Dulce's nonstop barking that had alerted her that there was something wrong next door. As soon as she had crossed the landing she'd noticed the broken lock. She'd pushed the door open and immediately seen poor Mrs. Dettwiler lying on the floor, a nasty gash across her forehead. Dulce was barking like mad and ran to her, trying to drag her towards her mistress.

After she called 911, Mrs. Herz had tried to dab some water on the old lady's face: Mrs. Dettwiler had been breathing raggedly and was dreadfully pale. The paramedics arrived just before the police.

Nadine came out of the apartment, talking on her cell phone. It looked as though she was calling the hospital. Mrs. Herz went closer to her, still holding the little dog. Nadine hung up and turned to her.

I watched as she talked to the neighbor. Apparently, Dulce's future was being discussed. I overheard Mrs. Herz saying she would come twice a day to walk and feed the little dog. I went over to Mrs. Herz and asked her: "So, what is going to happen to Dulce?" Mrs. Herz shook her head. She was still holding the small creature in her arms. Dulce seemed quite content there: she had settled down happily and obviously enjoyed her high vantage point. It gave her a view she rarely enjoyed and she watched everything around her with great interest. I scratched her behind one furry ear: while Mrs. Herz went on talking, I was thinking furiously.

I wanted to get a dog: not only for my own safety, but also for the company. I had to admit I sometimes felt a bit lonely in the evenings in my apartment. Maybe even lonelier because I was in a large building and there were so many unknown people around. When I saw my neighbors taking out their impeccably groomed dogs for a walk and saw the complicity they seemed to share, I sometimes felt a small twinge of jealousy.

My building accepted dogs, with, of course, some strict rules. I thought that I could take Dulce "on trial", while Mrs. Dettwiler was away. When the hospital released her, I could return the little dog and, if everything had worked out well, I could get one for myself. I voiced the idea to Mrs. Herz who smiled and said: "I'm not so sure, Alex: on the one hand, it would be great for Dulce to be in a nice home while Mrs. Dettwiler is in hospital. But what if you discover that you don't really want a dog? That you don't have the time or patience to look after her?"

I shrugged: "Then it's back to plan A. She goes back to Mrs. Dettwiler's apartment and we take turns walking and feeding her." Mrs. Herz shook her head: "There is another problem: you have never had a dog, so you don't know what it's like. But you might become so attached to this little bundle of love, that you could find it heartbreaking to return her to her owner!" Dulce was following the conversation, looking from one to the other. It seemed she had understood the last sentence, as she gave Mrs. Herz's face a very small and discreet lick.

See how lovable I am!

I laughed: "She really is wonderful. But I'm sure even when Mrs. Dettwiler comes back I'll see plenty of her. I mean, this is where I spend most of my day and I see them all the time. Besides, Mrs. Dettwiler might need help taking care of Dulce when she comes back: she'll probably need some time to recover completely.

Neither of us said aloud what worried us: that Mrs. Dettwiler might never recover, and never come back. Mrs. Herz thought about my proposal, obviously reluctant to let go of Dulce. In the end she said: "I would take her home if I could. But with Teresa and Paco it's impossible." I nodded: Teresa and Paco were Mrs. Herz's Persian cats. Two large and ferocious beasts, that had the great advantage of keeping the building's rodent population in check. But they would certainly not take kindly to the arrival of a small canine visitor. And Dulce weighed less than any of them: they would make mincemeat of her in no time. Mrs. Herz seemed to come to a decision: "Let's ask Nadine."

She went over to Nadine Dettwiler, who was giving her contact details to the detective, and asked her if she agreed to let me take Dulce while her mother was in the hospital. Nadine shrugged, without even looking at us and said she didn't care. She said we might as well take the dog's stuff, which would mean less things getting in her way. I went into the living room to get Dulce's bed. I had a pretty strong feeling though, that the dog usually slept on her mistress' bed. I went into the kitchen and took a look around. In the end, I decided I would buy Dulce some new things, so that she would find everything in place when she came back. Plus, it would annoy the unpleasant Nadine. I noted on my iPhone the brands of food Dulce ate, took a small quantity of dry food in a plastic bag, and then came out to get her from Mrs. Herz.

Mrs. Herz had put her down on the floor, and Dulce sat expectantly, waiting to see what would happen next. Although she wasn't with her mistress, she was surrounded by people she knew and liked, so she wasn't too worried. I put her on her leash and prepared to go downstairs. Mrs.

Herz bent down, and taking the little dog's face in her hands said: "Dulce, you'll be OK and so will your mistress!" She kissed her and watched as we walked down the stairs, the little dog bounding after me, turning one last time to look at Mrs. Herz.

"Bye Ma Herz! Thanks for everything!"

As I went downstairs I looked at my watch: I was quite late. "Tate" was supposed to open at two thirty and it was almost three. I arranged Dulce's bed in the back of the shop, found two bowls in which I put water and some dry food. Dulce came to inspect the offerings and then went on a tour of the premises.

"Hm. Got my bed, kibble and water: now I have to take a look around the place, find out where the enemy might come from, since I suppose I've got to watch this place, now."

Meanwhile, I unlocked the front door. I was dismayed to see there was a customer stamping her feet in front of the door, looking quite impatient. I opened to let the woman in, excusing myself for being late. The woman was dismissive and stepped in. Dulce, who took her duties seriously, ran up to her, barking.

"Hey, you! What do you want? This is Alex' house, you can't just barge in like this!"

My heart sank: this wouldn't work. If she started barking at every customer, there soon wouldn't be any left. I tried to restrain the small dog, telling her to shut up and was surprised when the woman's sour expression changed to a big smile when she saw Dulce.

She exclaimed: "What a lovely baby! She's beautiful! How old is she?" She bent down to tickle Dulce under the chin. Dulce, who considered she had done her duty as a watchdog, was now on her back, enjoying a tummy rub from the lady.

"I'm sorry that I barked at you, lady, but you know, I was just doing my job. Can you please scratch just a bit higher, under my pawpit?"

I answered: "She's eight months old: I'm taking care of her for her mistress, who was attacked this morning." I added, apologetically: "That's why I was a bit late opening this afternoon". The customer smiled: "That's quite alright, I understand." I let out a small sigh of relief, as the woman started looking through some costume jewelry.

My gallery is located on the Upper East Side of Manhattan, on Lexington Avenue. It reflects the personality of its owner, never giving in to fashions or trends, exhibiting only artists whose work I personally enjoy. It also carries a lot of art related articles, costume and real jewelry, books, small objects like mugs or T-shirts. It's neat, airy, uncluttered and pleasant. My friends keep on telling me to give the gallery a more defined identity, to stick to a style. I'm sure they are right and that it might work better if I was selling only one art movement. But I make enough money to live comfortably with what the gallery sells and I enjoy the variety.

Looking around me and thinking of my friends' advice, I sighed. They were right, like they were right in telling me I should lose some weight and do some exercise. I furtively looked at myself in the mirror. The only word that describes me accurately is "plump". No one would call me fat: I'm just...pleasantly plump. Which, I thought, explained the emptiness of my love life. Dulce came and gave me a small push with her nose, demanding my attention. I smiled: I didn't feel so lonely anymore.

I took care of my customer, who in the end bought two pairs of earrings. I was sure it was Dulce's presence that had swayed the woman to buy. She had walked in with the air of someone who is "just looking". After five years as a retailer, I knew exactly who was a potential buyer and who was just a "looker". Dulce had apparently changed that. I bent down and patted the little dog. I said: "We'll go and get you some food and toys at lunchtime" Dulce wagged her tail and gave a muffled bark.

"Sounds like a great plan, Alex! I like it!"

The morning went on as usual: a few customers came in and I made some sales. I noticed that Dulce always raised her head and barked when someone came in. As soon as I greeted the person, Dulce stopped barking and wagged her tail. But she remained alert, keenly watching the intruders and ready to jump at them at the slightest sign that they might be a danger to me. It wasn't a perfect situation and I wondered how to train the dog to react in a more friendly way with my customers.

CHAPTER II

At lunchtime I closed the gallery and went down to a pet shop to buy Dulce some equipment and food. I felt like a young mother buying stuff for her newborn! I listened carefully to the saleswoman's advice about what brand of food to give the dog, and ended up with two huge bags of dry food. Dulce also got a bagful of toys and a brand new leash, as the one she had been wearing was frayed and chewed. We then went to have lunch on the terrace of a café in the neighborhood. Dulce was brought a bowl of fresh water and I was amused to see how much attention the dachshund attracted.

I finally had time to observe the little dog quietly. When we had gone to the pet shop to buy her stuff, I couldn't help noticing how much handsomer Dulce was compared to the other doxies. She had a beautiful caramel coat, and the tips of her ears and tail were marked in black. She still had traces of her baby's black mask, which would be totally gone within a few weeks. She was very very furry, in fact much more so than any doxie I had ever seen and was extremely vivacious. But her main attraction was her expressive face: she didn't just stare in front of her, like many dogs do, or raise her ears when another dog passed. Her ears were constantly in motion and her sparkling eyes followed everything. She was extremely curious and from time to time commented on something with a small bark.

Looking at her, I reflected there was more intelligence in her small furry face than in many people I knew. Dulce gave a discreet snort, as if to say "Of course". I smiled and went on with my lunch. Dulce watched me attentively, wondering if some food would come her way. But she didn't beg or bark: she just sat, quite dignified. I had been admonished by the woman at the pet shop never to give her anything at the table and I intended to follow her advice. I sat back, enjoying the June sunshine and smiling as person after person exclaimed on Dulce's beauty and stopped to pat or talk to her. As I finished my delicious lemon pie, I thought I would drop by a bookstore to find some literature on the care of dogs, and dachshunds in particular.

By the time I returned to "Tate", I was panting: I was carrying an impressive number of bags, containing various dog paraphernalia, dog food, dog clothes, dog beds and dog books. Dulce was straining at her leash and tried to go to the building's door instead of the shop. I felt sorry for her: Dulce wanted to see her mistress. I had to pull her to come into the shop and I noticed that the little dog was a little less perky than usual.

"Hey, Alex! Thanks for the walk and everything, but I've got to go home, now! Mrs. D. must be waiting for me..."

I spent the afternoon taking care of customers and reading about dachshunds. I discovered I had taken on the king of dogs, one of the smartest breeds and among the most difficult to train. I also found out with dismay that, as a rule, you were trained by a doxie, rather than the opposite. As I looked at the small fur ball rolled up in her bed, I wondered how such a small creature could take the upper paw. I suspected that I would soon find out: under that adorable exterior lurked an iron personality, which would get its way, no matter what.

At closing time I started gathering Dulce's things to go home. Again, as we walked out, the little dog looked longingly towards the building door. I sighed and we walked off to Second Avenue, where I live in a high-rise building on the corner of 79th street. After she had looked back once or twice at her building, Dulce seemed to shrug it off and trotted happily next to me.

"We're not going home yet? Oh well...I guess I have to be patient. This is a new adventure..."

We were greeted with enthusiasm by the building's doormen, who welcomed the new resident. As we rode the elevator, Dulce was admired and patted by some neighbors. I reflected that I had never talked with so many people in my building. Dulce was a mixer. I had been carrying her, as the building's strict rules demanded. I let her down once we arrived on my floor. As soon as she hit the ground, Dulce ran off, sprinting to the end of the corridor at full speed. When she reached the end, she ran back, ears flying, passing me and running to the other end. I watched her, amused: my apartment was in the middle of the building, just in front of the elevator bank and the little dog was running through the full length of the corridor. After a while she stopped in front of me, sticking her small pink tongue out and with an expression meaning: "OK, let's go in now!"

"That was nice! It's almost as pleasant as running on the grass! Let's go in, now!"

I opened the door and Dulce ran into the apartment, slipping on the wooden floor. She ran to the bedroom and came running out again, exploring her new territory. I installed her bed according to the instructions I had read in the various books I had bought: against a wall, protecting her back and at a vantage point where she could watch everything. I wondered if the dog would understand that this was her bed and was relieved when, as soon as I had set it down, Dulce rushed to lie down in it.

Once Dulce was comfortably settled into her new home, I started making my own dinner. Later, as I sat eating spaghetti in front of the TV,

I watched Dulce in her small bed. She was snoring softly: I thought what a homey picture it made and how nice it felt to share my apartment with a living and loving creature. I took my bath and went to bed, wondering if Dulce would try to jump on it. Which, of course, she did. But to no avail. The floor was highly polished wood and quite slippery and the bed was very high. Dulce tried a few times, and then, being a philosophical dog, padded back to her own bed and stayed there for the night.

"I'd rather sleep with you, Alex, but the floor's too slippery. Never mind, my new bed looks quite comfy. Nighty night, now…"

***

The next day I decided to pay a visit to Mrs. Dettwiler. When I closed for lunch, I left Dulce alone in the shop, duly provided with toys and food, and took a taxi across town to Saint-Luke's Hospital, where they had taken Mrs. Dettwiler. The old lady was delighted to see me and even happier to get news of her little darling. I couldn't help noticing, though, that she seemed ill at ease when discussing the dog. In the end, she sighed and said: "Alex, I'm afraid I'm going to have to give her away." I jumped: "What?" Mrs. Dettwiler explained: "Nadine and her husband have been after me for months to move in with them. They have a huge house in New Jersey, in a very nice place called Saddle River. I love New York City and I never even considered moving in with them: but after what happened the other day…" Her voice trailed off. She was rumpling her covers with gnarled fingers and after a while she looked up at me: "Nadine is a bit difficult sometimes, but Ted, her husband, is a real sweetheart. And of course, there are the kids. It would be nice to be able to spend some time with them: they hardly ever come to see me in Manhattan." She sighed: "It would be a wonderful place for my little Dulce: huge lawns, she could run around…but Nadine hates dogs. If I go there, I won't be able to take her."

I saw a tear running down the old lady's face and felt my heart breaking: I'd only spent one day with Dulce and I already felt I couldn't live without her small furry presence. I could imagine how difficult it must be for Mrs. Dettwiler. And then it suddenly dawned on me that I had to take Dulce. There was no way I was letting this little bundle of love go away. I asked Mrs. Dettwiler, diffidently: "If you really want to give her away, would you mind if I took her?" I felt my stomach tightening as I waited for the old lady's answer.

Mrs. Dettwiler looked at me, her expression going from amazement to joy: "Would you? You would take Dulce, Alex? That would be so wonderful! I'd feel so much better if my little baby were with you!" I felt tears rise in my eyes as I said: "I would love to Mrs. Dettwiler! She's such a wonderful little dog…it's just that I'm so sorry for you, having to let her go…" Mrs. Dettwiler leaned forward and took my hand: "Don't worry Alex: you know, Dulce's only been with me for a few months. If it had been my dear Oscar, it would have been harder. No: it would have been impossible. As it is, I think Dulce will be much happier with a young person."

I smiled, at being called a young person: I'm in my early thirties, after all. And I kept on smiling as I recalled Oscar. Oscar had been Mrs. Dettwiler's previous dog, a large and hairy dachshund, who was as placid as Dulce was a bundle of energy. He had died some time ago at the respectable age of 18: I knew that in my mind I would always associate Mrs. Dettwiler with Oscar, rather than with the vivacious Dulce.

Things were going a bit too fast for me. I hadn't been ready to make that sort of commitment: after all, I'd intended to take Dulce on a trial basis. On the other hand, I couldn't bear parting with Dulce now that the little dog was in my life. I squeezed Mrs. Dettwiler's hand: "Then don't worry: I'll treat her like a princess!"

Mrs. Dettwiler laughed softly: "Oh I have no doubt about that! She'll twist you round her little paws!" I sat with her a bit longer, and we talked about the break-in. I asked if there had been any news from the police, but Mrs. Dettwiler told me that apart from a young detective who had come around to interrogate her, she had no news. She sighed: "I very much fear that since nothing of much value was taken and I'm almost recovered, they won't spend too much time and resources investigating this." After a while I looked at the time: "Better get going, I've got a shop and a small dog to get back to! " I bent down to kiss Mrs. Dettwiler: "I'll be back in two days."

Dulce was overjoyed to see me and gave me such a welcome, I felt guilty for having left her for almost two hours. I submitted myself to some doggy kissing and hugged the little creature. I thought I saw an interrogation in the dog's eyes, but didn't understand it.

"Alex, I'm really happy to see you, but I thought Mrs. D. would be with you. When are we going home?"

After closing the shop in the afternoon, I went to see Mrs. Herz to ask her for Mrs. Dettwiler's keys. I explained to Mrs. Herz that I was going to keep Dulce. Mrs. Herz burst out laughing when I told her about my visit to the hospital and its outcome. She looked at Dulce, who I held on a leash and who had her head turned in her old home's direction: "I told you you might fall in love with this little dog!" She gave me the keys and said:

"What do you need from the apartment?"

"Dulce's papers: I need them for her shots, etc. And I want to transfer her ownership: if she ever gets lost, her chip needs to have the right address and name on it." Mrs. Herz agreed: "You're right".

I opened the door to 2A and looked for Dulce's papers. I was going to ask Mrs. Herz if she knew what had been stolen, when it hit me: all the paintings I'd sold to Mrs. Dettwiler lately were gone. There had been two Australian aboriginal art dot paintings, and two collages by Denise Kübler. It struck me as very strange, especially since the small silver objects scattered through the apartment were still there.

I was more worried about Dulce than about the burglary. The little dog was extremely disturbed to be in the apartment without her mistress and when we came back home in the evening, she seemed sad. I played with her, gave her some belly and back scrubs: Dulce played along, but without her usual enthusiasm. I was a bit worried and tried to find something in my dachshund books. I realized Dulce missed her mistress but didn't know how I could help. I sighed and looked at Dulce, who looked back with melancholy eyes from her little bed.

"Alex, when am I going home? Why wasn't Mrs. D. there? I miss her."

I tried to brush the dog's hair and noticed that her tail was very tangled: she needed to be groomed. There was a dog groomer around the corner and I gave them a call to schedule an appointment. I was lucky and managed to get one for the next morning.

While I drifted off to sleep, I couldn't help thinking that the three break-ins in New York and the one in Switzerland had one thing in common: Denise's paintings. But what was there about them that attracted thieves?

CHAPTER III

At nine thirty the next morning, Dulce was brought to the groomer's. She wasn't overjoyed to see where she was going. There were already a few other dogs there and they didn't seem very happy. They were in various stages of washing, drying or grooming. None of them paid attention to the arrival of a new co-sufferer.

"What's this place and why are there so many other dogs? They don't look very happy, Alex! Are you going to leave me here?"

I had a few misgivings, until I met the young woman who took Dulce from my hands. The little dog relaxed immediately in her hands and even made a small attempt to lick her face. I left her and arranged to pick her up at lunchtime.

When I came back to get her, Dulce was a transformed dog, proudly flaunting her fluffed-up tail and her impeccable and shiny coat.

"Look at me, Alex! I'm the most elegant dog in the neighborhood!"

The woman who had taken care of her told me she was a sweetie. I smiled: "She is, poor little thing: even though she misses her mistress…" The woman, who had introduced herself as Jean, asked me what had happened. I explained and said I felt the dog was sad. Jean asked me: "Have you explained the situation to her?" I frowned: "No, I guess not." Jean put Dulce in my arms and said: "Take a little bit of time to explain to her what happened to her old mistress and that she'll be staying with you now. She'll understand everything. You'll see."

During the walk back to the shop, I thought about Jean's words. I wondered if Dulce would really understand everything I told her, but after all, I had nothing to lose. Back at the shop, I was kept busy all afternoon and had to postpone my heart to heart talk with Dulce until we returned home, later in the evening.

After we had each had our dinner, I sat Dulce next to me on the couch. I told the dog:

"Dulce, as you know, your mom was attacked. She is in the hospital now. She is getting better, but she doesn't feel she could come back to live at her apartment. She is going to go and live with her daughter, you know, the sourpuss who came that day?" I could have sworn Dulce nodded. I went on: "She can't take you there, as her daughter hates dogs. So she asked me if I could take you in, for good. And I said yes. So from now on, Dulce, we're going to live together. And I promise we'll try to see Mrs. Dettwiler from time to time. Do you understand?"

There wasn't the slightest doubt in my mind that the little dog had understood. It was plainly obvious. Once I had finished my little speech, Dulce came over and snuggled on my lap. I felt tears rising in my eyes: Dulce was mine now.

"I understand, Alex. Poor Mrs.D. So you and I belong to each other, now, right?"

Or was it the other way around?

***

I had a lot of paperwork to take care of because of the break-ins. Some of the paintings that had been stolen were at the shop on consignment: I had to call the artists to tell them their works were gone. But most of the artworks that had been stolen had been Denise's, as it had been her exhibition. The rest where in the smaller room where I kept the permanent collection.

Thinking about Denise reminded me I needed to call Edouard to find out how he was doing. He answered quite quickly. And his voice sounded firm and not too distressed. He thanked me for asking about him and then we got talking about the burglary. I told him I hoped that at least there hadn't been too much damage in the house for him to take care of, but he answered:

"Oh, but it wasn't in the house. The break-in was in Denise's workshop, in the old hothouse next door. She was a bit of an insomniac and she had a very keen hearing. She got up to investigate and apparently disturbed the thief while he was ransacking her workshop. He or they knocked her out with a blunt instrument and left her lying there, unconscious. I was sedated for the night and it's the cleaning lady who discovered her in the morning. Too late, unfortunately: she had been dead a few hours."

There was something very wrong: and that something had to do with Denise's paintings. My brain was putting together facts, almost unconsciously and these facts kept on adding up to the same conclusion. I said a few more words to Edouard and promised to call him again shortly.

I leaned back in my chair and patted Dulce, who was sitting on my lap. Then I went through the events that had happened lately, in chronological order.

First there had been the burglary and the murder of Denise, in Switzerland. Then, a few days later, there had been the first break-in at the gallery. All the paintings by Denise had been stolen, as well as quite a few others, all of them non-figurative. Then, the next day, the gallery was broken into, again. This time, they had stolen another couple of paintings and some papers. Amongst which, my big black sales book. And the next day, it was Mrs. Dettwiler's apartment that was broken into. And by a strange coincidence, the two works by Denise were stolen.

It was now obvious to me that someone was trying to get hold of her works: but why go through all this hassle? Why not simply buy them? It wasn't as if they were that expensive…I chewed my lower lip and wondered: was I letting my imagination run away with me? Still, it was extremely strange. As I tickled Dulce's soft ears, I had an idea. I had sold four of Denise's works. Two to Mrs. Dettwiler and the other two to other customers. I didn't know either of them, and one of them had paid in cash. But the other one had paid with a credit card. I remembered more or less when it had been sold and could find his name from the credit card receipts. All these details would have been in my black book which had been stolen, of course.

I put Dulce on the floor and went to look through my papers. It didn't take me long to find the receipt. I had hoped that the name wouldn't be too ordinary and was happy to see that it was a very long, Polish sounding name. I decided to try the name on Facebook, to see if I could find the person and if I recognized him. It took me two clicks to find the painting's buyer and I recognized him immediately. I then looked him up in the white pages: he lived in White Plains and there was also a business number listed for him. I looked at the time: it was almost lunchtime, but he'd probably be at work. I tried the second number.

He answered on the first ring. I had cooked up an excuse for calling him: I introduced myself and told him I was organizing a new exhibition of works by Denise Kübler, and since he had purchased one, would he like to receive an invitation to the opening? There was a silence on the other end of the line.

The man answered: "Strangely enough, I don't have that picture anymore. We had a burglary two days ago, and this picture is one of the few things that were stolen" I exclaimed, empathized and hung up.

I said to Dulce: "What do you think, Dulce? This is too much to be a series of coincidences, isn't it?" The little dog looked back at me and barked. I took this as an agreement. Reflecting about the situation, I realized that there was only one thing I could do: I had to go to the police with my suspicions. It would probably be better to call them early in the morning: the next day would be soon enough. But, as it were, my suspicions were confirmed in a violent fashion the same evening.

***

At eight o'clock, like every evening, I closed the front door of the gallery. I took the garbage bag in one hand and Dulce's leash in the other and went out through the door that opened into the lobby of the building. I lugged the garbage through the back door of the building, to put it in the dumpster in the alley.

I opened the door and Dulce suddenly started growling and the hair on her back rose. I bent down to see what was wrong with her, thinking she might have seen a cat.

"Alex! Be careful! I smell a stranger!"

Then I felt someone grab me from behind: the garbage bag fell from my hands and Dulce was now barking like crazy. I felt the cold steel of a knife against my throat. The person who was holding me tried to kick her, but the little dog was much too nimble. I had let go of her leash in the struggle and she was running around us, barking and trying to get a bite off my aggressor's leg.

"Leave her alone! Let her go! Damn it, I'll manage to get a bite out of you! Help, someone help! I'll get you, wait until I dig my teeth into you!""

He kept kicking around to keep her away and asked me in a harsh voice: "Where are the rest of Denise Kübler's paintings?" I tried to turn around to see his face, but he grabbed my jaw to keep my face turned away. I saw no reason to lie, so I answered: "I don't know what you're talking about! You stole all of them except for one which I sold to a client! I have no idea who he was! You should know that, you have my sales book!"

He growled very close to my ear: "We'll be back until we find them! And don't even think of going to the police: you wouldn't live one day afterwards!"

He pushed me violently sideway and I fell down: in one second he was gone, back into the building's lobby and out in the street. I only had time to catch sight of a hooded figure in jeans. Dulce, next to me on the floor, was going wild with barking: I had just managed to catch her leash before she shot off after the man.

"Let go of me, Alex! I'll catch him!"

Still sitting on the -not very clean- ground, I gathered her in my arms and calmed her down. I told her she'd been very courageous and had saved my life.

After a while she calmed down and stopped trembling with anger. It was a good thing that I was concentrating on her, since I didn't have time to think about my own fright. She was frantically licking my face.

"I'm so sorry, Alex! I wasn't able to defend you! But you're alright, aren't you?"

I stood up and dusted myself, checked we both were intact and went out to go home.

Back at my apartment I thought about my options.

Going to the police was out: I believed what the guy had said. I didn't think these people would hesitate one second in killing me.

But I had a feeling that it wouldn't end there: he had said that they would be back until they found the painting. I knew that there was one of them which I couldn't find. If, despite the fact that they already knew that from my sales book, they decided not to believe me…if they thought I knew where it was, or that I had other paintings hidden somewhere…it would never end.

I had watched every person I met on my way back from the boutique, wondering if it was one of "them". I couldn't live like that. I had to find out what it was all about and put an end to it. And most of all, I couldn't let Denise's murder go unpunished. Perhaps because I hadn't liked her very much and it somehow gave me a feeling of guilt, I knew I had to see this wrong righted.

One thing was obvious: it all began with Denise Kübler's paintings. In Switzerland. It had been some time since I had gone to Switzerland, where I still had some family and friends. I looked at Dulce: how easy was it to travel with a small dog? I had no idea.

I spent the afternoon wondering what to do. I felt compelled to see justice done for Denise. Besides, I certainly didn't feel like staying in New York, like a sitting duck: the incident in the alley had shaken me more than I cared to admit. It would be the beginning of July next week: I could close the gallery without risking losing too many sales. Or I could get one of the two girls who occasionally replaced me to come in.

I started searching for the best fare and discovered that if I left before the next Thursday, I could get quite good prices. Next, I found out what traveling with my new furry friend entailed: vaccines, travel bag, passport. There seemed to be no major problem, except that Dulce's ticket was going to cost almost as much as mine! I sighed and confirmed my bookings.

Lucie Williams

CHAPTER IV

Before leaving for Geneva, I went once again to see Mrs. Dettwiler in hospital. I was glad to see the old lady was almost fully recovered and looking forward to move in with her grandchildren. Although she asked for news of Dulce, I could see that the little dog wasn't her first priority anymore, and I was glad. In the evening, as I let Dulce take her run in the corridor in front of the apartment -which had become a daily ritual- I felt incredibly lucky to have this little being in my life.

I had organized to leave on Wednesday: on Monday, I called Edouard Kübler, telling him I was coming over to Europe and would he mind if I came to visit him. He sounded delighted to see me and we arranged to meet as soon as I could make it to Gruyères, where he had lived with his wife. I had decided to close the shop for two weeks, finding it would give me less to worry about. As I locked my door and hoisted Dulce's travel bag on my shoulder, I wondered what I was getting myself into. From all points of view. I shrugged and stepped into the elevator, tightly holding Dulce's leash. I thought: "Alea jacta est!" and pushed the button for the lobby.

***

The airplane trip with Dulce went better than I had feared. It was a night flight: once the lights were dimmed, I managed to sneak Dulce out of her bag and put her on my lap, hidden by the airline's blanket. It was great to feel the dog's warmth and her regular breathing. Dulce had fallen blissfully asleep and I was also able to sleep for a few hours.

The little dog was very happy to get out of the airport and stretch her short legs. She sniffed happily everything around her, discovering a new country and new smells.

"Alex, where are we? It smells different here?"

We took a bus to go downtown, as we were going to stay with one of my old friends, who had an apartment in a residential area of Geneva.

Dulce was as much a hit in Switzerland as she had been in New York. Her strong personality made an impression on everyone and she immediately made herself at home in Felicia's apartment. Felicia and I had known each other for twenty years. When she'd gone back to live in Switzerland, we'd kept in touch through Skype and we saw each other at least once a year, either in Switzerland or in New York. But we still had a lot to catch up on and we spent a very pleasant day together.

I always enjoyed spending time with her. Felicia was a tall, very handsome woman, with a strong personality and a keen sense of humour, and we both enjoyed exchanging news and gossip. I was very much in awe of the way she managed an interesting job, the education of two boys (alone, now that she was divorced), plus an active social life. I had trouble just taking care of myself, so I admired very much the way she handled her life. She asked me about my plans.

"I think I'm going to go to Gruyères for a couple of days and then I'll come back here, if you don't mind?"

Felicia exclaimed that of course, I was welcome to come and go, and stay with her as long as I wanted. She added: "I have to go to Paris next week: why don't you come with me? Or else, if you have things to do here, you can stay at my place alone…whatever you want!"

I was tempted: Paris was always a favorite of mine. I asked Felicia to leave me some time to give her an answer. In the meantime, I would go to Gruyères: looking at Dulce, I was sure the little dog would love this excursion. Plenty of grass and lovely new smells: a total contrast to Manhattan.

I packed a small bag for myself and a bigger one for Dulce and went downtown to rent a car. Switzerland has an excellent train system, but Gruyères is a bit more difficult to reach, and the Kübler's house wasn't anywhere near the station. I rented the smallest and cheapest car I could find and drove off to Gruyères, Dulce sitting on the back seat on her blanket.

It was a one hour and a half drive to Gruyères and I enjoyed being back in the country where I was born. I had lived in Switzerland on and off for a few years and always had a feeling of peace and contentment when I came back. Dulce was a perfect passenger for the first part of the trip, napping on her blanket. Once we got off the highway, though, she wasn't so happy: she particularly resented the twists in the road, which didn't allow her to sleep in peace.

"Are we there, yet? I'm very uncomfortable, you don't know how to drive, Alex!"

Gruyères is one of Switzerland's most picturesque villages. Even to me it looks like a fairy tale village, on a roc promontory, with its fortified walls and its castle. I had booked a room in the village, deciding to take advantage of my visit to Edouard to treat myself to a mini holiday. I left the car in the parking lot, beyond the town's gates and walked up to the hotel, Dulce in tow. The hotel was an unostentatious 3 star establishment, one of the buildings on the main street of the village. I was given a small room under the eaves, with a sloping wooden ceiling. There was an old fashioned but neat little bathroom and a bed with a plump eiderdown. I was thankful for it: I knew that despite the warm temperatures during the day, it could get quite cool in the evenings.

I settled Dulce in her bed, installed her food and water bowls and while the little dog had her meal, sat thinking about my oncoming interview with Edouard. I didn't quite know what to tell him: it would depend of his state of mind I supposed.

Sitting in this cozy hotel room, the whole episode in New York seemed very remote and the product of an overactive imagination. But then I was reminded of Denise's death and felt a twinge of unease. I took out my iPhone and found Edouard's address on Google maps. It would take me about half an hour to get to his house.

At five thirty I walked down the cobbled street to the parking lot, Dulce trotting happily beside me, delighted at all the smells on the street. Gruyères is a rural village and there was the occasional cowpat, whose rich scent intrigued her very much. I wondered if I had been right to take Dulce along.

"Hey Alex, I love it here! Why don't you stop and enjoy all these delicious smells?"

Despite the clear indications on my phone's GPS, I managed to get lost a couple of times before arriving at the Kübler's house. It was a converted farm, on the outskirts of the small town of Bulle. I parked in the driveway and rang the bell: I could hear shuffling footsteps inside. Edouard opened the door and let me in, bending down to pat Dulce, who greeted him with a small "woof". I was relieved: Dulce was accepted. I followed Edouard into the large living room, with its terracotta tiles and its wide fireplace. He went off to the kitchen to ask the cleaning lady to bring us some coffee while I settled down on the large leather couch in front of the fireplace.

While I waited for Edouard, I looked around me: the room was clean and, apart from a stack of papers in one corner, did not show any evidence of Denise's presence. There were just a few pictures of her and her family on the credenza, but apart from that, the room felt "his". There were books everywhere. Edouard's place must be the armchair near the fireplace: next to it there was a side table, on which there was a pile of books.

Edouard came back, followed by the cleaning lady, a jovial Swiss lady in her sixties. She served us coffee and returned to her duties in the kitchen. Edouard sighed: "I'm very lucky to have Mrs. Mueller. I don't know how I could cope without her! Of course, my daughter came and stayed as long as she could, but she had to go back to Paris. Once she left, Mrs. Mueller took over and she's been invaluable help!"

He was a polite host and asked me if I had had a good trip and how long I would be staying in Switzerland. I was watching him and wondering how to phrase my questions. In the end, I decided to be straightforward. Edouard didn't seem overwhelmed by grief -which, having known Denise, did not astonish me. And, above all, he was a man of superior intelligence, as witnessed by his three doctorates and the two University chairs he'd held until recently in London and Paris. I thought he would not be fooled if I told him anything else than the truth.

So I embarked on my narrative, telling him about all the incidents that had happened in New York. Edouard drank his coffee, listening silently. He remained quiet for a while after I had finished and finally said: "I knew there was something wrong about this break-in at her studio. It just didn't seem logical. Denise's work sells well, but no one in his or her right mind would steal dozens of her paintings. And that is precisely what happened." I asked: " Was anything else stolen?" Edouard shrugged: "To tell you the truth, I never checked. I was very shocked by the whole thing and I knew that there was nothing worth stealing in the workshop: so I never thought of looking through it." He rose: "I think we had better go there now, don't you agree?"

I followed him outside of the house, to a small side building. It had initially been a hothouse that Denise had converted into a painter's workshop. The glass panes that had been broken by the burglar had not been replaced. I lifted Dulce so she wouldn't hurt her delicate paws on the broken glass, and released her when we went into the workshop. Dulce sprinted off, stopping from time to time to sniff something unfamiliar. She sneezed a lot: there was dust in the workshop, coming from the piles of cut paper. Apparently all of Denise's work hadn't been stolen. I picked up a framed picture and looked at it thoughtfully.

Denise wasn't a proper painter: she didn't really qualify as an artist, more of a decorative artist. She came from the region known as the "Pays d'En Haut", where there is a long tradition of paper cutting. It is done by the women, during the long winter evenings, and is always black paper on a white background and represents traditional scenes of the region. The most frequent one is the "Poya": once a year the farmers take their cattle up to the mountain pastures. It is a beautiful spectacle, as the men and women dress in their traditional costumes and walk in a long line, which can stretch for miles. They drive before them their cows and heifers, who wear huge bells around their necks and flower ornaments on their heads. It is very spectacular, very quaint and attracts tourists from all over the world. This is the scene which is depicted in most paper cuttings in the region.

But Denise had deviated from the custom and created her own style of paper cutting. She used all kinds of papers both for the background and for the cuttings, and spray-painted or hand painted the paper. It was extremely ornamental work. According to her moods, she looked for her inspiration in the north or in the Orient. If truth were told, her work didn't have much to do anymore with the traditional Swiss paper cutting. In her recent works, the ones that had been stolen, Denise had used a lot of textured wallpaper, which added another three-dimensional aspect to her work

We inspected the workshop: Edouard looked around, trying to see what had been disturbed or stolen. It was difficult to assess, as the whole place was full of papers and materials. The only obvious thing was that the shelf where she'd kept her finished work was now empty. I looked in a corner: "Edouard, what about these pictures? They weren't stolen, why?" Edouard bent down and took three out of the stack. They had been kept upright, next to the shelves. We looked at them and Edouard remarked: "These ones are older: she made them ten years ago: look, here's the date!" I chewed my lower lip and went on looking around me.

Little by little, I was getting a sense of Denise's organization: I could see where she stocked her finished works, the ones she was working on and her materials. There was a half finished picture on the table, which had escaped the thief's attention. It seemed to be an experimental work, a new line: the background was a thin sheet of wood, and the cuttings were in fabric, some kind of silky material. We heard barking from the other side of the workshop and walked over to where Dulce was standing. I exclaimed: "Oh no, Dulce, what have you done?" looking at a pile of scraps of paper that seemed to have been stacked against the wall and was now lying on the floor.

"Alex, come here! Someone must have been hurt here, there is blood and everything is in a mess! I smell enemies…"

Edouard bent down to pat the little dog, saying: "It's not her fault: this is where they found Denise. These papers were spread around her." I looked more carefully and noticed, with a small shudder, a trace of blood on one of the papers. I picked one up and recognized a small piece of the type of textured wallpaper that had been used in the missing works. I gathered the scraps, looking carefully to see if there was anything special about them. But as far as I could see, it was just wallpaper, textured and printed on one side. The other side was cream, with a thin grey pinstripe and the name of the manufacturer printed in the same light grey color at regular intervals. Some of the paper had been auto-adhesive and still had the shiny, plastified paper on it. I stacked all the papers and put them on a table near me.

Edouard walked over to look at them and scratched his chin: "Alexandra, there is something here I think: I'm pretty sure they must have stolen several rolls of this paper. There was tons of it, I remember seeing it a few days before Denise was killed. And you knew her: she never threw anything away. If this paper is missing, it's because it was stolen. She definitely didn't use it in her latest works, she was experimenting with wood and fabrics."

I asked him, as we walked back to the house: "Could Denise have written something on one of those papers? Hidden something?" Edouard shrugged and smiled: "Much as I loved my dear wife, Alexandra, she was something of an egoist and she was totally involved in her art. What you're describing is not at all like her. No, the solution is elsewhere, it's in the paper itself."

We stopped before going into the house to let Dulce take care of her business on the gravel outside. I asked: "Where did this paper come from? Do you know?" Edouard nodded: "She got it from her friend Alice. Alice de Brousse. She was an old school friend of Denise's, who died a couple of months ago." I pricked up my ears: "How did she die?"

Edouard shook his head: "Don't go imagining things: she died of cancer. She had been sick for a long time. Anyway, shortly before her death Denise went to visit her in her house outside of Geneva. I didn't stay, as I had some things to attend to, but when I picked her up to leave, she came out with rolls of wallpaper. Alice knew that Denise used all kinds of paper for her work and she thought she could use these old rolls."

Back into the living room, we sat down and he added: "The de Brousse had one of France's largest wallpaper manufacturing company: in fact, I suppose Alice must still have owned a considerable amount of the company's shares. Her husband's been dead for some years now, and they had no children. Well, anyway, that's not the point. Alice had samples of de Brousse wallpapers dating back to the fifties, when she'd married de Brousse and asked to be sent all the new models. She said to Denise that the paper would probably be thrown away after her death, as the company had its own archives, so why didn't Denise use them in her work?"

Edouard sighed: "You know how stingy Denise was: she would have taken anything as long as it was free. Plus, I have to admit, these wallpapers worked well in her pictures. Anyway, I had to lug all these rolls of paper back home. She used quite a lot of them for your exhibition."

I said pensively: "What could there be in these papers that would make someone desperate to get them?" Edouard raised his eyebrows: "It could be anything...maybe something compromising written on the back of one of the rolls?"

We sat speculating for some time, until I finally said: "I think the solution lies at the de Brousse residence. The best thing would be if I could go there to find out why someone is so anxious to get their hands on them." I added: "Denise probably died as a result of someone wanting to get these wallpaper rolls, or something they contained. I consider it my duty to see that whoever did this is brought to justice."

Edouard smiled: "You are on a mission." I sighed.

"Yes. But don't think too highly of me, Edouard. I'm also terrified of these people and I hope that if I can unravel the mystery behind these papers, I will be able to go on with my life in peace. As will you." He nodded. I then asked him if he could give me an introduction to the household. He said that, of course, he could, and proceeded to give me some background about the family.

"I'm telling you what I know, which is not much: Denise and Alice went to school together in Paris. Alice came from the French bourgeoisie: her parents were from Bordeaux. She was sent to study in the same posh school Denise attended when her parents lived in Paris. They remained in touch throughout the years and saw each other from time to time. They used to meet in Paris, where Alice went on living after she'd married de Brousse: they had a beautiful house there, on one of the boulevards. They also owned a lovely little manor by the lakeside, near Geneva. In the last years they spent more and more time there, and when her husband died, she sold the Paris house and moved in for good at "Clair-Chant".

Edouard scratched his chin: "I think she became involved with some kind of charity in the last couple of years: Denise was very admiring of her involvement in it." He added sheepishly: "I didn't pay much attention, to tell you the truth." I smiled: "I understand. Who inherited the house and Alice's fortune?" Edouard answered: "I think the charitable foundation in question got most of it: the house I'm not so sure, as I seem to recall her nephew moved in after her death." He shrugged: "As you see, I don't know that much. When she died Denise was sent some things

Alice had left her in her will." I asked: "What kind of things?" Edouard got up and signaled me to follow him upstairs.

He took me to Denise's bedroom, explaining that for the last ten years they'd been sleeping in separate rooms. The bed had been made and the room was regularly cleaned, but apart from that nothing had been touched. He went to the chest of drawers and indicated a precious set of silver, ivory inlaid combs, brushes and mirror. There was a matching jewelry box. After asking for Edouard's permission, I gingerly opened the box. It was almost empty, containing only Denise's watch and three rings. I removed the top tray and looked in the lower compartment. There were a couple of brooches and a gold chain, as well as a few assorted buttons. I put back the tray and closed the box. Edouard and I looked at each other: nothing there for anyone to covet.

We went back downstairs and began thinking about how to get me into the Brousse property and ask some questions. I thought of an idea and said: "I could tell them you are writing a small memorial book about Denise's work and her life, and that I am collecting information from the people she knew, the places she went…I can ask them if they still have pictures from the time Alice and Denise were at school together. It will give me an excuse to ask some questions!" Edouard thought it was an excellent idea. He went to get Denise's address book and found the house's number.

I looked at my watch: I had spent much more time than I had thought at the Kübler's house. It was almost seven and I suspected it was past Edouard's dinner time. I took my leave to go back to Gruyères. As Edouard stood on the doorstep, watching me get into the car with little Dulce, he called out: "Alexandra!" I opened the window: "Yes?" Edouard took two steps to come closer: he had a slightly worried expression on his face: "Be careful. I don't know what all this is about. But one thing I'm sure of, is that whoever is behind this, is without scruples. It has already cost Denise her life and they definitely threatened you. I wouldn't want anything to happen to you." I smiled and said: "Don't worry. I'll be careful. Besides, I have a watchdog now!" Dulce, from her backseat, barked as if to emphasize the point. Edouard waved to us as we drove off.

Dulce and I had a quiet evening in Gruyères: we went to my favorite restaurant, the "Chalet de Gruyères". Their specialty is the "Chalet soup", a thick concoction made with vegetables, macaroni, potatoes, cheese and cream. I sighed as I thought about what it would do to my -already- plump figure, but couldn't resist.

I told myself sensibly that I would have only the soup. And maybe a small dessert. Except the soup is served in an "all you can eat" formula and I ended up downing the equivalent of a whole pot. Still, I reasoned, it was only soup: I allowed myself a dessert of meringues with fresh clotted cream, another specialty of Gruyères. In the end I thought Dulce would have to drag me back to the hotel, which, mercifully, was only a few yards away.

"Alex, stop eating: or if you're going to eat, give me something too! There...you've stuffed your face again and you can hardly walk! Pshaw!"

I spent the next morning playing tourist, walking in the fairy tale village with its myriad of tempting shops, and ended up buying much more than I'd intended. Dulce was treated to a beautiful black leather leash and harness, studded with golden metal figures and symbols typical of the region. Every time we walked into a shop, someone would see Dulce and exclaim on her beauty. I was a very proud owner.

I checked out of the hotel later in the morning and started on the drive back to Geneva. On the way down, I stopped for a quick lunch and called Felicia to tell her I'd be arriving in the afternoon. I thought I would try calling Clair-Chant the next day, in the morning. But if I got off the highway one exit before Geneva, I could pass in front of the house and at least get a glimpse of it.

A little before four o'clock, I went through the village of Versoix and then took the old National road, which followed the lakeshore. There were some formidable estates on this road, large properties owned by rich families or embassies. I checked the number on my iPhone and saw I was near Clair-Chant. I slowed down and went by the house's gates. It was on the opposite side of the road, but I saw it would be useless to turn around and get closer. All that was visible from the road was a tall wall covered in ivy, and an elegant wrought iron gate. It was forbidding and I thought it would take me some courage to weasel my way inside the property.

I sighed and drove on, arriving an hour later at Felicia's, tired and frustrated. I had got caught in the traffic, so that the short drive from Clair-Chant to Felicia's, which should have taken me no longer than twenty minutes, had taken more than one hour. I wondered once again how the people in Geneva managed: it had become practically impossible to drive from one place to another in the city. I finally made it, with frazzled nerves, to Felicia's street.

Dulce was showing signs of impatience: she was quiet during the drive, but when she sensed we were stuck in traffic, she looked as though she was ready to lower the window on her side and hurl insults at the other drivers. I wondered how the dog could tell. Another mystery.

In the evening we had a friendly meal with Felicia and some friends. I had brought back all sorts of delicacies from Gruyères. We ended the meal with meringues and clotted cream. I discreetly unbuttoned my jeans: if I went on eating like that, I wouldn't be able to wear even my "fat" clothes! I promised myself to be a little more careful in the future.

Felicia had invited some old friends , and it was a pleasure catching up with them. Amongst them was Francis, whom we had known for donkey's years. He was a lawyer, working in a bank. Francis was the most sociable person I had ever met: he had literally hundreds of friends, all over the world, and spent a large part of his time visiting them. He was also the world's greatest gossip and could be counted on to learn the latest local news. It was always fun talking to him.

CHAPTER V

In the morning, I dialed the Clair-Chant residence's number. A young woman's voice answered, saying: "Clair-Chant". I explained that I wanted to talk to whoever had inherited Alice de Brousse's personal effects: pictures, letters, etc…, as I was gathering material on her friend Denise Kübler's life. The girl said: "Could you hold on for a minute, please? I'll get Mr. Etienne."

I waited, wondering who Mr. Etienne was: probably the nephew. A few seconds later I heard a young male voice on the phone, saying: "Etienne de Brousse?". I rolled out my story once again and waited anxiously. There was a long silence on the other end. Finally he answered: "I don't quite understand what you want from me, but I guess you can come here and explain in detail." I sighed with relief and said: "Thank you so much: when would be a convenient time for you? Could I drop by this afternoon?"

We agreed on a time and I hung up, doing a small victory dance: I was in!

I took a long time selecting the clothes I would wear for the coming interview. I wanted to look professional but not too severe, so that people would confide in me. I was glad I was perfectly bilingual and that I still had a slight Genevese accent when I spoke. I didn't want to confuse the issue with my American residence and nationality or my professional activities. As far as Etienne de Brousse and the household were concerned, I was Alexandra Tate, an idle married woman living in Geneva. I was supposed to have been a friend of Denise Kübler -God forbid!- and to help her bereaved husband gather material for the small monograph this learned gentleman was preparing about his deceased artist wife.

I wondered whether I should take Dulce along: in the beginning I thought it wouldn't be such a good idea, as it would distract me from my purpose. On the other hand, a small dog would be a convincing accessory for the character I was playing. So I took her along, wearing her brand new Gruyères outfit.

This time it took me less time than I had expected to cross town and get to Clair-Chant. I decided to leave the car outside of the property. It had rental car plates and that wouldn't look normal for someone supposed to be living in Geneva.

As I walked on the sidewalk along the property, I noticed that the wall was well taken care of and everything seemed in good repair. There certainly was money there. I arrived at the imposing gate and rang: the wrought iron doors opened silently and I stood facing a long driveway, meandering through the property.

I immediately regretted having left the car outside, and more than anything, I regretted having worn high-heeled sandals! I looked down at my feet: the elegant thin sandals were beginning to make them feel like salami, crisscrossed by painful straps. I sighed and trundled on, glad to see that Dulce, at least, was enjoying the walk.

The little dog trotted by my side, stopping every now and then to inhale a delicious smell, and then running to catch up. It took us a good five minutes to reach the house, by which time I was wondering if my feet would have to be amputated.

"Nice place, Alex! Just give me a little bit of time to sniff everything and mark my territory, OK?"

The house was beautiful, a small turreted manor in bricks and white stone, in the style of the area. It was close to the lakeshore and had a small private jetty, which I could just see beyond the house. The driveway turned into a wide, white graveled courtyard in front of the house. I saw that next to the house there was a garage: the doors were open and there were three cars parked inside. As soon as I got near the house, the entrance door opened. A young woman peered out and waited for me to arrive. She asked: "Madame Tate?".

By now the exercise and the pain in my feet had left me breathless. I waited one or two seconds to recover and answered: "Yes. I'm here to see Mr. Etienne de Brousse." The young woman showed me in.

As we crossed the elegant entrance hall paved in black and white marble squares, I took the opportunity to look around. The house was beautifully furnished with what I knew were authentic antiques. There were small occasional couches dotted here and there, refurbished in gorgeous fabrics. There were some extremely precious objects, signs of excellent taste and ample means. I followed the young woman to the main living room, a large, bright room opening on a paved terrace, which lead to the lake. The view through the large bay windows was magnificent.

The young woman asked me whether I would like to drink something, and looking down at Dulce asked if the dog would like a bowl of water. I said yes to both: better to look comfortable and well installed. It would be more difficult to kick me out.

Etienne de Brousse arrived before the girl's return. I gasped when I saw him. He was a tall, slim and elegant young man, with wavy light brown hair and a very handsome face. He wore a pair of beige pants with a light blue shirt, which matched his eyes. In other works, a hunk.

He walked across the living room in a few long strides and bent down to shake my hand, introducing himself. Then he caught sight of Dulce and lowered himself to her level, exclaiming: "What a beauty! A real princess!" I felt myself blushing at the compliment and then kicked myself: he was referring to the dog, not to me! I said: "I hope you don't mind that I took her along? I haven't had her for a long time and I hate leaving her alone!" He tickled Dulce's ear and answered with a blinding smile: "Of course not! I love dogs and this one is especially beautiful!"

"I like this person: he appreciates my beauty and charm and he knows where to scratch me!

He sat down on the couch next to me, as the young woman returned with a tray laden with iced tea and delicious looking macarons. Etienne smiled at her and said: "Thank you Anny! Would you mind awfully bringing me a cup of coffee?"

I watched the girl: I could tell from her accent that she was Portuguese. She was quite tall and with a very good figure, but had a very homely face. She was dressed in everyday clothes, so it was hard to tell what her exact duties were. Anny went off to get Etienne's coffee and he offered me a macaron, asking: "What can I do for you, Mrs Tate? By the way, I'm very sorry about Denise's death. She was one of my aunt's oldest chums."

I bit into a delicious macaron.

"Yes, it was awful. Poor Edouard is devastated (now how was that for an exaggeration!) He wants to keep Denise's memory alive, for their daughter and son and for their friends, so he is going to publish a short book about her life and her work. Alice de Brousse was her closest friend when they were both schoolgirls in Paris and Edouard thinks she may have kept some pictures of that period." I quickly invented: "You see, Denise lost a lot of her own pictures during one of her parents' moves".

Etienne said: "I see. Well, I really can't help you there: I only moved in after my aunt's death, and, to tell you the truth, I haven't been through her papers yet. I think there are some boxes full of old photographs in her rooms. If you have enough patience, you could look through them. I wouldn't mind. But it's a long and dusty process!"

I repressed a small smile: that was exactly what I wanted. I thought it was time to turn on the charm and get into my listening mode. I'm an excellent listener and most of my friends confide in me. To the extent that it sometimes puts me into difficult situations, where I know too much about everybody. But in this instance, my particular gift was going to prove useful. I leaned forward and said: "It must be difficult for you to move into this house, with so many memories of your aunt. Did you grow up here?"

Everybody loves talking about his or herself. Etienne was no exception. He opened up under my skillful touch and told me his story.

"No, I didn't: I was born and raised in Paris. My mother was Jean de Brousse's younger sister and we used to come here for the summers, sometimes." He added, for clarification: "Alice and Jean didn't have children, which is why after my father's death, fifteen years ago, Jean asked me to change my surname to de Brousse. Otherwise the name would have become extinct."

Anny brought him his coffee: he thanked her, took a sip and went on: "My father was a doctor and wanted me to follow his footsteps: but I was much more interested in the de Brousse business, so my uncle let me work at the company."

I could see he was angry: he put his cup down brusquely. "I can't understand what happened. When oncle Jean died, tante Alice took over the management. I worked my way up through the company, and, two years ago, she handed over the reins to me. The company was doing well, and everyone took it for granted that I would inherit oncle Jean and tante Alice's shares, and that I would stay at the head of de Brousse."

I listened without saying a word, not wishing to break the thread. He ran a nervous hand through his hair and said: "You were a friend of Denise: was she as weird as my aunt? Because honestly, I don't understand why she did what she did!" I looked at him questioningly. He went on:

"Oncle Jean didn't make a will, because everything he owned would go to my aunt. I think he thought that she would simply follow his wishes. But then she fell into the clutches of these people, and look where it got me!"

I had to ask him for details: he was now talking as if I were aware of the whole story. I said: "Which people?"

Etienne shook himself, as if suddenly realizing whom he was talking to. He sighed: "I don't want to bore you with my story…" I shook my head energetically, sending my shoulder length hair flying: "Of course you're not boring me! What happened?"

"It seems Aunt Alice got trapped in a cult. They call themselves a Foundation, but I'm sure they are some kind of cult. They wheedled their way into her life and convinced her to change her will. As a result, the Foundation has inherited all her shares in the de Brousse company and the bare property of this house. There were various bequests to servants and friends and all I got was a small annuity and the usufruct of Clair-Chant. Just enough to live on, if I stay in the house."

He looked up at me, with anger and desperation in his eyes: "You know, it's not so much the question of the money that infuriates me: it's our family's patrimony falling into the hands of these unscrupulous people. Up to know they've contented themselves with replacing me as President of the Board by one of the oldest directors, which I guess is OK. But I don't know how long it's going to last and what they intend to do with the company."

I exclaimed: "But this is so unfair! How could your aunt do this to you?" Etienne shrugged: "I don't know. She had changed and in the last three months of her life she refused to see me. I couldn't understand why, because we always got along very well. I always thought she considered me as the child they didn't have." He added: "It really hurts: it's like a betrayal. And now, I'm idle, wasting my time in this big house, without a job, without a family!"

He stopped and I felt very sorry for him. I patted his hand and Dulce, with her unerring instinct, went closer to him to be patted.

"Oh, poor man! He seems upset: come on, let me give you some doxie comfort!"

He felt her cold nose pushing against his leg and smiled as he ran a hand through her soft fur. There was a short silence as I digested what he had told me. One thing was certain, these Foundation people seemed pretty formidable.

I took a sip of ice tea and restrained from eating another macaron. I didn't want to seem like a glutton: although looking at the devastation on the tray, that cause was already lost. I asked: "Was there nothing you could do to contest the will?" Etienne sneered: "Believe me, I tried everything. But it was watertight. My aunt had full control of her fortune and she could leave it to whomever she saw fit. I'm only her nephew, there was no legal obligation for her to leave me anything." He added: "Hell, the way things are, I should consider myself lucky to have gotten anything at all!"

I was thoughtful: I wondered if there was something in the lost papers that would justify the Foundation trying to get its hands on it. A proof of undue influence on the old lady? A threat? More than ever I was determined to solve this mystery. As I was about to ask Etienne another question, I caught a weird sight from the corner of my eye. I could have sworn I saw a veiled woman, carrying a vacuum cleaner, cross the landing. I must have looked very surprised, as Etienne, following my stare, laughed and said: "Ha! I see you've noticed our burqua team!" I looked at him inquiringly: "What the heck was that?

Etienne shrugged and said:

"Tante Alice's will stated that the Foundation is obliged to keep Anny, whom you have met, on the payroll of Clair-Chant, for as long as she wishes. It also provides a sum for the upkeep of the house, indicating there are to be two gardeners at all times. And finally, there is a proviso that the Foundation must undertake to hire as much personnel as necessary to maintain the house." He indicated the direction where the veiled woman had gone: "And this is how I come to have one or two of these veiled specimens in the house on an almost permanent basis!"

My eyes widened: "But why are they veiled?" Etienne raised his shoulders in another shrug: "Search me! I've tried to find out what this Foundation is all about: it's called the "Fondation pour la liberté de culte". The Foundation in favor of the freedom of religion…my foot! Let me tell you that the women who come here look anything but free, with their weird gear!" He added: "It's a nuisance having them around: I never know when I'm going to bump into one of them, and with those damned veils you can't tell one from the other." He sighed: "I have to say this for them, though: as cleaners, they are pretty thorough. They've been through every room of this house, even the ones that hadn't been used for years."

Etienne looked at his watch and said: "I'm sorry, I've kept you much too long talking about my personal problems. I don't know what impelled me to confide in you, it's really not my style." He ran a hand through his hair, in a gesture I understood was habitual in him. I answered: "Don't worry, I've got all the time in the world. Besides, your story is intriguing." I bit my lip: "intriguing" wasn't the right word to have used. But he didn't react to it and I went on: "If you do agree at my looking through your aunt's photographs…"

He jumped up and said: "Of course! Please do." He thought for a minute and said: "I'll ask Anny to come with you and give you some help. She is not the brightest person, but she does what you tell her"

He grumbled: "And you can see her face, which is more than you can say for some people in this house!" He walked out of the living room to find Anny. As I watched him leave, I caught a flash of a long skirt disappearing around the corner. I shuddered: the presence of these women was decidedly creepy.

Etienne returned with Anny, and explained to her what I was looking for and how she could help me. As I watched Etienne talking to the young woman, I understood what he had said about her not being "bright". In fact, it seemed as if he'd vastly understated the situation. Anny was on the thin line between normal and mentally retarded. She could function in every day life, but it was obvious that the slightest demand on her brain would have catastrophic consequences. Still, she understood what Etienne told her well enough and stood waiting for me to follow her upstairs.

Etienne said to me: "I don't know how long it will take you, but I doubt you can finish this afternoon. So please feel free to come back as often as you need!". I thanked him profusely and followed Anny up to the second floor, where Alice de Brousse's rooms had been.

Turning right when we reached the landing, Anny took me to a door, which opened into a private corridor. We walked to the room at the end. It was a pleasant and bright boudoir with French windows opening onto a balcony and a beautiful view of the lake. There were two rooms on the other side of the corridor, one which appeared to have been Alice de Brousse's bedroom, and another, smaller bedroom.

The boudoir was an oblong room, taking up half of the floor's façade on the lake side. There was a desk and two big chests of drawers on one side: the other side was organized as a small sitting-room, with little couches and a reclining chair in front of a fireplace. The furniture, like downstairs, was precious and antique. The room was very feminine and gracious, decorated in a range of warm pinks and beige.

Anny showed me some boxes which were carefully stacked against the wall on the "office" side. We opened them and discovered photographs and photo albums: there were five other such boxes and I understood what Etienne had meant when he said it would take me some time. Apparently everything had been piled in haphazardly: there didn't seem to be any kind of order.

We dragged one of the boxes to the other side of the room, where I could sit on a couch and sift through the material. We both coughed when I took out the first photo album and Anny offered to get me something to drink. I accepted with pleasure and reflected that Anny might not be very bright, but she had at least been taught to be a good hostess.

When the young woman returned with a tray laden with glasses and cold drinks, I made her sit beside me and take a glass. I began sorting through the albums, ostensibly searching for anything from the twenties and thirties, up to the Second World War.

While I looked and sorted, I talked to Anny. I asked her for how long she'd been working for Mrs. de Brousse. Anny answered: "Oh, I've been here since I was sixteen. My mother worked for Mrs. de Brousse and that's why I came to work here too." She added, sheepishly: "I wasn't very good in school, I failed all my exams: so I was very lucky to get such a nice job here." I asked: "But what is your job here?".

Anny shrugged and said: "I help." I thought that was about as much as I was going to get on that subject. I went on to ask Anny about Mrs. de Brousse: "Was she nice?" Anny shook her head: "She was wonderful, Mrs. Alice. A real lady. Poor thing, such a pity she lost so many people."

CHAPTER VI

I pricked up my ears: "Who did she lose? Her husband?" Anny answered: "Yes, but that was years ago. I mean old Caroline, and then Miss Rivière, and Giuseppe…" She let her phrase trail off. I was intrigued: "What happened to all these people?" Anny handed me another album, which I absently dusted and checked for a date. The young woman answered: "First she lost her husband, Monsieur Jean, of course. Then poor Caroline who was Mrs. Alice's nurse for years. She was run over by a car. And then Miss Rivière, the secretary, drowned here, in the lake, right in front of the property."

She fell silent. I coaxed her a little bit: "What about Giuseppe, who was he? Did he die also?" Anny answered absentmindedly: "Oh, no. He didn't die. Giuseppe was the gardener, he'd been working for Mrs. Alice for at least thirty years. He just went."

I was puzzled: "What do you mean "He just went"? Did Mrs. Alice dismiss him?" Anny shrugged: the question was obviously too much for her. She said: "I don't know. He just left."

It had taken a lot to get her to say that much. I soon discovered that Anny's limited capacities stopped at asking questions or trying to find reasons for things she didn't control. Which was just about everything. If she was asked to speculate on something, she panicked, which translated by a sudden mutism, out of which it was very difficult to coax her.

On the other hand, if she was asked a straightforward question about a fact, she answered quite readily. And there seemed to be nothing wrong with her memory. I asked her about her life and the last years of Alice de

Brousse's life.

***

Anny told me she'd been taken into the household when the de Brousse started coming more often to their Swiss home. She had stayed on even after her mother had returned to Portugal. Anny was a Swiss citizen, she had a well paid job in a nice house, there was no reason for her to go anywhere. Besides, Alice de Brousse liked her very much. She said with a bemused smile: "Mrs. Alice said my presence relaxed her."

I smiled back: I could understand that Mrs. de Brousse would appreciate the young woman's undemanding presence. Having Anny around was like having a pet: I looked down at Dulce, who was peacefully snoring on the marvelous Turkish carpet. I had an inkling that Dulce was much more curious and sharp than Anny. The young woman was now talking about Mr. Jean's death: she said that Mrs. Alice had often told her that in a way, it was a good thing he had died so suddenly and at that time, because he was grinding the company into bankruptcy. I was amazed that the young Portuguese woman would know that much: but then I realized she was just repeating what she had heard from Alice de Brousse, without speculating on it. Anny went on: "After he died Mrs. Alice came to stay here for good. That was when Caroline came to stay with us. The nurse. She was very nice too. She liked my cooking."

I asked: "Why did Mrs. Alice need a nurse?" A slightly bovine look answered me. Once again, Anny was lost. I tried another tack: "Was Mrs. Alice sick?" the young woman looked at me vacantly: "Caroline gave her shots and her medicine" I sighed: this was going to be difficult. I asked: "Anny, when was Mrs. Alice's cancer diagnosed?" I winced when I saw the young woman's vacuous look. Sighing, I tried to ask some questions about the Foundation.

57

It took me another three hours to extract some information from Anny. It was rough going, as the woman answered only to direct, factual questions. I took some notes. We had been working on the albums in the meantime and had gone through the first two boxes. There was nothing in there anterior to the eighties. We hadn't found a single photograph featuring Denise, who, thank heavens, Anny remembered well and could identify. Which justified my keeping her with me.

At some point during our search the door had opened and a veiled woman had walked in, carrying a dust rag. As soon as she saw the room was occupied by Anny and I, she silently oozed out. Anny hadn't paid any attention to her. But it had given me the opportunity to ask her about the Foundation and its people.

At seven I decided to leave: I had quite a lot of information to mull on. I thanked Anny for her help and told her I might be back the next day. There was no sign of Etienne downstairs. I let Dulce take her time on the way out, sniffing and running.

Cursing my high heeled sandals, I walked back to my car. For one step I took, Dulce went back and forth three times. I told her: "Yeah, yeah! I would be running too if I had your comfortably cushioned paws!"

It's not my fault if you wear these ridiculous shoes!

I was very pensive on the drive back to Felicia's. I had managed to get a lot of information from Anny. It all added up to a pattern of violent deaths and I didn't like it. Back at Felicia's, I remembered she had told me she was going out that evening. I was glad, as it allowed me to think about what I had learned.

I decided to write down the order of the events, from the time the Foundation had appeared in Alice's life. I looked at my notes.

After Jean de Brousse's death, Alice had had some health problems.

She had hired Caroline as a live-in nurse. Caroline, according to Anny, was a pleasant woman, very much appreciated by Alice. In fact, I got the impression that Caroline had become more of a friend then just a caretaker to Alice de Brousse. About two years ago, Mrs. de Brousse had gone with a friend to a charity event in favor of the Foundation.

It wasn't quite clear from Anny's explanations how the Foundation had wormed its way into Mrs. de Brousse's life. I gathered that there had been regular visits from various people Anny referred to vaguely as "these people". Caroline had disliked them it seemed. And then one day, Caroline died, run over by a car. Then a new nurse had come in and Mrs. de Brousse had spent less and less time outside of the house. The only people who visited regularly from the outside were the house's personnel, among them Florence Rivière, the secretary, the gardeners, the cleaning company and Anny herself. Plus, later, the veiled women.

Then, there had been that awful accident with Miss Rivière, who drowned in the lake. The next day, Giuseppe had left. Denise Kübler had been one of the only and last visitors Mrs. de Brousse had.

I sighed: whichever way you looked at it, something was wrong in this household. I decided to try to find out some details about the deaths of Caroline and Florence Rivière the next day. I went to bed but had trouble falling asleep: it was only by concentrating on Dulce's soft and regular breathing that I managed to finally drift off to sleep.

CHAPTER VII

The next morning was another warm and sunny July day. I was thankful I could open all the windows and get some fresh air into the apartment. I sat at Felicia's computer and tried to find out details about the two deaths and about Giuseppe the gardener. I found out the date of Caroline's funeral from the local newspapers. Apparently, Caroline had no family left: the only person who had put an announcement in the paper had been Alice de Brousse herself, and she had written a line about "her dear friend" Caroline. From there, I worked back to the article about the nurse's accident.

It had happened not very far from the property, on a side road, where Caroline was on the way to her bus stop. It wasn't very late in the evening, but it was already dark, as the month was December. The short article said it was a hit-and-run accident and that the guilty party had fled the scene. Caroline had apparently been crossing the road. She had been found within minutes by another driver who came along. She was still alive but unconscious when the ambulance came and died on her way to the hospital.

I chewed my lip: there was not even a hint of foul play. According to the police it had just been another accident, where the driver had panicked and left. I ran a hand through my hair and, catching myself, smiled: I was becoming like Etienne. I allowed myself five minutes to daydream about the handsome young man.

After a while I shook myself and went on with my research. Giuseppe di Natale was apparently alive and kicking. At any rate, his name did not appear in the obituary columns after his leaving Clair-Chant. I looked for something about Florence Rivière's accident and there I struck gold.

There were several articles about the accident, as well as photographs and interviews. Miss Rivière's death had made the headlines for a couple of days. I took a pad and wrote down the salient facts.

On the afternoon of April 6th, Miss Rivière had been working at the property, like every day. She had left work at her usual time, six thirty. Apparently no one had noticed the fact that her car was still in the garage during the night. One of the gardeners found her body the next morning, caught between the rocks next to the private jetty. She was fully dressed, wearing the light raincoat she'd had on when she left the house.

The police had first leaned towards the suicide theory. But when they interviewed Miss Rivière's sister, the girl was adamant that her sister could not have committed suicide. When the coroner's report came in, Florence Rivière's death was ruled as an accident. They had found a bump on the side of her head, which could have matched the stones near which she had been found. The police concluded that, for some reason, Florence had taken a walk along the lake, slipped on the moss covered stones and knocked herself unconscious. She had fallen face first in the lake, as they had found her, and drowned.

As I read the articles, I got a feeling that the younger sister had not been satisfied with the verdict. I decided to try to see her. Maybe she could shed some light on the mystery. I looked her up in the white pages and tried to call her at home. An answering machine took the call and I left a message, saying I wanted to talk to Sylvie Rivière about her sister's death.

Dulce was gently pushing me to remind me she wanted to go out for a walk, so I obliged. I was strolling along, admiring my marvelous little doxie running on the small patch of grass in front of the building, when my cell phone rang.

It was a Swiss cell phone number. A young and musical voice asked: "Madame Tate? This is Sylvie Rivière. You called me about my sister…" I was caught short: I hadn't thought the young woman would call me back so quickly and hadn't prepared anything to say. So I just asked: "I would like to discuss some things with you, but it's difficult to explain on the phone. Would you mind meeting me somewhere for coffee?"

Sylvie's reply was immediate: "When do you want to meet and where?" I had noticed that Sylvie Rivière lived not very far from Felicia's apartment, so I suggested we meet at six thirty at a tearoom in the area. Sylvie agreed enthusiastically and without asking more questions. I was intrigued: apparently Sylvie had issues with her sister's death: otherwise she would just be grieving and not too willing to talk about it with strangers.

The next thing I wanted to research was the Foundation. I Googled it up and found their site. It was an unappealing and bland website, which gave the Foundation's aim and purpose, showed a picture of their main offices, which were in Paris, and a few more photographs of their "missions". It looked as though they helped local communities throughout the world build churches, mosques and synagogues, as well as one Buddhist temple in Norway.

Their mission, as they described it, was to "encourage the diversity of religions, beliefs and faiths throughout the world." On the whole, it looked pretty innocuous, one of so many similar associations or foundations.

I went further into the Google pages and another picture began emerging. There had been several complaints about the Foundation, and it even looked as though they had been sued by families a couple of times, regarding inheritance problems. They had been accused of using undue influence to persuade members of the Foundation to make wills in their favor. Just like Alice de Brousse. But from what I could see, they were smart enough never to have been convicted.

I thought it tallied with what I'd seen at Clair-Chant. I tried to find out where they were located in Geneva: but there was only a phone number and no address. I wrote the phone number down and decided to try it later.

I still had no information about Giuseppe di Natale and it annoyed me. I decided to try find something on him through old, trusty Facebook. At first I was stumped, as there was a football player by the same name and he kept coming up in my searches. I thought he would probably not be on Facebook, but his family would…sons, nieces, grandchildren. It took me almost the whole day to track him down, but in the end I was pretty sure I had found the right Giuseppe di Natale. In Parma.

He wasn't listed in the phone book, didn't appear on any search engine: but by a miracle of deductions, looking at pictures, finding which di Natale family had links to Switzerland, I had found him. I bent down to scratch Dulce's head and told her: "Dulce, you have a very smart owner!" The little dog sighed and went back to sleep. So much for congratulations!

"Yeah, yeah, Alex…"

I prepared for my meeting with Sylvie. I had decided the only way to tackle her was to be straightforward. I just couldn't invent a reason for asking her questions and anyway, I thought that Sylvie would also be anxious to find out more about her sister's death.

The tearoom where we were meeting was just across the street. I had told Sylvie I would have a small dachshund with me and as soon as I walked into the room, I saw a pretty young woman waving at me.

As I walked towards her, I thought the word "pretty" didn't quite do the young woman justice. "Exquisite" would have been a more precise term. She was sitting down but rose when I arrived and we exchanged handshakes. She bent down to pat Dulce and smiled at me: "What a gorgeous dog!"

We sat down and I took stock of her: Sylvie was a slim 5'8, with Nordic blonde hair that curled naturally around the prettiest face. She had full lips that always seemed ready to smile and the most beautiful turquoise eyes I had ever seen, underlined by naturally dark lashes. She was extraordinarily pretty, but what made her even more attractive was her pleasant, open expression. She had come straight from work and was wearing a light grey jacket with a matching skirt and high heeled shoes.

Once we had done the introductions and ordered some tea, I tackled the delicate subject of Sylvie's sister. I decided to be quite blunt about it: the girl looked as though she could take it. I said: "Miss Rivière, I don't know how you feel about it, but I think there is something…not quite right about your sister's death." I took a big breath: "In fact, I think she was murdered." A shadow crossed Sylvie's sunny face. She stirred some sugar into her tea, and after a couple of minutes looked up at me. "I think so too."

CHAPTER VIII

For the first time, she asked the question I had been waiting for: "Why are you interested in Florence's death?" I had had time to assess her: I decided to follow my instinct and trust the girl.

I didn't tell her the whole story though: only that while talking to the nephew and maid of Mrs. de Brousse, I had thought there was something very strange about those two deaths, Florence's and the nurse's. So much so that I had wanted to find out more, out of personal interest.

I knew it was lame and thought most people would have sent me to hell for interfering in something that was none of my business. But Sylvie was also searching for answers, so she didn't question her unlikely ally. She explained to me how Florence had come to work with Mrs. de Brousse.

"Flo was a first rate assistant to a partner in one of Geneva's Private Banks, who was a good friend of Mrs. de Brousse. He retired just when Mrs. de Brousse started looking for an assistant, so he recommended Flo. Alice de Brousse wanted someone to help her to go through her old personal papers, pictures, correspondence, etc…and with the household bills and all that stuff. Mrs. de Brousse was very sharp and she'd always taken care of her administrative work herself, but she was beginning to have problems with her eyesight. Also, she needed help with the old stuff, which she wanted to get in order so that her heir wouldn't have to worry about it."

I interrupted her: "By "heir", you mean her nephew Etienne, of course?" Sylvie nodded: "Yes. At the time she hired Flo, Etienne was still her heir. I mean, she hadn't made a will or anything, but it was clear everything would go to him." Sylvie interrupted herself : "You have to understand, that although we loved each other very much, there was a big age difference between Flo and me. We didn't have the same friends or the same lifestyle, and we didn't see each other that often. But we'd talk a least two or three times a week and have lunch or dinner every couple of weekends or so. So I followed her from a distance, in a way. Anyway, she was quite happy working for Alice de Brousse, until a couple of years ago when this Foundation appeared in the old lady's life"

Sylvie narrowed her eyes: "I'm sure, that one way or another these people are behind Flo's death." I nodded: "I feel that way too." Sylvie finished her cup of tea and went on: "There was a lot of tension between Alice and my sister when these people appeared. She used to rant about how they were influencing her and one day when she called me, she was furious. Apparently the Foundation had managed to persuade Mrs. de Brousse to make a will in their favor. Flo was so angry, she almost quit. Afterwards, things seemed to calm down a little."

She shook her pretty blonde hair: "In fact, during the last weeks, Flo was quite happy, as if she were hugging a secret to herself. She told me once or twice that they would see, that Mrs. de B. was going to put one over them." She was silent for a moment and then went on: "She said something like "and the best thing about it, is that I'm going to make a tidy sum in the process…".

I asked her: "How long before her death did she say that?" Sylvie answered: "Oh, about one week."

We ordered two more cups of tea and I said:

"Can you tell me about the "accident"?"

"The police said she went out of the house that evening, and that instead of taking her car right away, she went for a walk on the lakeshore, in front of the house. Which, to begin with, is ridiculous: it was a chilly April evening, the lakeshore is not lighted. I mean, it wasn't as if it were a pleasant summer evening. It was cold, dark and humid. Unless she was meeting someone, there is no earthly reason why Flo would have gone there. And believe me, she wasn't the kind of person to put in extra hours at her job. Her hours were her hours, full stop. She left at six thirty every day and nothing would have kept her longer on the premises. She gave her employer full value for her money, but if Mrs. de Brousse had wanted her to stay on for some reason, it would have been as extra hours. And it never happened."

I asked: "Could she have been meeting someone there?" Sylvie shrugged: "Why? I mean, if it were someone from the household, she was with them all day long. And someone from the outside would have had to ring the bell and be admitted to the property, which didn't happen."

The waitress brought us our cups. I stirred my tea and asked: "Did anyone see what happened? Or see her outside?" Sylvie sipped her tea: "That is one of the strange things. There were three of the Foundation women working in the house during that evening. They all said they didn't see her: but the house isn't huge and half the windows look out on the lake side. Although it was dark, there was still enough light for anyone looking out of the window to see her, especially since she was wearing a light yellow raincoat."

"What about Mrs. de Brousse? What did she say?"

"That is even stranger. I thought she was quite well, the last time we had talked with Flo, she told me how the old lady was in very good shape. But her doctor didn't allow the police to interview her, saying she wasn't well enough. And the strange thing is that she didn't even bother to send me a card, or call me. And she knew me, I'd been up to the house twice. From what Flo told me, it wasn't her style not to do the "right" thing for a funeral, or any formal occasion. I can understand her not going to the funeral, but I can't imagine her not calling me, especially under the circumstances."

"I read the police thought it was a suicide at first?"

"That's ridiculous. Flo had never been in better spirits than the two last weeks before her death. Besides, even if she had wanted to commit suicide, I can tell you drowning would have been an impossible choice. She was an athlete and an excellent swimmer. Swimmers just can't drown, it would be a ridiculous way to try to kill yourself! That's what I told the police. Then they found the wound on her scalp and decided it was an accident."

Sylvie added, visibly angry: "I can't prove that she was attacked, but I'm pretty sure of it. They didn't find any evidence either way: there was blood on one of the stones near the shore and they thought that it was the one she knocked herself out on when she slipped and fell."

She shook her head and said: "It could be that, or someone could have knocked her out and left to drown. I think the Foundation wanted her out of the way and I'm almost sure they killed her."

She fell silent and I reflected on what she had said. It made sense. I tried to figure out what role the wallpaper rolls played in this. If I remembered well, Denise's visit had taken place shortly after Florence Rivière's death. Could it be that the secretary had been gotten out of the way so the Foundation could have free access to these papers? But at least four days had elapsed between her death and Denise's visit. Plenty of time to get hold of them. On the other hand, it looked as though whoever was trying to get hold of them only started to search after Mrs. de

Brousse's death.

The more I thought about it, the less I understood the order of events. I asked: "Sylvie, did your sister ever mention any specific papers? Something precious in the house?"

I was met by a blank stare: "No, not that I remember. It may have been what she was talking about when she said Mrs. de Brousse was going to put one over them, but I really don't know. As I said, she never gave me any details. Why, do you know something?"

I decided it was time to tell her everything: I didn't see any reason not to. Besides, she might know something which might put her in danger. Whoever was looking for the papers was totally unscrupulous and apparently did not hesitate to wound or to kill. If they thought Florence had confided in her sister...I shuddered. I watched the girl across the table: she was slim and looked fragile. But I guessed there was an iron core in her and the blaze in her turquoise eyes when she talked about her sister's death was proof enough that she would not let herself be intimidated.

There was movement from underneath the table and Dulce's small head emerged, with a look which clearly said: "Are you finished? I'm fed up of sitting here!" I smiled and patted her, murmuring: "Be a little patient, Dulce. We'll go for a nice long walk afterwards."

Sylvie suggested: "Why don't we continue this conversation outside, while you walk her? It's lovely outside and we can go to the Park Bertrand, which is very close." I exclaimed: "Great idea!"

"Well, thank goodness someone thinks about my wellbeing, Alex! I can't count on you!

We chatted about Sylvie's job during the walk to the park. She told me that she worked in the back-office of a bank: an undemanding and well-paid job, which left her plenty of time for her social life. I gathered from what she said that she had tons of friends and went out a lot. I waited until we had reached the park and sat on a bench to tell her how I had become involved in this story. I explained:

"I own an art gallery in New York City, where I organize exhibitions. One of the artists I exhibited and whose pictures I sold was Denise Kübler."

I glanced at Sylvie: apparently the name did not ring a bell. I went on: "Denise Kübler was an old friend of Alice de Brousse. It seems that a couple of weeks before her death, Denise went to visit her at Clair-Chant and Alice gave her a trunkful of old wallpaper rolls from the de Brousse manufacture. Shortly after Alice de Brousse's death, Denise Kübler's workshop near Bulle was ransacked and she was killed by the intruders. All her recent pictures were taken, as well as the de Brousse wallpaper rolls. Then, a few days later, my gallery in New York was broken into. The thieves took only paintings, and only non-figurative works. They stole all of Denise's work. Then, the next day, my gallery was again broken into. They stole two or three paintings they'd missed the first time, and my book of accounts.

The next day, my upstairs neighbor at the gallery also had a break-in. Unfortunately for her, she was in the apartment and must have interrupted them, as she was knocked out. She was one of my customers and among the few things that were stolen in her apartment were a pair of paintings by Denise Kübler I'd sold her recently."

Sylvie whistled: "Wow."

I went on: "I had to call Denise Kübler about her pictures being stolen and that's how I learned about her death. I thought there was something very strange going on. I decided to check if the customers who had bought works by Denise from me still had them. I managed to find one of them: he told me his house had been broken into and the picture by Denise was one of the things that had been stolen."

Sylvie exclaimed: "Oh no! Did you go to the police?"

I shrugged: "I thought about it: but the fact that Denise's death occurred in Switzerland…and it was all wild speculation on my part…well, I didn't think it would be useful. There was something else also…" I wondered if I should tell her about the guy who tried to intimidate me in New York, but thought better of it. I went on: "At any rate, I didn't want to go: not until I had some concrete evidence about this whole thing. Now I'm sure it's not about Denise's work, but rather about the de Brousse papers. And your sister's death confirms that, don't you think so?"

Sylvie got up to pace in front of the bench. Dulce, seeing some movement on our side came running back, hoping we were going home. Sylvie bent down and found a small branch, which she threw for Dulce. I felt like laughing when I saw the expression on the little dog's face.

"Oh, OK. It's below my dignity, but if you like throwing sticks, I'll go and get it!"

She ran off to get the branch and brought it back, wagging her tail happily. But she didn't bring it to Sylvie, preferring to sit down and keep it between her front paws.

"There, I got it for you: but since you seem to be rather careless about your stuff, I'm keeping it, OK?"

I laughed: Sylvie went to retrieve the branch and threw it again. I sighed wistfully as I looked at the girl's figure. She had taken off her suit jacket and wore a plain white sleeveless shirt underneath. She had a perfect figure and her short flared skirt showed off her long tanned legs.

71

I looked down at my own: they were marmoreal and chubby. I sighed again and Sylvie, coming back to sit next to me, looked at me curiously: "What's wrong?" I ran a hand through my hair and said: "Nothing, I was just thinking…"

Sylvie asked: "What did you do next?"

"Well, I had some holidays coming up, I usually close the gallery for two weeks in July. So I decided to come to Switzerland to try to find out more. Edouard Kübler, Denise's husband, was kind enough to see me and show me the workshop where Denise had been attacked. That's where I learned about the wallpaper. So I came back to Geneva and managed to get into the house. Clair-Chant. I spent the afternoon there, yesterday, and that's where I learned about your sister."

Sylvie jumped up again - catching Dulce's attention - and crossed her arms. She said: "I think we ought to go to the police with this."

I chewed my lower lip, thinking. I watched Dulce, who had now decided to run around in wide circles, ears flying. The amusing thing was that the dog ran furiously, but she managed to keep an eye on us in the meantime. It was quite funny. I gave my attention to Sylvie's question: "Not yet, Sylvie. It's all so…nebulous right now. I don't think anyone would take us seriously. Not unless we have more solid evidence to bring to the table."

Sylvie sat down again, frowning slightly. I felt a twinge of jealousy as I watched her: how could she manage to look so pretty, even frowning and pouting? I thought of what my own face looked like when I pouted and it was definitely not an attractive sight!

Sylvie asked: "So what do you propose to do?"

I had thought about my answer and said: "The friend I'm staying with is going to Paris in two days: she's offered that I join her, as we can share her hotel room and she would enjoy the company on the trip. So I was thinking I'd go there and try to find out more details about the Foundation. Everything seems to point to them. I want to know who they are."

Sylvie turned her bright blue gaze on me: "It could be dangerous."

I shrugged: "I don't think so. I don't have anything that they want. They've already stolen from me anything that contained some of the famous wallpaper, so I don't see what they would want with me. And it's a public Foundation, with offices in the middle of Paris. I don't see what could happen to me if I go there and ask a few questions."

We got up and Sylvie, slinging her jacket on her shoulder, said: "As you wish. If you need any help, in any way…don't hesitate to call me. And good luck!"

I watched the tall svelte girl walk off. I sighed and called Dulce, who came barreling down, eager to go back to home and dinner. On the way back, I wondered if I should try to return to Clair-Chant the next day. I reasoned that I might get some more information there: if only the confirmation that the Giuseppe di Natale I had found was the right one. The truth was, I didn't want to admit it to myself, but I was dying to see Etienne again.

CHAPTER IX

In the evening I told Felicia I would join her on her trip to Paris. Felicia was taking the TGV, the high speed train that takes 3 hours from Geneva to Paris. I booked my ticket online and checked that the hotel where Felicia was staying accepted dogs.

I was beginning to realize that my life was now dictated by this small, furry bundle of love: I just wouldn't go anywhere that didn't accept dogs. It was a feeling of responsibility that was totally new to me, but it was now part of my way of thinking. It was me and Dulce, or nothing. I dug my nose in the little dog's fur, inhaling her wonderful smell: it reminded me of toasted bread.

Dulce rolled on her back to get her evening belly scratch and once we had gone through our personal bed time rituals, we met in the bedroom, and went to our respective beds.

In the morning I called Clair-Chant and told Anny, who answered the phone, that I would be coming to the house a bit later that morning. I didn't ask about Etienne and the girl didn't tell me anything, so it was with some trepidation that I arrived at the house at mid-morning.

I had returned my rental car and took a bus down to the house. The bus stop wasn't too far from the house, but it was unpleasant going. The sidewalk was narrow and there was a lot of traffic on the road: the cars moved at great speed and from time to time there were trucks. Dulce kept carefully close to the high walls of the properties we passed before reaching Clair-Chant. She was disturbed by the noise and the sensation of the traffic on the other side.

This time I had the foresight to wear reasonable shoes, low heeled sandals with wide straps. We walked to the gate and rang: it took quite a long time for someone to answer and open the gates, and I could have sworn the voice who had asked my name wasn't Anny's.

But it was Anny who waited for me at the door. I noticed there were four cars in the garage this time. There was the little red car, a grey sportscar that had been there the last time and two other ones.

I followed Anny into the house and asked her it it was OK for her to help me that morning. I asked: "I hope I'm not taking you from your other duties?" Anny looked back at me with small, blank eyes: "Duties?" I shrugged and followed her upstairs. I decided to ask if Etienne was there: after all, it would only be polite to greet him. But Anny said he had gone out. She didn't know when he would be back. I sighed and trundled up the stairs.

It was only one floor, but I was so out of shape that I was panting by the time I arrived on the landing. I stopped for a second to get my breath back and caught sight of a silhouette on my right. I frowned to get a better look at it: it was one of the Foundation women, who was standing at the end of the corridor opposite of the one where Alice de Brousse's rooms had been. She was staring at me, with an intensity that made me uncomfortable.

I made a move towards her and instantly the woman turned around and vanished into one of the rooms. Despite the fact that the woman was gone, I had the uncanny feeling of being observed. It never left me again in the house.

I followed Anny to Mrs. de Brousse's boudoir and we began sifting through piles of old photographs again. This time we were luckier, as the box we tackled was full of very old material, from Alice's birth to approximately her twentieth year. We found quite a few pictures of her and Denise: we sat looking at them for some time, commenting on the fashion in the twenties. Anny kept exclaiming how pretty they were, and I had to admit she was right. Both girls had been tall and slender, Alice a handsome redhead and Denise a delicate brunette. The fashion of the time, with its mid-long skirts and tiny waists suited them both and made them look even slimmer. There were so many pictures of the two girls, that it would take me some time to select a few for the –mythical- book of Edouard.

I tried to pry more information out of Anny during that morning. The one positive thing I got was a confirmation of Giuseppe di Natale's identity. When I asked Anny if he had a son called Sandro and a daughter called Lila, she said that yes, that was their names. I was now sure I'd found them and that they lived in Parma. I would try to find them and give them a ring later.

A couple of hours after we had started working on the photograph boxes, Etienne suddenly made his appearance. He knocked on the open door and said: "Hello, hello! How are you Mrs. Tate? Are you making some progress?"

I raised my head and smiled at him: "Yes, absolutely. Look at what we found!"

Etienne walked into the room and pulled a chair near the table on which we had spread our findings. He looked through some of the pictures and commented on the two girls' beauty. "They were both very pretty! And they seemed to happy, so carefree!"

I nodded: "It was shortly after the war. I think there must have been a feeling of exhilaration, of freedom…something none of us has ever experienced. And hopefully never will!"

While we went on looking through the box, we began a discussion about the current political and economic situation in the world. I found him a well read and intelligent interlocutor, with whom it was both pleasant and instructive to discuss. I glanced at Anny, who during this conversation had assumed her bland, absent expression.

I realized that it wasn't only the topic that she didn't understand: she was missing half of the words. I felt sorry for the girl: sometimes when you talked to her about everyday, ordinary things, like the length of a skirt or a recipe, she could seem almost normal. But as soon as the discussion became more esoteric, she closed down and retired to an uncomplicated world of her own.

Etienne looked at his watch and said: "It's almost lunchtime. Why don't you stay here and have lunch with me? Anny is an excellent cook."

I was very tempted: it would be an excellent opportunity to learn more. On the other hand, I didn't want to impose myself on Etienne. There was also Dulce, who had strict meal schedules. In less than an hour she should be fed and I hadn't taken her food along. I hadn't counted on staying for lunch. I told Etienne that my dog was my number one priority. He laughed and said: "I'll ask Anny to prepare some chow for her. All the dogs I know thrive on rice, carrots and meat and I'm sure Anny can make that."

I was embarrassed, but he insisted, with what seemed genuine enthusiasm, so in the end I accepted. When we went in to eat, Dulce got two beautiful Sèvres bowls, in which there was her lunch and some water.

"Wow, classy outfit they got here, Alex! And the food is great!"

We had lunch in the small dining room on the left of the main living room. It was a pleasant room, with walls covered in the de Brousse wallpapers I was beginning to know well. This one was particularly beautiful, a pale cream color with a textured pattern of flowers in ivory. The mahogany chairs were upholstered in the same fabric with the pattern inversed: ivory background and cream pattern. It was a beautiful room and I said so to Etienne, who nodded: "Tante Alice had wonderful taste and she always tried to integrate de Brousse fabrics and papers in her decoration. In fact," he added, "She always asked for a sample roll of the new wallpapers and fabrics."

I thought this was my opening: if I mentioned the rolls Alice had given to Denise, how would he react? I said: "Yes, and apparently she gave a whole stack of them to Denise, shortly before her death. To use in her cuttings, you know." Etienne didn't seem very interested. He just said: "Oh yes? I didn't know that." and changed the subject. I could have sworn he hadn't known anything about the wallpapers and he truly didn't seem very interested.

Lunch was cooked and served by Anny. It consisted of an excellent mixed salad, followed by a cold roast beef with perfect French fries. It was a simple meal, but very tasty. I congratulated Anny, who beamed at me. Apparently her cooking was her greatest pride, and justifiably so.

Once she was out of the room, I asked Etienne: "What does she do, exactly? Is she the cook?" Etienne shrugged: "Tante Alice used to ask her to do whatever was within her capacities. She discovered that she enjoyed cooking, so she did that from time to time. Basically, Anny does what you ask her to do, within her limits. I don't have much work to give her: I don't need someone to organize my shoe closet or do small errands. So these days she mainly does the cooking and serving, especially when I have guests. Which is not very often."

I got the feeling that he was a bit lonely in Geneva. He had been living in Paris until his aunt's death and it couldn't have been easy for him to move to the quiet -and boring- Swiss city. I asked him about it and he said that at first he had hated it there, but that he was beginning to enjoy the quietness.

He was setting up a new business from the house. He didn't want to give me details but I understood it was something to do with the de Brousse business. He talked to me about the company, explaining its history.

The de Brousse company had been created in the 18th century, producing the famous Toile de Jouy at first, like many other manufacturers of the area. The company had then diversified into wallpapers. They were the first company to be able to produce matching fabrics and wallpapers and it was a huge success. There had been de Brousses at the head of the business until Jean de Brousse. Or rather, until Etienne de Brousse, since he was out of the company now.

Obviously he felt very strongly about that. And even more obviously he felt strongly about his aunt's betrayal. I asked him why he hadn't intervened before, when the Foundation had started to make its influence felt. Etienne ran a hand through his hair: "I had no idea about what was happening! I was very busy at the company and I didn't have time to come to Switzerland. I used to talk to her every couple of weeks and I didn't see it coming. Once I had Caroline, her old nurse on the phone. She told me she was worried, that there were these new people in Tante Alice's life and that she didn't like the way they were influencing her. Unfortunately I didn't pay too much attention: I suppose I thought Caroline was jealous of whoever these new friends of Tante Alice were. By the time I realized something was seriously wrong, it was too late. They had brainwashed her so much that she didn't want to see me anymore."

Etienne finished his glass of wine and remarked: "They worked very fast. It took them just a few months to do it."

I had noticed the presence of one of the Foundation's women just outside of the dining room, ostensibly doing some dusting. I indicated her with a gesture of the head to Etienne, but he shrugged: "Oh, I don't give a damn if the burqua team hears me. They know very well I'm licked. They've inherited everything and there isn't a damn thing I can do about it…"

Which made me ask: "Your family had no shares in the company?" He answered: " My mother had some shares: she had inherited about 14% of the shares. But my family had all kinds of financial problems and they sold most of them. Now I own less than 1% of de Brousse. "

I nodded. We went out to have coffee in the living room: while we were sipping our espressos, I told him I was going to Paris the next day. At the mention of the City of Lights, his face suddenly lit up. He asked me if I knew Paris well, and when I told him I hadn't been there for years, proceeded to give me all the best places to go to, the new trendy restaurants, the shows…everything. I laughed and said I wouldn't have time to make all the list and he said wistfully: "I wish I could go with you!" My heart did a little summersault. But I soon realized it was Paris, not me that he longed for. I sighed and finished my coffee. Looking at my watch I realized it was later than I had thought. I told Etienne I ought to go and let him return to his obligations.

Watching him, I felt like laughing: he had picked up Dulce and sat her on his lap. The little dog was contentedly digesting her rich meal, while being scratched behind the ears. The two of them looked very comfortable and I was reluctant to interrupt their postprandial bliss. I told Etienne I should be leaving and he sighed: "Are you sure?" I smiled and he lowered Dulce reluctantly to the floor.

He followed me outside, asking me where I had left my car. I said I had come by bus and he exclaimed: "You must let me drive you back then!" I accepted, thinking to myself that he either had taken a shine to me or he must really be feeling bored. We walked to the garage to his car: it was the grey sports model I had noticed before. He opened the passenger door and I sat down with Dulce on my lap.

While I fastened my seatbelt, I suddenly felt the little dog stiffen. Dulce pricked up her ears and emitted a low growl, looking in the house's direction. I turned to see what had attracted her attention. I vaguely saw the silhouette of a woman standing on the doorstep in the dark, looking fixedly in our direction.

"Alex! Watch out! I don't like this person!"

I said to Etienne, who was manoeuvering to back the car out: "These women give the creeps! Don't they bother you?" Etienne turned the car in the driveway, catching a glimpse of the veiled woman on the way. He said: "I've had these freaks in the house since I moved in. I don't notice them anymore"

That, I thought, might be a big mistake…

CHAPTER X

During the afternoon, I tried to get hold of Giuseppe di Natale's family in Parma. I managed to find his son, Sandro, who seemed very suspicious of me and didn't want to give me his father's address. Who in fact, didn't want to admit he knew where the old man was. My Italian was pretty basic, but I did manage to convey to him that I needed Giuseppe's help and that I really wanted to talk to him. I said: "Mr. di Natale, I absolutely need to talk to your father. If you won't give me his address or his phone number, can you please at least ask him to call me? Tell him it is about Mrs. de Brousse and her nephew."

There was silence at the other end. Then Sandro said: "I'll give him the message. But don't expect him to call you." I thanked him profusely and hung up. I sat looking at the view outside Felicia's apartment. There were two women discussing outside: I knew them, they were Felicia's cleaning lady and her cousin. Both of them Italian. Both of them had lived all their lives in Geneva, worked, raised their children…and they had stayed. What had made Giuseppe return to Italy and hide there? Because there was no doubt in my mind that Giuseppe di Natale was hiding. But why and from whom?

***

The TGV train to Paris left early in the morning. Felicia and I spent the evening packing our stuff for the three days we'd be there. Felicia laughed when she saw my and Dulce's bags: the dog's bag was twice the size as mine. I shrugged when Felicia commented on it and replied: "It's like a baby…she has to have her own special food, her toys, her blanket.

And I'm not even taking her bed!"

Felicia shook her head and patted Dulce, whispering in her silky ear: "You spoiled princess, you!" She was rewarded with a delicate lick on the hand.

"Yes, my dear."

Dulce then went back to her bed: she had heard we wouldn't take it along and probably thought she should enjoy it as much as she could while she still had it!

The TGV is the most comfortable way to get to Paris from Geneva: it takes just over three hours and arrives in the center of Paris, at the Gare de Lyon. I took the opportunity of these three hours to tell Felicia everything about my "mission", as I'd begun to think of it, in Switzerland.

I hadn't told her anything previously, because I was still not sure that there was anything behind my suspicions. But the last two days had convinced me and I wanted to talk to my best friend about it. Felicia was smart and I wanted her input. It took me the greatest part of an hour to tell her everything from the beginning.

I saw Felicia's expression change as I went on with my story. I could see my friend was worried, even frightened. In the end Felicia asked: "And you're going to Paris to see these people? The Foundation?" I nodded. Felicia gave me a worried look: "I'm not really sure it's a good idea, Alex. They sound as if they could be very dangerous. Especially if they are the ones who threatened you."

I shook my head so impatiently that it made my hair bounce on my shoulders: "Oh come on, Felicia! Don't be such a wuss! What do you think could happen to me? Their offices are in the middle of Paris, and I'll make sure they know someone knows where I am! And what's more,

I can't be certain they're behind the thefts and the guy in New York!"

Felicia sighed and didn't insist. She looked at Dulce, who was happily seated on my lap and watched with undisguised interest the scenery outside. She said: "Well, at least you'll have your fearless defense dog with you!" I buried my nose in Dulce's fur, telling the little dog: "You are a brave dog, aren't you? You'll make mincemeat of anyone who tries to bother your mummy, won't you, Dulce?"

The dog sighed and I was sure I saw her shrug.

"Well, if you get yourself into trouble, I can at least try!"

Felicia laughed and we started talking about our plans in Paris. We would be spending three days and two nights there. Felicia was going there for her work. She had several interviews during the day and one dinner that evening. She told me: "I'm having dinner with Laurent, the photographer, tonight. He said he'd be delighted if you joined us."

I accepted the invitation with pleasure: Laurent was a professional photographer, a good friend of Felicia whom I had met a few times.

We arrived at the Gare de Lyon at midday and went directly to our hotel on the Place des Vosges, in the trendy Marais. We had both been going to this hotel for years and had seen it change from a 3 star boutique hotel to its present more prestigious 4 star status.

Dulce was welcomed with a bowl of fresh water in the room. She disdained it, preferring her own which had been brought along. It was her lunchtime though and she fell nose first in her chow. We watched her with curiosity: she must have had some very pushy brothers and sisters, if one could judge by the way she gobbled up her food.

Once we had opened our bags and installed our stuff, we thought we should take care of our own lunch. Felicia's first rendez-vous was at two thirty, so it left us a bit of time to find a place to eat and enjoy the sunshine.

In the end, we stayed on the Place de Vosges and had a light meal at one of the cafés around the square. I could see Felicia was mulling over the story I had told her in the train, and not too happy about it. She asked me what I was going to do that afternoon. I smiled and said: "Visit the Foundation, of course!"

Felicia sighed unhappily but didn't comment. She knew me well enough to realize nothing would make me change my mind. We ordered some ice cream and sat eating it in the sun, while Dulce was busy discovering all kinds of interesting new scents. At a quarter past two Felicia left for her meeting and I went back to the hotel.

I had to get dressed for my mission. I hadn't wanted Felicia to see me getting ready, as my friend would have said I was crazy. I put on all my gold jewelry and a Chanel jacket: it was an old model, but still shouted undoubtedly "money". I slung on my shoulder my equally old Hermès bag and left in quest of the Foundation. The address I had was somewhere in the 5th Arrondissement, not very far from the Place des Vosges.

It was a beautiful day and I decided to walk: Dulce would welcome the exercise after being cooped up in the train for three hours.

I love Paris in July and August, when a lot of Parisians are on holidays and the city is empty, save for a few tourists. I strolled along, without hurry, enjoying the comments on Dulce and the occasional chat with a particularly fervent dachshund lover.

It was almost four by the time I arrived at the Foundation's address, a bland, non-descript building which nothing distinguished from its neighbors. I stood across the street for a moment, observing the comings and goings. It didn't take me long to realize that all the people who came in or went out of the Foundation seemed pretty harmless.

After a moment I walked in, assuming my most innocent and gullible expression. There was a large hall, and a reception desk on my right. On my left I saw a billboard, towards which I walked, to try to get a sense of what was happening there. I didn't make it very far: a female voice said sharply: "Madame! Where are you going? Dogs are not allowed here!"

I turned around and saw that the woman behind the counter, who had been speaking to someone when I walked in, was half raised on her seat and looking at me with a thunderous expression on her face. I smirked: at least one could see it. She wore a veil on her head, but it left her face visible. I sauntered over to the reception desk, trying to look as asinine as I could, holding Dulce's leash tightly.

By now, I felt more unfriendly eyes on me: the men who came by seemed to want to spit at me and Dulce, or worse...It was a very unpleasant feeling of hostility and I had to make a big effort to keep from just walking out. I took Dulce in my arms, deriving some comfort from the warm feeling of her small body, and bleated: "Oooooh. I'm so sorry! I didn't realize! I was interested in your good works and I thought I'd come to get more information. I'm really sorry if my little baby is a nuisance!"

Nastily, I brought Dulce's nose closer to the woman's face and watched her recoil. The receptionist said in a high pitched voice: "Get her out of here! Now!" She was becoming slightly hysterical and I saw two or three men looking menacingly in my direction. I was about to leave, when a tall, impressive man came over from the other side of the hall and said: "Now what's the problem, Salima?"

The girl indicated us with a movement of her chin and said: "This woman here, she came with her dog! She says she is interested in the

Foundation. I told her dogs are not allowed here..." The man took one look at me and suddenly became all smiles. I patted myself on the back: my disguise had worked perfectly, the fish was baited. The man said: "But I'm sure this nice lady didn't know that before she came here, did she, Salima? We can show a bit of tolerance for our fellow human beings who love their pets, especially when it is such a handsome specimen as this one!"

All this was said in a mellifluous voice and he bent down to pat Dulce who was still nestled in my arms. I was amazed when the small dog bared her teeth and let out a low growl. I had never seen her do that yet to someone who approached her to pat her. It sent the woman Salima screaming "Get her out of here, she's ferocious!" and the man backed up, saying with a not so bright smile now: "Indeed! We have a small savage beast here!"

"You, there, get away from Alex! And don't you dare touch me! I don't know who you are, but I don't like you!"

I clutched Dulce protectively, mumbling: "She's just defending me!" The man had regained his composure and smiled smoothly: "But yes, of course, it is perfectly understandable: but tell me, Madam, what was the purpose of your visit here?"

Trying to quiet down Dulce, I was scratching her back. I replied: "I heard about your Foundation through an acquaintance of mine, and I thought it was lovely". I left my voice trail off...Lovely was a carefully chosen word, just what an idle woman with time and money on her hands might use. I added: "I lost my husband recently and I have a lot of time on my hands...Freedom of faith is something that has always seemed something essential to me, so I wondered if there was any way I could contribute to your work."

As I ran a hand through Dulce's fur, I made sure the light caught my huge zirconia ring, which looked more authentic than a real diamond. The man was looking at me appraisingly. I could see myself in his eyes: a chubby, solitary widow, with ample means. I went on: "Of course, I didn't realize my poor little Dulce would provoke such an incident, I'm really sorry!" I smiled ingratiatingly at Salima, but the woman kept her resentful and hateful expression. The man seemed to come to a decision.

He said, bowing slightly: "Of course. We are always grateful to get support." He said graciously: "Why don't you come back tomorrow…alone " he glanced at Dulce, " and I can show you around and tell you about our wonderful dedicated people and the fantastic work they do for the Freedom of Belief around the world."

I was thankful for this way out and said gushingly: "Yes, of course! I'll be back tomorrow morning without my baby and I'll be delighted to hear everything about this wonderful Foundation!" I batted flirty eyelashes at him and said: "And I do hope Mr.?" He exclaimed: "How inexcusably rude of me! I haven't introduced myself: My name is Michel Damien and I am in charge of the Foundation. You were saying?"

I simpered: "I'm sooooo delighted to meet you Mr. Damien. My name is Sophie Martin, and as I was saying, I do hope that you will be there tomorrow morning to show me around?"

I saw in his eyes the unmistakable look of the man who thinks he's made a conquest, together with something subtler and much more unpleasant that I identified as the slightest hint of contempt. It suited me perfectly. He accompanied me to the door as I said: "I'll see you tomorrow then, Mr. Damien!", all the while batting my eyelashes madly at him.

I set Dulce down on the pavement and stomped off, trying to get my eyes focused again as all this eyelash batting had made me cross-eyed. Dulce pulled on her leash, relieved to have been let down and glad to be at sniffing level again. We strolled back to the hotel, doing some window shopping on the way and a lot of sniffing for Dulce.

CHAPTER XI

I looked at the shop windows, but my mind was elsewhere. It was more and more clear to me that the Foundation, was a suspicious outfit. It was obvious from their attitude towards dogs, amongst other things. It was only rabid idiots who thought dogs were "impure", or dirty or dangerous or goodness knows what else, and the receptionist's attitude had been eloquent enough. I looked at my iPhone as I walked on. There was a message from Felicia: she said that Francis happened to be in town and that he would have dinner with us.

It took me another hour to reach the hotel, after numerous stops in boutiques, pit stops for Dulce and a cold drink halfway to the hotel, at the pleasant terrace of a café. The temperature had risen quite a lot during the afternoon and by the time we reached the hotel, I was glad to be able to take a shower and rest my feet.

Felicia returned quite late from her last meeting and had just enough time to shower and to change before we left for the restaurant. We had decided to go to the Quartier Latin for a couscous, an old tradition of ours.

After careful consideration, we had decided to leave Dulce at the hotel: the little dog was comfortably settled on cushions and her blanket and she would certainly be happier sleeping in the quiet hotel room than under a table in a noisy restaurant.

We made our way through the lively streets of the Quartier Latin, to the "Au Bon Couscous", our favorite couscous restaurant in Paris. We loved the atmosphere of the area, and even if our restaurant of choice wasn't the best in Paris, it had become a tradition to go there.

Laurent was already waiting for us at the table and Francis met us later. We ordered the Couscous Royal and some red wine. It was a pleasant reunion: Laurent told us about his latest exhibition in a gallery not very far from the Place des Vosges. I told him I would visit it the next day, after my visit to the Foundation.

Francis asked what Foundation I was talking about and Felicia told him. Before I could stop her, she had summed up the whole story to them. Francis asked: "What did you say this outfit is called?" I told him: "Fondation pour la liberté de culte". Francis speared a merguez and took a thoughtful bite out of it. He drank a sip of wine and said: "They sound dangerous. I think you should be careful. If you want, I'll ask around."

I agreed thankfully: Francis had such a huge network of friends and connections, he could get information in no time.

They all asked me why I had undertaken what I now called my "mission". I took some time to think: it was a question I hadn't asked myself and now I was faced with it. Finally I answered: "At the beginning I was plain scared and I realized if I didn't do anything about it I'd be looking behind my back forever. But above all, I think it was outrage at the injustice…the injustice of Denise's death, of my poor neighbor being attacked…and now at the death of these two other women. Something has to be done about it. I'm not sure if the two series of events are linked. Maybe the two deaths in Geneva really were accidents? But I'm sure Denise's death is linked to the wallpaper rolls…"

This opened a debate as to what there could be in the papers: it went from incriminating letters, a will or a secret recipe for extra easy to use wallpaper. I hadn't thought it could have something to do with the de Brousse company, but it made sense. Laurent piped in: "Maybe it was a contract between the original de Brousse and an associate? And the de Brousse company belongs to someone else? Felicia said: "What about a will? What if Jean de Brousse had made a will in someone else's favor and that was the paper they were looking for? Wouldn't it trump the will in the Foundation's favor?"

It was Francis who answered: "It would be a complicated case…I'm more in favor of compromising documents: something that would prove the Foundation's actions were reprehensible!"

Laurent said: "Why are we fixated on the Foundation? Maybe they've got nothing to do with this? After all, they inherited from this old lady, but their acquaintance with her is quite recent. It's quite possible that this whole thing is related to the de Brousse history and not to these people?"

They all had their opinion and in the end I said: "I think the only way to find out is to look a bit deeper into the Foundation…"

There were various admonitions and advice to be careful from my friends. I told them I would be as careful as possible. Which got me a sigh from Felicia, who took this kind of statement with a pinch of salt.

We stayed out quite late and I was wondering what Dulce had been doing while we were away. Of course, she heard us in the corridor and was waiting in front of the door when we got there. She greeted me as if I'd been away for days, not hours. I had to take her in my arms to prevent her from barking her welcome. She wriggled like a worm in my arms, demanding to be let down.

"Alex! I missed you! Where were you? I was bored, here, alone! Let me kiss you!"

***

I dressed as carefully the next day as I had for my first visit at the

Foundation. Felicia watched me suspiciously and inquired: "Why are you disguising yourself as a Christmas tree? I've never seen you wear so much jewelry?" I smiled: "I want to impress the people at the Foundation..." She shrugged and said: "You're looking for trouble!"

After breakfast I took Dulce for a long walk, since she was going to have to stay in the hotel room during my visit to the Foundation and the exquisite Mr. Damien. It was another warm July day and Dulce seemed to find that the heat brought out some stronger and more delicious smells. I took her back to the hotel and told her I'd be back by lunch time. She watched me quietly, sitting on her furry behind and her intelligent eyes followed me as I went out.

"Be careful, Alex, and come back soon."

On my way to the Foundation I wondered if I would find out something interesting. I couldn't ask them anything about Alice de Brousse, of course, but I wanted to know how they operated. Maybe if I found that out I could get an idea of what they might be looking for in the wallpapers.

I discovered I missed having Dulce walking next to me. I had become accustomed very quickly to having to stop at street corners or places which looked promising for a dog. Now I was just walking straight ahead and I felt...bereft...

The great hall of the FLC, the "Fondation pour la Liberté de Culte" was empty when I got there, save for the unpleasant receptionist. She glared at me when she saw me coming in, but greeted me politely and said she would call Mr. Damien.

While I waited for him to come down, I wandered in the hall, looking at the photographs on the walls. They represented all kinds of places of worship, churches, synagogues, mosques and a Bouddhist temple in a snow covered landscape: presumably the Norwegian Buddhist temple. As I looked closer I noticed that all these buildings had two things in common: they were small and seemed to be built very shoddily.

Mr. Damien hadn't showed up yet, so I walked over to the announcement board I hadn't been able to look at the previous day. There was a schedule of meetings for the members of one of the committees, recent photographs of a small protestant church that was being built somewhere, and a list of names. I tried to commit two or three of them to memory: they were members who had been elected to something named the "Account verification committee".

I heard footsteps behind me and Mr. Damien appeared, arms stretched to take my hands in both of his. I hated the gesture and what it implied, but recognized some advanced manipulation techniques. He put a hand around my shoulder and wheeled me towards the elevator, all the while saying how glad he was to see me again.

We went up to the second floor where he took me to his office. I watched with interest the carefully selected décor. It was a serviceable office, furnished with sturdy and unremarkable items. It said "This is the place where I work: we cannot afford luxurious furniture or anything extravagant, but we believe we need to be comfortable to work. There was a photograph of a handsome blonde and two children on his desk. They wore jeans and T-shirts and were somewhere by the seaside. There were various awards on the credenza behind him, two of them on their sides, as if he didn't really care about them. There were three enlarged photographs of the places of worship I had seen downstairs, except that in these pictures there were people in front of them. They had been autographed by several people, probably those in the photographs.

The largest picture, on the right hand wall, represented a Greek

Orthodox pope looking on as an official cut the ribbon in front of a small, brand new Orthodox church. There were tears running down the pope's grizzled face. It was a very moving picture. I felt like smiling, but managed to look appropriately touched and impressed by these displays of the FLC'S actions.

Damien noticed me looking at the picture on the wall and produced a carefully calibrated smile which conveyed discreet satisfaction, modesty and sensitivity. I could only admire this masterpiece. He said, in a modest tone: "Ah, you're looking at Father Spiros: we built this church in the South of Italy. There is a small community of Orthodox Greeks there and they could not afford to build a new church. So the Foundation financed it: I have rarely seen so much joy in someone's face!"

I simpered: "How wonderful! Tell me more, it seems fascinating!" Damien sat behind his desk and joined his hands in front of him in a small pyramid shape. It was my turn to smile: that is one gesture to avoid, as it indicates that the speaker is about to tell a lie. Damien offered me a drink and I accepted: he took his phone and called someone, ordering two coffees.

While we waited, he told me about the FLC. He said he had created it after having renounced a successful career in finance. He had had an "awakening" he said, while visiting a client in the north of Greece. There, he said, he had become aware if the plight of the muslim community in Thrace, who could not afford to build a new mosque.

He added: "It might surprise you that I am an agnostic. But I have always thought people should be not only free, but encouraged, to worship where and how they want. That day it struck me that I was just another parasite in this society. I resolved to use the modest fortune I had built to try to help people gain freedom of cult. I also decided to use my extensive network to tap into my acquaintances to find more money for this cause. I created the Foundation, and with the help of our members and staff we have been doing some remarkable work these last years"

I nodded, trying to look fascinated: "Do you have many members?"

He smiled: "Never enough, unfortunately! That's why we are always glad to welcome new ones!"

Then came the question I feared most: "My dear Mrs. Martin, how did you hear about us?"

I had done some feverish research on the internet in the morning to try to find a suitable answer. In the end I settled for " a friend of a friend" It was very weak, but I couldn't afford to use a name he could check, especially not Alice de Brousse's. As I answered, I saw something in his eyes I didn't like. However, he didn't comment and went on with his presentation of the Foundation.

There was a knock on the door, which had remained open, and the unpleasant woman from the reception walked in, carrying a tray with cups of coffee and some sugar. I was amused to see that the cups were mismatched and the coffee was instant. There were some dry biscuits -the cheapest supermarket brand - on a plate. Damien said, with a smile of excuse: "I'm sorry for the quality of our coffee, but we try to keep our costs low, so that a maximum of funds go towards our goals."

I had to bite my lip not to laugh. The staging was a bit overdone. I murmured something admiring and stirred sugar in my coffee: no cream, of course. Damien went on telling me about the Foundation. After a while he said: "The best way to introduce you to our mission is to show you our small movie. If you would please follow me, I will take you to our conference room."

We went out of his office and back down to the ground floor. There was a large conference room which occupied the rest of the floor and opened into the entrance hall. It had a screen on the far wall. We sat around the conference table and Damien made me watch a movie about the FLC.

Once again, I admired these people. The movie was a work of art. It seemed to be a montage of amateur and professional images, showing the building of various places of worship around the world. There were cunning shots of "poor" people, saying how they could not afford to build their chosen religion's place of worship, and then the same people once it was being built and once it was finished. The narrator had a youthful and enthusiastic voice. From time to time, the voice would choke with emotion. Even though I understood perfectly well the mechanisms behind this remarkable marketing tool, I could not help a few tears running down my face.

Which was exactly what I needed, to convince Damien that he had taken me in. Once he turned on the light I discreetly wiped a tear and said in a choked voice: "Mr. Damien, what you are doing is extraordinary and more than ever I want to help. What can I do?"

There was a gleam in his eyes as he rose and took my elbow to show me out. While we went back to his office, he explained: "There are various ways in which you can help us, Mrs. Martin. We have volunteers here working at the administration. There are other volunteers doing work on location, helping us build the places of worship."

He looked at me inquiringly, as if expecting me to jump up and say: "Yeees! Of course! I'll go tomorrow to Mexico to help lay bricks for a Protestant church!" I just smiled and let him continue. He pulled the chair in his office for me and went back to sit behind his desk. There was a pile of brochures on it and he gave me one, adding: "Then, of course, you can contribute financially to our cause."

Aha! That was my line. I gushed: "Of course! I don't really see myself with a trowel or a paintbrush! And I'm afraid I don't have any accounting or secretarial skills!" I simpered: "In fact, my late husband used to say I couldn't add 2 and 2. And it was only a slight exaggeration!"

Damien smiled and said: "Well, I'm sure your children help you balance your accounts?"

I took an appropriately forlorn expression: "Sadly, Mr. Damien, we did not have children. I'm all alone now: I was an only child and even though my husband had quite a big family, he was estranged from them long before we met." I decided to pad my story a little:

"My husband was quite a few years older than me. He was a notary public in Courchevaux: as you can imagine, he was very wealthy when he died. But our marriage did not last very long, he died two years ago and we had no children. So there is no one. This is why, if I can help such a worthy cause as yours and meet people…like you…it would give me the illusion of a family."

Damien looked at me soberly and understandingly. He jumped into the opening: "I understand you perfectly. I too wanted to fill the void in my life, to find a new family: and the Foundation has given me just that. I hope it will be the same for you."

I decided he was ripe for some more in-depth questioning. I said: "I'm very enthusiastic about all this. Can you tell me how your other members contribute? Do they give you monthly amounts, or lump sums? Do they contribute to specific projects or to the Foundation in general?"

He was shrewd and wasn't going to answer immediately. He said, opening his hands: "It all depends. We don't want our members to give us money without knowing exactly where it is going. So we usually organize a field trip to one of our current projects. And once the person is convinced, they decide how they want to contribute. I am happy to say that a few of our members, after having shared some wonderful experiences with us, have seen fit to put the FLC on their will."

Ha! I knew that! I said sweetly: "Of course, after finding a family like this, it would be normal…"

He nodded: "Absolutely. You understand perfectly." He took a sheet of paper from a tray and pushed it towards me, saying: "I would really love to have you joins us. Would you like to fill our membership application? It is free and that way we will have you on our mailing list. You can decide at a later stage how you want to contribute."

I took the sheet of paper and nodded enthusiastically: "Of course, I'll fill it right now!"

Which I had no intention of doing: I had enough information for the moment and wanted to get out as soon as possible and never see these people again. I pretended to look at my phone to see what date it was and to notice the time and exclaimed: "Oh dear! It's very late! I have to run to feed my little darling, she has very strict meal hours!" I snatched the paper in front of me and got up hurriedly, saying: "I have to run back to the hotel, Mr. Damien: but I will fill this in and bring it back to you this afternoon or tomorrow morning, as you prefer. I'm a Paris for a few days and I won't leave without becoming a member of your wonderful foundation, Mr. Damien…" There I inserted some eyelash batting, which Damien must have found convincing, since he followed me outside of his office without protesting.

He accompanied me to the door and as I made to leave, took both my hands in his and looked me in the eyes, murmuring: "I look forward to seeing you again very soon, Mrs. Martin."

I smiled weakly and sauntered off, with a feeling of relief. I shuddered: the man was decidedly creepy. His seductive smile probably worked with most women, but it gave me the willies.

CHAPTER XII

It was still early - and definitely not Dulce's lunch time yet, so I decided to stop by the gallery where Laurent was exhibiting his work. The gallery was located on the rue Beautreillis, which leads to the Place des Vosges: so that even someone as directionally challenged as I was could not get lost.

I wasn't walking very fast: in order to look "lady like" I had worn relatively high heels and they weren't very comfortable. I stopped from time to time to look at shop windows - with a preference for delicatessen and bakeries, which had the most delicious displays! After a while I had the uncanny feeling that someone was following me. I shrugged, thinking it must be my imagination.

When I walked into the gallery I was greeted by Laurent flashing away at me with his camera. Apparently he took pictures of everyone who came into the gallery: he told me he would use these photos -,with the agreement of the subjects - to do a wall sized composition. He said the repetition of people stepping in from the street through the door would be quite striking. He added with a smile: "You look charming today, Alex! I'll send you these pictures as soon as I transfer them to my computer."

I appreciated the compliment: coming from our gay friend it was certainly sincere! He walked me through the exhibition. It was a series of black and white shots, on the theme of light. I turned to Laurent: "Very striking! You've done an excellent job! We should organize an exhibition for you in New York one of these days!"

We chatted for a while and Laurent asked me how the visit to the

Foundation had gone. I shrugged: "All I can say is that the guy I met seems like a pretty formidable character and I'm sure he's totally devoid of scruples. It looks as though the Foundation is really building places of worship throughout the world. On the other hand, Alice de Brousse's fortune alone would have been enough to build ten times more than what they're showing…and it looks like she wasn't the only gullible old lady they took in. The thing is, I suppose it must be very difficult to prove they're crooks and took advantage of her. Unless there is a letter somewhere: which would justify their mad search for it."

I sighed: "Right now, all I've found out is that they give me the creeps! This guy Damien, in particular."

Laurent asked: "Did Francis get back to you with some information about FLC?" I looked at my email: "No, not yet. I'm sure he hasn't had time yet."

After I left Laurent I went straight to the hotel. It was near Dulce's mealtime and she made me understand it by her enthusiastic welcome. I took her out for a long walk around the Place des Vosges and then let her have her lunch in the hotel room, just before Felicia arrived.

We checked out and had lunch before going to catch our train back to Geneva. Once we were sitting on a terrace on the Place de la Bastille, I took out my phone to see if there were any messages from Francis. There was nothing yet, but Laurent had already sent me the series of five pictures he'd taken of me walking into the gallery. I showed them to Felicia, who was delighted. She exclaimed: "They're fantastic! Look at the way he caught the movement, the sway of your skirt! And you look absolutely gorgeous!"

I looked at the photograph: It showed me walking through the open door, in a ray of sunlight, with the people walking on the opposite pavement in the background. I had rarely had such a good picture of myself.

We finished our lunch and hopped into the subway. It was only one stop to the Gare de Lyon where our train was waiting. Once we had found our seats, I noticed I had a message from Francis. It gave some interesting information about the Foundation and Michel Damien.

I read the message out loud for Felicia's sake:

"Dear Alex! Please find herebelow what I've managed to find about your "friends".

The FLC was created and is run by Michel Damien, a French citizen. It is a Panama Foundation, with offices in various countries of the world, the largest being in Paris. They employ a dozen people, most of them in Paris. There have been several complaints about them, mostly from disgruntled families who were cut out of wills. Apparently the Foundation preys on rich elderly people who have no close family and persuades them to put them in their will. They also have a brigade of single, divorced or widowed women who regularly donate large amounts of money to the "cause".

All this is not very ethical but not illegal and none of the people who have tried to sue the Foundation have been successful. Damien has on his payroll some of the world's best lawyers.

Given the amounts they have inherited or acquired by various methods during the last years, the Foundation must be sitting on vast amounts of cash.

There have been all kinds of rumors and allegations regarding their methods, but nothing has ever been proven. Which makes the theory of a compromising document the most likely.

All in all, this Damien sounds like a very unsavory character, and I'd advise you to keep well away from him and his outfit.

Hope this helps!

Best to you and Felicia,

Francis"

I looked up at Felicia, who had listened carefully: "I guess he was hoping to enroll me in his "widow and divorcee brigade!"

Felicia was worried: "I hope you didn't get yourself in trouble! What if they go after you once you don't show up again at the Foundation?"

I smirked: " I'm not stupid enough to have given my real name! They'll be looking for Sophie Martin, widow of a notary somewhere in the Alps! There is no way they can find me again!"

Felicia sighed: "I don't like it"

Looking out of the window, I tried to see the station's clock to see how much longer we had until the train left.

I started saying "Oh, come on!" to Felicia, when something caught my attention on the platform. I frowned and took out my iPhone: I looked through my email messages, until I found Laurent's.

A cold sweat ran down my back: the man who was standing at the end of the platform, watching fixedly in our direction, had been standing in front of the gallery when Laurent had taken my picture.

I didn't want to frighten Felicia, so I said nothing and moved away from the window. I went on talking nervously to her, basically blabbering. She frowned and asked me what was wrong. I said: "Isn't this train ever going to start?"

At that precise moment it started moving: I looked in the man's direction. He was still on the platform, looking in my direction, but now he was talking on his cell phone. I shuddered.

Thankfully, Felicia was reading her own email and didn't notice my reaction. I thought about what I'd just seen. So Damien had sent someone to keep track of me. Or was it something totally different? No, it didn't make sense. It had to follow my visit to the Foundation. I reflected that, once I'd baited the fish, it made sense for them to try to find out more about me. Maybe they wanted to check at which hotel I was staying: and the guy had seen us leave with our suitcases and probably phoned Damien to tell him they'd lost a prospect.

I was slightly reassured by my reasoning. It seemed reasonable. I would probably never hear from them again: except, of course, in Geneva.

The incident had unsettled me but in no way did it make me change my mind about getting to the bottom of the "Wallpaper mystery!" I was resolved to find out more. I couldn't help it: there were too many unanswered questions and my curiosity was overwhelming.

I looked at Dulce, who was peacefully snoring on her blanket on the seat next to me: I wished I could be like her and simply enjoy life. Instead of getting myself into bizarre situations.

Geneva was as we had left it: sizzling hot and full of arab tourists. We went back to Felicia's apartment: like most apartments in Switzerland it wasn't air-conditioned. The trouble is that with global warming, Switzerland now has some pretty warm summers.

During the night, the atmosphere was stifling. We had all the windows open, but despite this there wasn't the slightest breeze. I couldn't sleep and kept on thinking about the lost papers. Dulce was stretched out on the floor, avoiding her bed.

In typical dog fashion she tried to make herself as flat as possible, to get maximum advantage of the slightly cooler floor. She sighed in her sleep and turned to lie flat on her back. I laughed: she looked like a very furry pelt like that.

A few hours later and after an almost sleepless night, we all got up. Felicia left for work and I took Dulce to the park, where I hoped it would be a bit more pleasant under the trees' shade. I sat on the bench where we had sat with Sylvie Rivière and thought about calling her. But I didn't have anything new to tell her and I doubted she would either. I sighed: what to do?

That was when my iPhone rang: I looked at the caller ID: it was a number in Italy. My heart beat faster: could it be the gardener?

CHAPTER XIII

I answered, gingerly: the voice on the other end was masculine and rather hoarse. It was Giuseppe di Natale, at last. He said: "My son told me you were looking for me. What do you want?" He was speaking French, with a heavy Italian accent. I replied in the same language: "Mr. di Natale, I think you worked for the de Brousses for quite a long time?" He replied gruffly: "Yes, so what?" I didn't know quite how to ask him what I wanted: not on the phone anyway. I told him: "Look, I'm a friend of Sylvie, Florence Rivière's sister: I'm trying to help her find some answers."

He knew perfectly what I meant. He didn't reply for a long time and I thought he'd hung up. I was about to lose hope, when he finally said: "I can't talk on the phone. Could you come here?"

I jumped at the occasion: both to see him and to get out of sizzling Geneva and Felicia's apartment. I asked him when and where we could meet. He was living near Parma and told me to call him at that number once I was there.

I hung up with some trepidation: Giuseppe di Natale's attitude made it perfectly clear he knew something to do with Florence's death. I wondered if he had been interviewed in connection with it. I hadn't thought of asking Sylvie the last time and decided to call her to find out.

She answered on the third ring and said: "Alex? How are you? Have you found anything new?"

I said that, unfortunately not, except I had met Damien and visited the Foundation in Paris. I told her I'd be going to Parma to visit the gardener and asked her if he'd been interviewed during the inquest about her sister's death. She answered: "Yes, of course, especially since his assistant was the one who found her body. But he had nothing to say, except he'd left at four, as he had to go and buy some fertilizer and stuff and didn't return until the next day, after they found my sister."

I chewed my lip: "I see. Well, I get the feeling that he knows more than he said. That's why I'm going to see him"

I hung up and called Dulce, who had been playing with two other dogs. She ran up to me, tail wagging, tongue lolling. I wondered how she could stand the heat with her fur and no way of sweating except through her tongue. I gave her some water from a small fountain and we walked back home.

"It's pretty hot, here, Alex! Thanks for the drink! I wish I could jump into the fountain, though..."

The area of Florissant, where Felicia lived, is pretty quiet. There aren't that many people in the streets. So it struck me when I saw the same woman walking out of the park behind me that had followed me in. Unconsciously I must have noticed that she didn't have a pram or a dog on a leash and that she was alone. She wasn't wearing athletic clothes either and it wasn't lunchtime, when the people who worked in the area came to the park.

She carefully avoided looking in my direction, and seemed to stroll in a relaxed way down the road. The woman looked perfectly ordinary, one of dozens dressed in the same way at that time of the day: business attire and pumps. I tried to see her face more clearly, but she managed to keep it turned away from me.

I began to feel very uneasy and hurried back to the apartment. Once there I started making plans for my trip to Parma. I decided the best would be to rent a car: it would give me more freedom and depending on where di Natale organized our meeting, it might be indispensable. I called the rental agency and arranged to pick up a car later in the day.

Next I located a hotel in the center of town which accepted dogs and seemed very nice. It was an old "Palazzo" right next to the Baptistery of Parma, which is its most notable monument. The hotel gave detailed directions as to how to get there by car. I sighed: no matter what, I'd still get lost.

I gave Felicia a call, telling her I was going to Parma for a couple of days. She was suspicious and asked me why: I fibbed and told her that the heat on Geneva was really unbearable and that I'd always wanted to visit the home town of Verdi and Toscanini. And I would bring back some Parma cheese and ham and some violet flavored sweets.

The culinary aspect seemed to convince her more than the cultural one: in which she did me an injustice, as I was firmly decided to take advantage of my short visit there to catch an opera, if possible.

Next I had to find a way to lose my follower: I was sure the woman I had seen was still lurking somewhere outside. There was only one way out of the building, so she couldn't miss me. But the car rental station was near the station and I knew I could lose her there. Maybe even make her think I'd taken a train!

I packed Dulce and my bags and went to take the bus that would take me directly to the station. The tearoom where I'd met Sylvie Rivière the other day, was just across the front door of the building. And lo and behold, I recognized my follower, who was sitting on the terrace with a cup of coffee and a newspaper meant to hide her. As soon as she saw me coming out she perked up and straightened the newspaper. Either she thought I was very stupid or she didn't really care if I saw her. At any rate, she was clearly recognizable.

I didn't pay attention to her and walked towards the bus stop, wondering how she intended to follow me there. There were rarely more than five or six people at this bus stop and at this time of the day there was no one. I crossed the street to the bus shelter and watched, as she hovered across the street, pretending to look at the window of the dry-cleaner's.

My bus arrived and I watched from the corner of my eye as she hesitated, then risked her life running across the road and jumping at the last second into the bus, through the back door. She tried to make herself as small as possible. I didn't look in her direction.

The train station in Geneva and the area around it, have been in the process of being renovated for the last thirty years. Lately, it has become so difficult to navigate that even seasoned Genevese go nuts. There are a warren of tunnels and arcades around it and it wasn't difficult at all to lose my follower. I went to the agency to get the car key and then took the car from the underground garage. She was nowhere in sight.

I drove out in the direction of France, to take the Mont-Blanc tunnel across to Italy and then drive down to Parma. It was a 4 to 5 hour drive, depending on the speed. It was just after twelve when I left and there was very little traffic.

After one pit and lunch stop on the way, to feed the dog, the driver and the car, we arrived at Parma shortly after five. By then I was absolutely sure I hadn't been followed, which relieved me quite a lot. I had walked Dulce for a long time when we had stopped at the gas station, making sure no cars with Swiss plates stopped after us.

Dulce traveled in great comfort, in her small bed, which I had installed on the back seat. She seemed to enjoy the car trip, except for the part going up and down the mountain from the Mont-Blanc tunnel. On the "autostrada", she was one happy and relaxed dog. I could hear her sighing contentedly from time to time.

Getting to the hotel was another story. I followed to the letter the hotel's instructions, expecting at any moment to be stopped by the police. The instructions involved driving into the pedestrian zone and taking several one-way streets the wrong way. I finally made it to the hotel door, and parked the car in front of the door, conspicuously the only car in the deserted street.

Dulce was glad to jump out of the car and shake herself.

"Are we there, finally?"

I walked into the small reception area and was relieved to learn that the hotel had a special permit for its clients, to drive in the pedestrian area and to park there. The guy at the reception told me to leave the car where it was and to check into my room and that he would take me to the hotel's parking lot later.

The Palazzo Dalla Rosa Pratti is a charming boutique hotel in a beautiful palazzo, where the rooms are tastefully decorated and appointed. The price was within my limited budget and, best of all, they accepted dogs! Our room was tiny but precious. My first priority was to install Dulce in her new quarters and give her some water. Once everyone was settled down, I called Giuseppe di Natale's number. It rang for a long time before he answered, in a wary voice.

I told him I was in Parma, and could we meet later in the day or the next morning? He hesitated and said: "I'd prefer it if we met in the morning. Can you come to the village?"

"Yes, of course. Is it very far from Parma?"

"No, it's only a few kilometers, a small place called Certosino. Call me once you are at the village and I will tell you how to get to the farm."

I spent the rest of the afternoon walking through the beautiful streets of Parma and doing some shopping. In the evening I treated myself to a nice trattoria, as there was no opera on. The trattoria I had chosen was just across the square. I had left Dulce in the hotel after feeding her.

Going back, the square was ill lit and very empty, surrounded by impressive deserted buildings. I crossed it in a hurry, wondering if the footsteps I heard behind me were coming nearer too fast. Once I was back in my room, holding Dulce in my arms, I realized my heart was beating wildly.

This couldn't go on: I needed answers and an end to this business.

CHAPTER XIV

The appointment with Giuseppe di Natale was at 10 the next morning. I decided to have breakfast and check out, so that I could drive back to Switzerland directly after the meeting.

It took me less than quarter of an hour to get to the tiny village of Certosino. I called di Natale, who gave me instructions to reach his house.

It was a farm, set in the middle of fields. It looked totally isolated, and you could see anyone arriving from miles away. As I approached, I could see someone waiting for me. He signaled me to drive into the farm's courtyard.

I parked and got out of the car, followed by Dulce. Giuseppe di Natale was waiting for me, keenly watching. He was a short, powerful man, with a weathered face and small, inquisitive eyes. He shook my hand and bent down to pat Dulce, who greeted him with a small friendly woof.

Di Natale invited me into the farm. We went to the kitchen and he offered me some coffee. I noticed he looked carefully outside, to see if there were other cars.

I told him: "Mr. di Natale, I've become involved in a story which doesn't concern me. But I've been threatened, I'm scared and I want to get to the bottom of it. Will you help me?" He creased his eyes: "What happened to you and what is it you want exactly?

He was sitting with his elbows on the table, watching me. Giuseppe had the weather beaten face of a man who had worked outdoors all his life and an intelligent expression.

I told him my story, a short version, without all the details he didn't need.

He sighed and ran a hand across his mouth: "I think you are dealing with very dangerous people. Mrs. de Brousse was sure that they had killed Miss Rivière."

"Can you tell me more? What happened exactly?"

"I'd been working for the de Brousses for more than thirty years: in fact, ever since they bought the house. I had an excellent relationship with Mrs. Alice: she loved her gardens and spent a lot of time discussing with me, giving me instructions, exchanging ideas. Sometimes she invited me into the house for tea and once or twice even for dinner. I think I had become more of a friend for her than just a gardener, just as her nurse Caroline had become very close to her. We were the people who shared her life the most, after all.

At some point, she got involved with this Foundation outfit and she spent less time in the garden. In the beginning, she seemed elated, she was happy to help them, she felt useful. Caroline and she got into arguments about it. Then, when poor Caroline had her car accident, another nurse came in. A very unpleasant woman. Mrs. de Brousse changed. She was having fights with her secretary: Florence almost quit.

Then, one day, Mrs. Alice called Anny and me into her office, upstairs. She asked us to witness the signing of her will. It was about one week later that Florence died. The day after her death, Mrs. Alice called me in her office. She gave me a very large amount in cash, the equivalent of five years' salary. She told me to leave immediately, to go back to Italy."

He had his head lowered while he told me this and now he looked up at me, with fear in his eyes. "She told me to leave immediately, not to pack my stuff, to do it later, much later, once she had been dead for some time. She knew she had not much time left. She said to me "Giuseppe, I'm sure these people are behind Florence's death. It's because of the will, and I don't want you to be in danger. So you have to leave, now.""

I asked him: "Do you know in whose favor the will was written? Was it in favor of the Foundation?" He shook his head: "I don't know. She asked us to witness her signing it and then to sign below: but she had covered the writing. I didn't ask her: it wasn't my place. Then we left to go back to work. She was…she looked both furious and frightened. I've never seen her like that. While we were signing, there was a knock at the door: it was her nurse. Mrs. Alice asked her to wait, that she was busy: we finished the signing very quickly and we left through the other door. When, after Miss Rivière's death, she told me to leave, she told me it was for my own safety, that maybe my life depended on it. I trusted Mrs. Alice totally; I didn't hesitate for one second. I went home and packed what I could and drove to Italy."

There was a silence and I saw his eyes filling with tears: "It was the last time I saw her, poor Mrs. Alice."

I asked him a question I'd been asking myself several times: "Giuseppe, do you think Mrs. de Brousse might have been killed? I know you weren't there when she died, but…"

He shook his head: "As you say, I wasn't there. But I'm pretty sure she died of natural causes. We all knew she had cancer at a very advanced stage and she could die any time. The last time I saw her, she looked very tired and somehow…close to death."

It confirmed what everyone had told me. I asked him about Florence Rivière's death. After all, his assistant had been the one who found her.

"Giuseppe, did you see her in the water?"

"Yes I did. And I can tell you one thing: if you slip on a mossy stone, you fall on your butt. You might hit the back of your head. But I really don't see how she could hit the side of her head and fall face down. Just tell me how it could happen, and then I might believe it was an accident."

"Did you tell that to the police?"

"I only saw them once: I arrived just after them at the house. They only asked me when I'd seen her last and let me go. The next day I left for Italy. But I followed the investigation on the Internet, with my son's help. I was flabbergasted when they said it was an accident. And I can understand her sister's questions. On the other hand…"

His voice trailed off and the fear was back in his eyes: "Look: someone killed her sister. Mrs. Alice said so and I'm sure she was right. Even if she hadn't said it, I saw the body. I've taken a fall or two on these bloody stones myself." He smiled with a kind of sad humor: "It was Mrs. Alice who insisted on keeping the lakeshore rocks mossy. She said it looked more romantic. I don't know about romantic, but it was dangerous. Still, the most that could happen to you was to fall on your bottom."

I said: "Giuseppe, Mrs. de Brousse sent you away for your own safety: why didn't she do the same for Anny, if this was related to the will you witnessed?"

Giuseppe grinned: "Have you met Anny?" I nodded "Well, you don't need more explanations. Anny is a nice girl, but" He made a sign with his finger near his temple: "she's not all there. I suppose if someone asked her if she had witnessed a will she would just look at you with those empty eyes of hers!" I had to laugh: the description was pretty accurate. I added: "Yes, I suppose you're right."

Giuseppe sighed: "You know, I was sure this whole thing wasn't over and that someday someone would come to ask me questions. But I rather thought it would be the police, not..."

Again his voice trailed off as he looked at me: I saw myself in his eyes, a plump and fresh faced brunette in a pink t-shirt and jean shorts. I shrugged: "I didn't ask to be involved in this. But I am, and I'm going to get to the bottom of this. From what you told me, I think the will you witnessed may have changed the beneficiary from the Foundation to someone else: I think Mrs. Alice might have hidden it in the papers they're trying to get their hands on."

I sighed: "Giuseppe, are you sure you don't know in whose favor the will was? She didn't give you a hint?"

"No, absolutely not. But I can tell you one thing I'm sure of: during the last weeks I was there, Mrs. Alice was under great pressure. She hardly ever came down to the garden, which she loved to do in the past: and there were practically no visitors at the house."

I thought for a moment and asked: "When did the change happen?" He turned his cup in his hands and reflected: "Well, I would say there were two periods. First, when she met this person, from the Foundation...I don't remember his name, but she made him visit the garden and she introduced me to him." I interrupted him: "Was this a tall, dark man, whose name is Damien?"

Giuseppe exclaimed: "Yes, that's the name and the man! He wasn't very interested in the garden and kept on talking to her all the time. During that first period, she was very happy, chatted with me all the time about the churches and temples and whatnot the Foundation was going to build with her money. I kept my peace, because it was not my place to comment on it, but I thought it was all very...silly." He sighed.

"Then, about a year later, she suddenly changed. She didn't talk about the Foundation any more and she was preoccupied. I put it down to the evolution of her health. She told me she didn't think she had more than a year to live. But, thinking back, I wonder if it wasn't something to do with the Foundation that had changed. I wanted to talk about it with Miss Rivière…but she was always very standoffish…kept to herself and wouldn't talk with "the help". And then, a few weeks later, Mrs. Alice made her will and asked me to leave, after Florence was found dead."

I reflected about what he had told me: it looked as though the new will had resulted from a change of heart towards the Foundation. Had Mrs. de Brousse found out something that had changed her attitude towards the Foundation? But what and when? I could try to find out the "when": "Giuseppe, do you remember when Mrs. de Brousse changed and stopped talking about the Foundation? More or less?"

"It must have been at the end of October: I had just planted the tulips and I remember it struck me that she wasn't mentioning the Foundation's building works at all."

We sat for a moment, lost in our thoughts. I was wondering if this will was the one that had been executed or another one. If it was a different one, in favor of Etienne de Brousse, for example, it made sense for the Foundation to try to get its hands on it before someone found it and invalidated the first one.

I didn't know what would happen if a post dated will were found now? I had to ask my lawyer friends. But Giuseppe didn't know in whose favor it was. It might very well have reinforced the first will and left everything to the Foundation. Or to someone totally different.

It was a complex problem and Giuseppe had given me all the help he could. I thanked him and asked him if he needed anything from

Switzerland. He smiled: "I never thought I'd miss Switzerland, I had been talking about returning to Italy for so long...But now, strangely enough, I miss it. I hope, if you manage to put an end to this story, that I will be able to go back as a visitor."

I smiled: "Well, I can understand you would miss a country where you spent all your life!" I rose to leave and Giuseppe followed me to my car, saying: "You know, I feel guilty. When Mrs. Alice told me to leave, for my own safety, I just did what she told me. I didn't think twice, I just went. But maybe I should have stayed near her, if she was in trouble."

I took his hand in mine: "Giuseppe, you did right. Mrs. de Brousse, from what I can see, was a very smart woman. If she told you to leave it was to protect you. If she had thought you could help her, I'm sure she would have asked."

He shrugged and said: "Maybe. In any case, Miss Tate, please be careful. There is someone very unscrupulous out there."

"I know. And I'm going to make sure they won't be a menace anymore: to you, to me, or to anyone else."

CHAPTER XV

During the drive back to Switzerland I wondered how I could find out the date on the will that had been executed. I couldn't just walk up to Etienne and ask him: he would find it strange, to say the least. Then I remembered that wills are public in Switzerland and that I could ask to see it. There was a bit of procedure involved but it could be done. I took out my iPhone and called Francis: by luck, he was in Geneva. I asked him to do me a favor and find the date of the will.

He asked me if I wanted to see it and I said no, that I just needed the date. He said he'd get back to me within an hour.

It took him less than that and he gave me the information. It was dated as of April, about ten months before the one Giuseppe and Anny had witnessed.

There was no doubt in my mind now: whoever was after these papers was after the later will.

What I couldn't understand was why hadn't Mrs. de Brousse simply called her notary? Why the need for secrecy? She could simply have given it to her secretary to take to the notary.

I wondered: was that why Florence Rivière had been killed? Did she have the will with her at the time of her death? Obviously not, or whoever killed her would have found it. Why had that will been hidden? It didn't make sense. Whatever influence the Foundation had on Alice de Brousse, if she decided to change her will, they couldn't prevent it.

What if the will favored someone else, someone who knew it and was desperate to get his or her hands on it? For example Etienne. But in that case, wouldn't he just go looking for it? There was no need for violence. If he knew there was a will in his favor somewhere in the papers his aunt had given to Denise, why not simply ask? Denise would never have denied him access to the wallpapers and nor would anyone else. If he had come to my shop asking to see Mrs. Kübler's paintings and explained why, of course I would have let him look at them. As would most people, I guess. Besides, he complained he lived on a "small annuity", but I was sure he could have afforded to buy all the works of that specific exhibition.

The most obvious solution was that Alice de Brousse had had a change of heart concerning the Foundation and decided to make a new will. For some reason, she hadn't deposited it with her notary: maybe she wasn't quite sure about what she wanted to do? At any rate, the Foundation must have been aware of its existence and had been trying by all means to get it back.

I stopped for lunch somewhere on the autostrada: because of Italy's strict rules regarding pets, Dulce and I ate our sandwiches outside. It was nice in the sun and I watched Dulce enjoy a run in the grass. When she came back, I took her on my lap and held her close to me, digging my nose in her fur. I wished she had some ideas to give me.

I had no way of getting the missing picture back: and it looked more and more likely that it was the one that contained the will…if that was what they were looking for. And if Denise had not simply thrown it away, without realizing what it was. I wouldn't put I beyond her not to read the paper. On the other hand, I doubted she would ever throw anything out. At all.

But I could try to find out in whose favor this will had been made: something had triggered the making of this new will. I had to find out what. And the answer was probably at Clair-Chant. I had to go back there. It was just a matter of calling the house when I got back to Geneva.

The temperature had abated slightly since I had left the previous day. I stopped at Felicia's first, to leave my stuff and rest a bit. Then I drove the car back to leave it at the station. I had the windows of the car open and Dulce's ears were pricked up. She watched with interest the crowds on the Mont-Blanc bridge and then on the quays. In a couple of weeks there would be the famous "Fêtes de Genève", with fireworks and all kinds of events. This attracted the middleeastern tourists in droves and they had already started arriving. Geneva is centered around its lake and the pretty quays, with their colorful patches of flowers and grass. The Jet d'Eau, Geneva's landmark fountain peaking at some 450 feet, was spouting straight up: not a good sign, as it meant no wind.

I drove to the station and decided to walk back home, at least part of the way. Dulce would enjoy it and it would do me good. It was a brisk half hour walk and by the time we reached our destination, we both had our tongues out!

Felicia was home and glad to see us. We decided to make ourselves a light and cool meal and I took out the Parma ham and cheese I'd brought back. We tossed a salad of greens and tomatoes and added some chunks of parma cheese. On the side we made some crostini, with fresh tomato and basil, topped with thin slices of Parmesan cheese and a trickle of olive oil. It was a delicious meal.

I told Felicia about my trip and its results. She agreed with my analysis of the situation and warned me again about taking on very dangerous people. I shrugged and mumbled through a large bite of crostino:

"I totally agree with you, Felicia. But what am I supposed to do?

They said they'd be back until I found the damned picture and I have absolutely no way of locating it. I'm not going to go back to New York and just stay there, a sitting duck! If I can find more about this will, maybe I can do something about it...At least, have sufficient grounds to call the police."

Felicia wiped the bottom of her plate with a piece of bread and licked her fingers.

"You have a point there. So what do you propose to do?"

"I called the house yesterday and told Anny I would be back in the morning to look through the last two boxes of pictures. I'll see if I can be alone in Mrs. de Brousse's boudoir for a moment and try to find a clue about the will."

Felicia shrugged and didn't comment: she didn't have to. I could see from her body language that she disapproved.

I thought I should call Sylvie, if only to tell her I was back. I didn't have anything positive to tell her. But I was able to tell her that Giuseppe, at least, had not believed in the thesis of the accident, and that most probably Mrs. de Brousse hadn't either and that was why she had sent Giuseppe away.

She was excited about what I told her and once again asked how she could help. I told her that the best thing for the moment was to stay put. I asked her if she had the impression she was being watched or followed. There was a silence on the other end and she said: "Um...no. I don't think so. But to tell you the truth, I haven't paid much attention. I'll be more careful in the future."

I hung up, sighing: Sylvie was the type of girl who would notice a man looking at her in a crowd of hundreds...but who wouldn't notice a woman if she stuck to her like scotchtape.

***

The next morning I left quite early for Clair-Chant. At the back of my mind was the small hope that if I got there early enough I'd see Etienne.

I was right: he was preparing to go out to a business meeting when I arrived and was clearly happy to see me. He looked at his watch and told me he'd be out for a couple of hours, and why didn't I have lunch with him?

Being the polite girl I am, I tried to invite him out myself, but he laughed and said we'd do that another day. I took advantage of his presence to ask him to tell Anny I wouldn't need her all the time. I made up the excuse I felt I was making her waste her time, while hinting that I would work faster if she weren't there. Etienne smiled and said he understood. He gave Anny instructions to let me work alone in the boudoir.

Anny took me upstairs and after bringing me a tray with a pot of tea, returned to whatever her mysterious duties were. I made sure she had left and the door was closed, to begin looking through the old lady's desk.

I had noticed a diary on the desk the last time and indeed, there it was. It was a heavy leatherbound affair, which covered the last year. I looked at the entries, hoping to find some clues to Mrs. de Brousse's state of mind. Unfortunately, all she wrote in her diary were appointments, small reminders, birthdays, etc. There wasn't a single personal note or anything that could give a hint as to how she felt at any given time.

I thought back to what Giuseppe had said about her change of attitude towards the Foundation: it had happened at the end of October. Maybe I could find out whom she had been seeing at the time?

In order to do that, I had to find the previous year's diary. It wasn't easy and it took me the best part of an hour. I kept on pricking up my ears, expecting someone to come in and to have to justify what I was doing, rooting through Mrs. de Brousse's personal papers instead of her photographs.

I finally managed to locate the old diarys and took out the last one.

As I flipped through the pages looking for the month of October, I glanced at the previous months. It made for interesting reading, as most of the appointments were with Damien. The man had been coming to see her on a regular basis, at least once a week, sometimes more often.

I noticed that the more she saw him, the less she saw other people. Little by little, he had isolated her, becoming the focal point of her life. I shuddered, and read on. It wasn't too difficult to find out who she had seen in October and November. Apart from Damien and other meetings which were obviously related to the Foundation, she had only had three appointments.

Taking out my phone, I noted the names. I thought the most likely ones were a couple, who had been invited to dinner at the house on the 23rd of October. The other names where apparently two ladies who had come to tea, one in November and one in December.

I took advantage of that morning to go through all the papers I could get my hands on. I didn't think Etienne would mind. On the other hand, I thought it was pretty much pointless, as the Foundation women had already been there and had probably been very thorough in their research.

What I did find out, though, was that Alice de Brousse had effectively taken over the management of the de Brousse company, albeit from Geneva. There were notes and reports, a whole wall of business papers. I looked quickly through the yearend reports: from the time her husband had died to the time Etienne had been named CEO, Alice had managed to bring back the company from the brink of bankruptcy. During the years Etienne had been there, the company had been making slow but regular progress.

What it added up to, in my eyes, was that Alice de Brousse was not just a dithering old lady, a bit gaga and with no idea about money. She was a smart businesswoman, and that made it stranger that she would be taken in by a guy like Damien. But then, Damien was a smooth operator. He must have found her weak spot and exploited it.

I did spend about one hour looking through more photographs, to justify my presence there. Now I was looking at them with different eyes, trying to read in this handsome woman's eyes how she could have fallen prey to the FLC:

It was another sweltering day in Geneva and I was very glad I was at the house. Clair-Chant was surrounded and protected by trees and the lake brought in some cool air. I had all the windows looking out on the lake open, to try to catch a little bit of breeze. Dulce had chosen a spot in the sun and had stretched out, enjoying the combination of warmth and light breeze on her fur.

While I looked through papers and pictures, she occasionally got up to sniff around, sneezing from time to time when there was dust. I had brought her water and food bowls with me, and she occasionally went to have a small drink. She had been extremely quiet and well behaved.

So I was very surprised when, all of a sudden, my smooth longhaired doxie became a small porcupine. All the hair on her back were raised and her muzzle was contorted in a ferocious growl. She rushed to the door, barking furiously.

"Alex! Come quickly! It's the guy! The same guy! Quick!"

I ran up to her and swept her in my arms, opening the door to see what had made her so furious. I hadn't been quick enough, as I saw a man's silhouette walking off down the corridor. He didn't turn around when he heard the door open and Dulce's barking become louder. He disappeared down the stairs. Dulce was squirming in my arms, desperately trying to jump down and go and take a bite out of him. I was mystified: why would my peaceful little dog get in such a state with a perfect stranger? The only other person I'd seen her being hostile with had been Damien, and that was definitely not him.

I calmed her down and resumed my search, looking at the time: Etienne should be back shortly. I left Dulce on her blanket, asking her to behave, and went to the bathroom I'd been shown by Anny.

It was down the corridor, on the other side of the stairwell. I went past three doors on the way. In one of the rooms I saw one of the Foundation women, with her signature grey veil. She didn't look up when I went by, busy shining some silver.

In the bathroom, I took out my war paint: I wanted to look perfect for lunch with Etienne. I took out some make-up and after five minutes gave up, sighing: no amount of make up could make my round face oval, or give my chubby face gaunt and elegant cheekbones. It could add some color to my pale face though, and sparkle to my brown eyes, which had often been characterized as "mischievious" by nice people who liked me.

I gave my glossy brown hair a good brushing and walked back to the boudoir, just in time, as five minutes later I heard someone walking down the corridor and knock on the door.

It was Etienne, who peeped through the opening and asked with a wink: "Ready for some chow?" Dulce ran to welcome him, recognizing a friendly face. She was thoroughly scratched and belly rubbed and enjoyed it very much. I commented: "She likes you".

Etienne laughed as we went down the stairs, preceded by Dulce bouncing down: "All dogs love me! It's my charisma".

Once she reached the ground floor landing though, Dulce stopped to sniff at some trail and instantly began to growl again. She must have picked up the scent of the man I'd seen earlier. I told Etienne: "She obviously likes you, but there is someone in this house she seems pretty hostile to: there was a man upstairs, earlier today and I'm sure if he had come closer she would have bitten him. Which is totally unlike her. I've never seen her behaving like this."

Etienne pulled back my chair at the table and replied: "That must be the guy the Foundation sent to fix the plumbing. He's been around for a couple of days. No wonder Dulce doesn't like him, he's one tough type."

Lunch was spent talking about Paris: we compared addresses and things we liked. It was nice talking to Etienne and I tended to get lost in his blue gaze, forgetting the purpose of my visit. He asked how the photograph hunt was going and I told him I'd soon be finished.

Etienne topped off my wine glass and said, looking into my eyes in a way that made me melt: " I hope this doesn't mean I won't be seeing you again? I enjoy your company very much and I'd love to have you as a friend, here in Geneva."

Oops. How to tell him that I didn't live in Geneva? Oh well, I'd cross that bridge when I came to it. I told him I'd have to come back once or twice anyway and that I owed him a dinner sometime. He shook his head and smiled: "As you wish"

As I drowned helplessly in his aquamarine gaze, I wondered if he was hitting on me. I couldn't help looking at his handsome face, his tall, muscular frame and wondering what the hell could attract him in little me?

As lunch went on, I decided to sit back and enjoy the ride. After all, some men found me attractive, in my pleasantly plump way: so why not him?

We had coffee in the living room and after an hour or so I decided to leave. I couldn't take the man's whole day! We walked to the entrance hall and his cell phone rang. He signaled for me to wait, but I could see it was a business call and likely to last, so I just whispered to him that I was going to visit the facilities and I'd let myself out.

Still on the phone, he smiled and made a sign with his hand, meaning "See you tomorrow". I walked to the small visitor's toilet next to the corridor.

When I came out, Dulce was patiently waiting sitting next to her bag and the hall was empty. The house was strangely silent. I let myself out of the main door and bent down to put on Dulce's leash. She let out a small bark and jumped away from my hands, making me take a step forward to catch her. That was what saved me.

CHAPTER XVI

"Alex, mooooove!"

I felt a whoosh behind me and then a crash and I was spattered with earth and flowers. My heart was beating wildly as I saw the huge stone flower pot that had landed inches behind me. If Dulce hadn't run off, it would have landed right on my head. And seeing the size and the weight of it, it would have flattened me right out. I grabbed Dulce, who was shaking as hard as I was and stayed there, trying to get my wits together.

"Jeeeezz…that was a close call!"

I looked up at the façade of the house: there was an open window just above me. The stone planter was missing. There was no one in sight. I was shaking so hard that I was paralyzed. I don't know how long I stood there, until another window on the second floor opened and I heard a voice saying "What was that noise? What happened?" and I saw Etienne leaning out.

When he saw me standing there, with the huge mess of broken stone and earth and plants, he gave a shout and disappeared. Within seconds he was by my side, asking me if I was OK, running his hands along my arms to make sure I was unhurt. I had managed to get myself under control by then and told him I was OK: shaken, but OK.

He looked up at the open window: "Did you see anyone? Did you see how it happened?"

I shook my head: "No. I had to take a step forward to catch Dulce, and then felt this…thing…landing behind me. I looked up but there was no one at the window."

Etienne ran a hand through his hair: "Of course, whoever is the idiot who did this wouldn't stay to claim his clumsiness!"

I mumbled: "Clumsiness. Yeah. Maybe."

Etienne looked sharply at me: "You don't think it was an accident?"

I shrugged: "Etienne, I'm in no state to think anything. I didn't see anyone or anything. All I want right now is to go home and rest."

"Of course, I understand! Can I take you home?"

I watched him closely. It had dawned on me that he could perfectly well have been the perpetrator. The window he had leaned out from was just next door to the one the planter had fallen from. On the other hand, unless he kidnapped me and disposed of my body in the Genevese countryside, I didn't see what he could do to me during the short trip home.

I nodded wearily. He told me to wait for one second and went inside. He came out with Anny and one of the women from the Foundation, all the while shouting and demanding to know who was responsible. When Anny saw the mess, she exclaimed, putting her hands to her cheeks and saying that I could have been killed. The woman stood silently and went back inside the house, coming out a few seconds later with a broom and a big bag.

Etienne asked Anny if she had seen anything, which the young woman denied vehemently. He brought her close to tears and in the end I put a hand on his arm and said: "Let's go please, Etienne? Or let me call a taxi?"

He looked at me with a worried look: I think it must have been obvious that I could hardly keep on my feet. He took Dulce from my arms in one hand and my elbow in the other and we went to his car.

As we drove down the driveway, I looked in the back mirror. Anny was still standing there, wringing her hands. I thought that I'd never seen anyone actually doing that. Next to her, the woman in the veil was silently cleaning up the mess. The man that had upset Dulce so much was nowhere in sight.

I was silent during the drive home, cradling Dulce in my arms and taking comfort from her warm little body. Etienne asked me some questions, but I answered in monosyllables, not trusting myself to say more. He left me in front of Felicia's building and I thanked him. He asked me if I'd come back the next day. I shrugged. He didn't insist and said he'd call me later in the day to find out how I was feeling.

As soon as I got home, I put Dulce on the floor, realizing that I almost hadn't let go of her since the planter had fallen. I was hanging on to her for dear life and the sweet little dog was enduring it, calmly. I think she knew perfectly how I was feeling and knew I needed her comfort. Once she was on the floor, she trotted off to her bed and curled up with a sigh: she had had enough emotions for one day.

"Pheww...poor Alex! That was frightening, wasn't it? Thank goodness I'm here to comfort you!"

I decided to take a long, bubbly hot bath to relax and think.

The bath did relax me and my brain started to function again. The incident had absolutely terrified me. Yet, strangely enough it didn't make me change my mind. On the contrary, I was more than ever resolved to get to the bottom of this story. There was no doubt in my mind that someone had just tried to kill me. There was no way this huge stone planter could have fallen all by itself.

The problem was who had pushed it? Of course, I immediately thought about the Foundation guy: he was certainly muscular enough to do it. But so was Etienne. Or, for that matter, anyone, even Anny: the planter was very heavy, but it was on the edge of the ledge and needed only a push to come crashing down.

I blew some bubbles at Dulce who had come to inquire why I was staying in the bathtub for so long. It landed on her long doxie nose and she snorted. I asked her: "Dulce, why would anyone want to kill me? Who am I threatening?"

At that point, I had talked to quite a few people and "they" must know I was on the track of the elusive will. If it was in favor of Etienne, the Foundation would want both me and the will out of the way. If it was in favor of the Foundation, but cut out all the other heirs, then it might very well be Etienne who was anxious to eliminate the will...and me. If the will was in favor of someone totally different...

I let myself sink to the bottom of the tub: it was too complicated. I wanted to trust Etienne and I wished I could confide in him. But the truth was that I didn't totally trust him. I wasn't so confident about my charms that I thought he'd fallen for me, and his lightly flirty manner at lunch made me cagey. I found it strange that he'd decided to come closer to me just before this botched attempt to flatten me out.

But if it was Etienne, it would mean he knew about the new will. How could he, if he hadn't spoken to his aunt for at least six months? Yes, but I had only his word for it. Maybe he had had a fight with her and that was the real reason why they weren't speaking. And maybe it had gotten worse and she'd decided to cut him out completely in this new version, and told him so.

I stepped out of the tub and started drying myself. I slipped on a pair of jeans and a shirt and went outside on the balcony to dry my hair in the sun. As I ran a brush through it, I looked down at the street. My heart missed a beat: the woman I'd seen the day before was there again, across the street. I went back into the apartment, a cold sweat running down my back. This was beginning to be stressful. I had to get answers, quickly.

CHAPTER XVII

I took out the names of the couple Alice de Brousse had seen in October the previous year and found their phone number. I sat for a long time, wondering how to approach them. Then I thought I would just play it by ear and called them. It was the husband, Mr. Lombardini, who answered. I told him I was calling about a friend of theirs, Mrs. de Brousse, and would he mind seeing me a few moments.

Mr. Lombardini, from his voice, was an old gentleman. He was probably very bored and was glad for the distraction. He asked me to drop by the next morning.

Later in the afternoon, to my great surprise, I got a call from Etienne. He wanted to know if I had gotten over the shock and how I was feeling. I was a bit curt with him, but told him I was OK and would call him back.

It was a good thing Felicia had invited some friends in the evening for an impromptu pasta party. At least, with all the others chattering around me, my silence wasn't so noticeable.

When I went to bed later, I made an exception to the rule and took Dulce with me in bed. She snuggled close to me and rolled herself in a ball. In a few seconds she was asleep. Her warmth and the feeling of her soft fur under my hand gave me infinite comfort: I hated to admit it, but I was still shaken.

In the morning when I woke up, though, she was snoring softly in her small bed.

The Lombardinis lived in the area of the Eaux-Vives, not very far from Florissant. I walked down sedately, Dulce trotting happily beside me. Without having to look, I knew there was someone behind me. I was very careful each time I crossed the road and tried to avoid deserted streets and keep to the main thoroughfares.

I wasn't too worried about being seen entering the Lombardinis' building. Their name was one in thirty others and would only ring a bell with someone who had known Alice de Brousse sufficiently well to know all her friends' names.

Once in the building, and as further insurance, I took the lift two floors higher than their floor and tiptoed down two flights of stairs.

The gentleman who opened the door was still very tall and good-looking. He must have been in his eighties but his hair was still mostly dark and his green eyes sparkled with intelligence. His wife came to greet me, a placid and handsome grey haired woman with a warm smile. They both greeted Dulce with pleasure, admiring and petting her.

We sat down in the living room and I looked around. It was a good-sized apartment, especially for Geneva where space is at a premium. The furniture was excellent quality, in classic design: nothing extravagant, nothing cheap. Mrs. Lombardini had prepared a tray with coffee and sweets, and served everyone. Mr. Lombardini raised an eyebrow, urging me to begin. I hesitated.

"Mr. Lombardini, I'm very sorry to disturb you and this is a bit of an unorthodox visit and request. Of course, you are under no obligation to talk to me or to reply to my questions and…"

He frowned: "What is all this about?" I decided to cut to the chase:

"Mr. Lombardini, I have become involved in a series of incidents, some of them pretty unpleasant, having to do with Mrs. de Brousse's death and her testament. I know it's very cheeky of me to come and ask you questions, but I'm in a difficult position and I really need to have some answers. In particular, some insight into Mrs. de Brousse's last months."

He looked at me and said: "I suppose you have your reasons for not telling me more, so I won't ask. I know that the last time we saw Alice she was very upset and I suppose this has to do with it. Alice was a great lady and we will help you if we can, won't we, Carla?"

His wife, who hadn't said a word, simply nodded. He went on: "What do you want to know?"

"When was the last time you saw Alice de Brousse?"

He thought back and said: "Sometime late last year, October or November. She invited us for dinner at her house"

"Would that be on the 23rd of October?"

"Yes, I think so. Why?"

"Did anything in particular happen that evening? Was she upset about something?"

Mrs. Lombardini piped in: "Not at the beginning of the evening. She was in good spirits and we had a nice dinner. But then she asked my husband a few questions, about his work. By the time we left, I had the impression that she was furious. Not with us, but about something he had told her."

Lombardini confirmed:

"Once we had finished dinner and were sitting in the living room, she brought over some pictures of a small chapel or church that was in the process of being built. Apparently, it was in Mexico. She showed the pictures to me: it was the church at various stages of completion, until it was finished."

He took a sip of his espresso and went on: "Alice knew that I'd been a civil engineer and managed projects in Mexico. I worked until recently on Swiss projects abroad. She asked me, since I knew the country and construction costs there, how much it would take to build such a small church or chapel. I looked carefully at the photographs and gave her an estimate, with a range of about 20% give or take. She asked me three times if I was sure: she went quite red when I told her the price and I was afraid she was having a problem with her heart. We knew she could go any time. I confirmed the price and she asked if there was any possible way this building could have cost fifteen times the price I had given her to build. I said to her that, as a Swiss engineer, I tended to overprice not underprice and that unless the walls were gold plated and the church was in the center of the best area of Mexico City, the cost could not exceed more than 10% the upper quote I'd given her."

Mrs Lombardini took up the conversation: "She was furious, I could see that. She was keeping calm and courteous because we were there, and that was her education. But if it was someone else, I think she would have thrown something across the room." I asked: "Did she say anything else?" Mrs. Lombardini shook her head: "She just said "I thought so!" and then she clamped her lips and changed the conversation. Of course, we knew it had something to do with this Foundation she was mixed up in, but we did not dare ask her. She was very reserved, always, not the kind of person you can ask about her problems."

Mr. Lombardini said: "That was the last time we saw her. I told her if she needed any kind of help she could rely on me, but she didn't take me up on the offer. And later, each time we tried to call her, the nurse said she was busy or not well enough to come to the phone."

I asked them: "Did you get the impression that she was under any kind of pressure or duress?"

They thought about it and in the end it was the wife who answered:

"Now that you say it, it's obvious. I think it had something to do with her new nurse, the one that had replaced Caroline. She was always there, hovering and I could see Alice was not happy about it. After the meal she told her very harshly to leave us alone. That's when Alice showed the pictures to Mauro."

Mauro Lombardini looked hesitantly at me and then at his wife: "Do you think we should have insisted? Tried to help her? Was she in trouble?"

I sighed: "I think she was, yes: but it seems she didn't want to get anyone else involved, because the people she was dealing with are extremely dangerous. So no matter how much you would have insisted she would never have accepted your help. Don't feel guilty."

Mrs. Lombardini was stroking Dulce. She said: "I hope you and your wonderful little dog won't get in trouble."

I got up and ran a hand through my hair: "I'm afraid that's already the case!" I thanked them both for their hospitality and for having the kindness to reply to my questions. They were obviously curious to know more, but were wise enough not to ask.

CHAPTER XVIII

When I came out of their building, I walked down to the lake: the street they lived on ended on the lakeside. There were quite a lot of people strolling along the quays. I stopped to buy an ice cream and a bottle of water. I took them to a bench and sat down, giving Dulce some water in the little plastic bowl I always carry with me. I sat for a moment looking at the Jet d'Eau and eating my ice cream.

It looked more and more as if Alice de Brousse had had a change of heart regarding the Foundation. At any rate, all the evidence pointed that way. It looked like she'd discovered that a large part of the money the members gave to the Foundation was overspent. This was probably the reason which had made her change her will, so the chances were that the new one was made either in favor of Etienne, or some other person or institution.

Either way, I would think Etienne had nothing to lose if a new will was found. On the other hand, the Foundation would be desperate to get its hands on it and destroy it. That version made much more sense.

I gave Dulce the tiny tip of my waffle cone, which she seemed to enjoy very much. There was a slight breeze on the lakeside and the Jet d'Eau was blowing eastwards. We were close enough to get a few droplets from time to time. I looked at the Jet d'Eau dispassionately: it always amazed me that a city as rich as Geneva would have, as its main landmark, a simple water fountain. It said something about the city and its inhabitants, but I didn't know what...

Dulce woofed: she was fed up of sitting down and knew there was no more biscuit forthcoming.

"Come on, Alex: let's go! We've been sitting here long enough!"

I got up with a sigh and we began the long uphill walk back home.

While I walked, I tried to get my thoughts together: I was now pretty sure of my scenario: there were still some unanswered questions. Such as why hadn't Mrs. de Brousse entrusted her will to a notary or the local courts? And above all, how would anyone be able to get back the missing will, since it was probably hanging in some New Yorker's living room?

One thing was certain, though, I had to talk to Etienne. Even if I wasn't a hundred percent sure that he wasn't involved in the attempt to kill me - or at least flatten me out... at the house, it seemed pretty unlikely. And after all, he was the main person to be concerned by a new will.

I decided to go and visit him in the afternoon. As it was, I didn't need to call him, as he called again to find out how I was. I told him I'd drop by later on and that I had some things to tell him. He said he'd be busy until late: he suggested that I come around seven, if I had some boxes to look through, and that we could go out to dinner afterwards.

Being in the house alone without him wasn't something I relished, but I thought that if Anny was around and stayed with me, it would be ok. And I did want to look at Mrs. de Brousse's later diaries to see if I could find out more. So I agreed and told him I'd be at the house around seven.

Next was operation "get ready for an evening out with a gorgeous man – who might, or might not have tried to kill you". It was complicated: I didn't want to look as though I was making a big effort for him, but I didn't want to seem too casual either. Finally I decided to wear white jeans which set off the best part of my anatomy, a nice rounded butt. I wore a dark tunic in shades of turquoise and navy over it, and some high platform shoes which would make me look taller without cutting my feet in small pieces.

If only I had a suntan! But how was I supposed to get a tan, when I spent my time chasing a vanished will and being shadowed by villains. Which reminded me that since the planter affair, I hadn't seen my follower anymore. Maybe she had been replaced by someone more skilled and more discreet.

I decided to leave Dulce at home: whatever the evening developed into - and there were quite a few possibilities, very different from each other - I thought I would feel more at ease if I knew she was safely at home. I fed her and left a note for Felicia, telling her I was invited to dinner.

When I arrived at Clair-Chant I felt some anxiety. It was Anny who answered the bell and opened. I walked through the park to the main entrance. It was very quiet inside the gates, and it always came as a surprise after the incessant noise of the national road just outside. Despite myself I was shivering, with the uncanny feeling that someone was watching me.

When I arrived at the door, I stepped quickly under the graceful awning, remembering the last time I'd stood under the windows. I had noticed when I walked up to the building that the stone planter had not been replaced.

Anny opened the door and let me in. I watched her as I followed her upstairs. She was a tall girl, with medium long brown hair caught in a ponytail. She was neatly dressed as always in black pants and a white shirt. Her long face was plain, not quite ugly but just plain. Her deep set eyes were just a little bit too small, her nostrils too flared. She had a mouth that was long but not sensual, a heavy, masculine jaw and lackluster skin. There was the shadow of a moustache on her upper lip. A bit of make-up and a nice haircut could have done something for her. But no makeup on earth could give her face an expression of intelligence.

She asked me if I wanted to drink something. I knew she was slow, so I asked her for some tea. She would have to boil some water and that would give me time to riffle through the diaries.

As soon as she left to go downstairs I looked for this year's diary. I did not find anything interesting in the weeks following the Lombardini's visit.

Anny was back much faster than I had thought, and she caught me reading the diary. She did not make any comment and nor did I. I simply put it down and went back to sorting photographs.

Twice during the session I saw a silhouette go by the doorway. I was glad Anny was with me. I asked her if they had found out how the flower planter had fallen. She looked at me with blank eyes and said that no, no one had seen it fall.

I heard Etienne arriving, and a few minutes later he came into the boudoir. He suggested we have a drink before leaving. We went down to the living room and Anny brought us a couple of sherries and some nuts.

Etienne said he needed a little bit of time to catch his breath and relax before we left. He'd had a tough day, discussing with potential investors for his venture. I repeated to him what Anny had said about not finding the person who had pushed the planter. He frowned and said he'd interrogated every one who was in the house at the time and no one had owned up.

I decided to drop the subject and asked him where we would be going to eat. He asked Anny to bring him a glass of water and said: "I thought we could go up to the Salève, There's a new restaurant there which got some good reviews."

"That's a great idea. It's a long time since I haven't been up there!"

The Salève is Geneva's mountain. It's a big chunk of rough stone, with large white wounds on its side where there are quarries and a great view of Geneva from the top. Although it is situated in France, the Genevese consider it as their mountain.

We finished our drinks and Etienne went upstairs to change into more casual clothes. He had been wearing a dark suit which looked beautiful on him, but I had to say he looked equally handsome in dark jeans and an open necked blue cotton shirt.

I sighed as I watched him: I had the niggling feeling I was falling in love.

As we went out I involuntarily stepped forward a bit faster and he laughed. He took my arm and we went to the garage, where his car was parked next to the small red one and two other non-descript grey cars.

We arrived at the foot of the mountain when the sun was beginning to go down. Etienne was a good driver and he went relatively fast in the hairpin curves. Here there was hardly any traffic, we met three or four cars coming up and I didn't see any in front of us. I was mulling about what to tell Etienne. There was still a tiny doubt in my mind concerning him. I didn't know just how soon I was to have an answer to that.

CHAPTER XIX

It all happened very fast and all I could do was hang onto my seat for dear life.

Just as we were arriving at one of the most dangerous curves of the road, a large SUV came barreling up behind us and crashed into our small sports car from behind. The impact pushed us over the edge. For one short second, I saw the void opening under us. And then in a desperate effort to avoid hurtling down, Etienne turned the wheel and sent us crashing into a fir tree. The car was halted by the tree and settled on the slope just below the road.

After the noise of the crash there was a prolonged silence, as Etienne and I came to terms with what had just happened. He put his head on the wheel and I tried to stop trembling.

We heard a car stop on the road above us and voices exclaiming, asking if we were alright. Etienne finally raised his head and looked at me: "Are you hurt?"

I checked myself mentally: "No, I'm OK. What about you?" He shook his head and began trying to open his door. He managed to get out and came round to help me out. But the car had landed on the side and my door was completely blocked by the tree against which it was resting. I scrambled over to the driver's side and made it out of the car safely.

There was now a small crowd on the road and someone shouted that they had called the police and an ambulance. It was rough going climbing up the slope back to the road. Since I wasn't exactly fit and despite Etienne's help, by the time I made it up I was completely out of breath.

The police was arriving and the ambulance followed not far behind.

It was Etienne, of course, who talked to the police: he told them that he'd been driving normally, going up, when a car had come at full speed from behind and pushed us off the road. That set the police on their toes. They asked us the brand of the car, its color, any details we could remember.

We both gave them as much information as we could, but it wasn't all that much. We had both seen a grey SUV and that was all. Neither of us had seen the driver, or the plates.

One of the policemen who had been looking at the tracks on the road came back and said: "There are tire marks a bit higher up on the road: it looks as though he did an about turn just after the accident."

The policeman in charge told us that he was putting out an APB on any suspicious grey SUV. We all knew it was perfectly useless, as there were so many vehicles of that description in the region.

Someone in the crowd piped up. It was a man who had been driving behind us and had stopped when he saw the accident. He said: "I saw a car like that coming down: just before I arrived here! It was speeding down so fast it almost missed the next curve."

The gendarme asked him whether he'd seen the driver. The man shook his head: "Not very well: but I'm sure it was a man, light skinned and with blond hair. He was really speeding."

Etienne was answering questions from the gendarme and the paramedics came to me. They asked me a few questions, checked my pulse and various other things. They said that seeing the violence of the shock, we should both go to the hospital to get checked out. Looking down at the license plates of the car they said that they could take us to a hospital in Switzerland if we preferred.

Etienne looked at me and I nodded. Once the gendarmes had finished taking down our particulars, we got into the ambulance. It took us to Geneva's hospital, the HUG: I wasn't too happy about it, as the emergency unit was always crowded. I knew we were in for at least two hours of waiting.

Once we were in the waiting room, I stopped Etienne, who had been talking non-stop and insulting the driver who had almost killed us. I was getting a headache. During the drive down in the ambulance, I had had time to think about the one thing I had learned: that Etienne was in the clear.

Now I had to tell him everything: I had put his life in danger and he needed to know why.

We were sitting on the blue plastic chairs of the waiting room. No one paid much attention to us and from time to time someone was brought in, in more or less bad condition. I went over to get us some warm drinks from the vending machine and came back to sit next to him.

I sighed: "Etienne, I haven't been quite honest with you. There is something I need to tell you."

He looked at me warily: after the accident, he must have wondered what was coming. I ran a hand through my disheveled hair and went on:

"I'm not gathering material for Edouard Kübler. I'm trying to find out something that has to do with your aunt Alice, and more specifically, I think, with another will she made after the one that was executed"

Etienne exclaimed: "What! Why? Who are you?"

"I was born in Switzerland, but I currently live in New York, where I own an art gallery. Some time ago, I organized an exhibition of works by Denise Kübler. I sold four of them. About a month ago, someone broke into my gallery. They stole all of Denise's pictures, as well as some other

147

paintings. Then, the next day, the gallery was broken into, again. This time they took three or four remaining paintings and they also stole my sales book. I didn't really make much of it, until the very next day someone broke into my upstairs neighbor's apartment. Unfortunately she was there and they knocked her out. She had to be taken to the hospital, and this is when I took in her dog, Dulce. The old lady was not only my upstairs neighbor from the gallery, she was also a customer and had bought two paintings by Denise Kübler."

I had Etienne's full attention now. He leaned forward to listen better. I went on.

"Those were stolen, as well as some other non-figurative art she had in her home. It crossed my mind at the time that it was a strange coincidence, especially since I had learned in the meantime that Denise Kübler had been killed during a break-in at her workshop near Gruyères. I realized something was going on around her pictures. So I tried to locate the two other ones I had sold. One of them will be impossible to find: I sold it in cash to a customer I don't know. I managed to track the other buyer, through his credit card: he told me he'd had a burglary at his house and the painting by Denise was one of the things that had been stolen."

Etienne whistled: "Wow."

I nodded: "Wow it is. Especially since the next day a man threatened me. He cornered me in the evening in the back alley, when I was taking out the garbage. He wanted the last picture. I told him that I had no way of finding it. He answered that they would be back until I found it. So I decided to come here to get away from them and to find some answers."

Someone was called into the emergency room: there were still several people ahead of us. I took a sip of my hot chocolate, which seemed to be made of hot water and half a spoonful of chocolate and sugar.

"When I got here, I went to see Edouard Kübler, Denise's husband. He told me he had always found this burglary very strange. We looked through Denise's workshop and we deducted that what the criminals are after is a bunch of wallpaper rolls that your aunt gave to Denise. And which she used in her pictures."

Etienne frowned: "Why? Why would anyone want them?"

"I think that your aunt may have hidden a new will in one of these rolls."

"What?!!!" Etienne almost jumped from his seat. He exclaimed: "In whose favor?"

I had to tell him that, unfortunately I didn't know. I told him about my visit to Sylvie and her certainty that her sister had not died in an accident. Then I told him about my visit to Damien in Paris. His eyes widened as he said: "You actually went to see that creep?"

With a deep I sigh I confirmed that, yes, I'd been to see Mr. Damien in his offices, pretending to be a rich widow. Etienne burst out laughing and then winced, putting his hand to his ribs.

"Ouch: I think I must have hit the wheel during the accident. That was very gutsy of you to go into the monster's lair!"

I looked at him curiously: "Would you call him a monster? I think he's just a despicable crook."

Etienne laughed again, holding his side. He bent down to kiss my cheek: "I love you, Alex!"

My heart did a triple somersault: he loved me! Of course the elation lasted only for a second, as I realized the jocular tone of his remark. Etienne asked: "What happened there?"

I shrugged: "Nothing much, really. But I wanted to get an idea of who I was against. After I'd been there, I decided to try to talk to Giuseppe, the vanishing gardener."

Etienne exclaimed: "Giuseppe? You managed to find Giuseppe? How is he? I used to spend hours with him and aunt Alice in the garden when I was a kid!"

"He's OK: he was asked by your aunt to witness her signing a new will. Him and Anny. When Florence Rivière, your aunt's secretary, was killed in that so-called accident, your aunt sent Giuseppe away the next day, telling him it was for his own safety. She gave him a sizeable sum of money and told him to disappear."

"So there is proof that there was another will made after the one that's been executed?"

"I guess so, although I'm pretty sure it's not much use if you can't get hold of the will itself."

"Did Giuseppe know or suspect in whose favor it was? Or where it was hidden?"

"No: your aunt hid the contents of the will when they signed. And he couldn't tell me more. The chances are that Florence knew where it was and its existence and that she got killed for that reason. I suppose she was meant to take it to the notary or deposit it at the bank, but got murdered before she managed to. And so your aunt smuggled it out in the wallpapers she gave to Denise, hoping her friend would give it to the new rightful heir."

I added: "I would think she made the new testament in your favor. At any rate, it looks like at some point she became disillusioned with the FLC."

Etienne frowned: "Really? How do you know that?" I told him about my visit to the Lombardinis.

"I think the Foundation must be cooking its books: I don't know why, but it appears they are vastly overpricing their building works. Maybe someone is siphoning off the money...I don't know. At any rate, she was very angry and my guess is that the new will she made a few days later was in someone else's favor."

Etienne was funny to watch: he looked like a parched flower that's been given water. He was, literally, blooming under my eyes. I saw that I'd given him an immense new hope and I felt I had to make some reservations.

"Look, Etienne: I'm at least 80% sure that your aunt's new will was not in favor of the Foundation. But there is no way to tell in whose favor it was. As far as we know, the new will could cut you out completely. In fact, I wasn't too sure about you...until today's accident. I wasn't sure you weren't behind the planter thing..."

His eyes widened: "Of course! I'd forgotten about that! It's the second time they've tried to kill you!" He mulled on what I'd told him: "I can understand you'd suspect me. You don't know me, and as you say, I could also be after that will to destroy it. But how would I have known about it?"

I shrugged: "I only know that you weren't talking to your aunt because you told me so. For all I knew, you might have talked to her and had a fight, and she might have told you she was making a new will that cut you out completely. Of course, after today, it all seems absurd."

Etienne ran a hand through his hair: "We have to notify the police. That's the second attempt on your life."

"Do as you wish: but as far as I'm concerned, I don't think the police will either believe us or help us. And it would mean a huge waste of time, I 'm sure"

"I understand what you say, but what are you suggesting to do now?"

I sighed: "I don't know Etienne: I'm stumped. I think I know what they're looking for, but no one can find it. Unless the person who bought the last painting suddenly shows up at my gallery brandishing the will and asking who to give it to…I don't know what to do."

"You're sure you can't find this customer?" I shook my head: "No. I'd never seen him before and he paid in cash. I don't even know whether he was a local or a tourist. I'm sorry."

I was indeed very sorry: Etienne looked so crestfallen that I felt terrible, having given him hope and yanking it away. He sighed: "I guess that's it, then? What are you going to do now?"

I hadn't really thought about it: all my energy had been concentrated on the wallpaper chase. Now that I was pretty sure I knew what was in them and why the Foundation wanted to get them back, I had to decide what to do.

Just then our names were called by a nurse. We went up to the counter. They took each of us to different examination rooms and we were subjected to prodding, testing, pinching and scanning.

They finished with me quite quickly: the only thing wrong with me was bruising. I watched with interest as it spread minute by minute. They gave me a prescription for a salve that would accelerate the healing process and told me I could go off.

Etienne was kept a bit longer by the doctors, as he had a cracked rib. When he came out he was sporting a bandage around his middle and looked very sexy.

CHAPTER XX

What a pity I'd come into this man's world and turned it upside down. I could very well understand if he never wanted to talk to me again, after what I'd (unwittingly) done to him.

But he was as friendly as ever and asked me what I wanted to do next. I looked at the time and was amazed to see it was twenty past eleven. I told Etienne I'd take a taxi home, feeling awful that he'd lost his car because of me. I told him so and he shrugged: "Don't worry: I've got excellent insurance, because the car was brand new. I'll be able to get the model they sneakily brought out just after I'd bought mine! Let's get a taxi, and I'll drop you off on my way."

It wasn't quite on his way but not that much out of it either, so I accepted. When we arrived in front of Felicia's building, he came out to open my door.

"Alex, can I invite you for lunch tomorrow? We never did get our dinner today. In fact, I'm starving!" At these words my stomach emitted a loud growl. Etienne laughed and said: "If this wasn't Geneva, I'd suggest we have a late dinner. But you know how it is in this city!"

It was my turn to laugh: "Don't worry. And yes, I'll be delighted to have lunch with you tomorrow."

We arranged to meet at a restaurant in the center of Geneva, the Relais de l'Entrecôte. It had been a favorite of mine when I lived in Geneva and I learned with dismay from Etienne that it was about to close down, for good. He said I should jump on the opportunity to go there while it still existed.

Felicia was asleep when I got home, but Dulce had known I was arriving and was waiting for me behind the door. She wagged her tail madly but refrained from barking when I picked her up and told her to be quiet, as there were people sleeping.

I took a quick shower and was horrified to see the extent of my bruises. During the accident I hadn't realized how much we'd bounced around. I dried myself and applied some salve from the sample tube the hospital had given me.

Dulce was watching me curiously, wondering why I was applying this foul smelling stuff on myself. She had attempted a tentative lick on my leg and recoiled with a disgusted expression on her small furry face. I laughed and scratched her behind the ears.

"What the hell have you been doing in my absence, Alex? I can see you've hurt yourself! Yuk...if you thing this horrible tasting stuff is going to help..."

It downed on me suddenly that if Dulce had been with us during the accident, she might very well have been killed. I grabbed my little dog and squeezed her close to me, whispering endearments in her ears.

After a few seconds of patience she got fed up of this squeezing and wiggled out of my arms. I looked at her as she settled back in her little bed, mumbling under her breath.

"OK, OK...no need to squeeze me that hard!"

I had been stupid. Very stupid. I was putting everyone in danger: Dulce, Etienne, myself...On the other hand, I had no proof that the Foundation and the foul Mr. Damien was behind this.

The night was long: my bruises hurt every time I turned and I couldn't sleep. Having two attempts made on your life does that sometimes.

What I couldn't understand was why they would want to kill me? What kind of danger was I to them? It only made sense if they thought I had found out about the will: but how could they know that?

The other question that kept on bothering me, was how they could have followed us up to the Salève without my noticing. I was very much aware of my environment these days, and I was sure I would have seen them.

One thing was sure: these people were totally ruthless: if murdering me meant killing someone else on the way, it was no skin off their nose.

It meant that I was becoming dangerous to the people around me and that was worse than anything else.

My vacation was coming to an end: I had three more days in Switzerland and then I'd be back in New York, with no solution and the fear that they could be back any day. I tossed and turned, trying to find some way to get out of my predicament. There was no obvious solution and I ended up falling asleep at dawn.

When Felicia saw me in the morning she let out a cry of disbelief: "What the hell happened to you! Did someone beat you up?"

I looked at my arms: I shouldn't have worn a short sleeved shirt. On the other hand, the temperature was already in the high eighties. With a lot of humming and hemming, I told her about yesterday's accident. I didn't tell her it was a deliberate attempt to kill us, though, just that a careless driver had pushed us by accident off the road.

Thankfully, Felicia believed my story and didn't ask more questions. I told her I was having lunch with Etienne. I must have blushed, because she shook her head knowingly and told me good luck.

Dulce got to wear her brand new leash, and we walked down to the restaurant. The Relais de l'Entrecôte is near the lake and it was only a ten minutes walk from Felicia's apartment.

After five minutes I started to regret my decision not to take the bus. I was beginning to feel aches in all kinds of weird places and walking was not as easy as it had seemed.

We finally made it to the restaurant, where Etienne had booked a table. It had the advantage that, even when it was crowded – which was most of the time – you could hear yourself and your table companions speak. The all wood décor muffled the noise and made for a nice cozy place to spend lunch. Dulce was brought a bowl of water.

Looking at her sniffing at the fresh water, I thought, once again, how much more civilized Switzerland was compared to New York as far as dog policy is concerned. There are very few places in Switzerland where you are not welcome with a dog. Dogs are a part of life and everything is organized to make their, and their owner's life happy. I had yet to see a restaurant which did not accept dogs. As for hotels, most of them accept dogs, and the ones that don't are the ones you wouldn't want to go to, anyway.

I sighed: in New York I'd have to leave Dulce home when I went out.

Etienne arrived a few minutes after me, looking as gorgeous as ever in a dark business suit, striped shirt and Hermès tie. He wasn't very sprightly, though, and walked a bit sideways, like a crab on a beach. I watched with interest as he folded himself carefully in his chair. He winced and I grinned in return:

"Same here! I looked at myself in the mirror this morning: I think I might call myself a Pict very soon…I'm blue all over!"

Etienne bent over to greet Dulce, who was manifesting her pleasure at seeing his friendly face with some energetic tail wagging.

"Thank heavens she wasn't with us, poor little creature! She might have been killed!"

Dulce barked her approval.

"Tell me about it!"

I shushed her as the waitress was coming over to take our order. One of the things I liked at the Relais de l'Entrecôte, is that the only thing you had to decide about your meal was whether you wanted your meat rare or medium. They served exclusively entrecôte with a Café de Paris sauce, with a side of delicious French fries and a salad. Dessert was another story, as they had quite a few of them to choose from.

I looked around us: there was the usual crowd of impeccably attired bankers with assorted clients from various places in the world. The bank employees, account officers and hedge fund managers, male and female, were easily recognizable by their suits. They had the arrogant, self-satisfied look that comes with an overpaid, cushy job. The clients, of all creeds and races had in common the reverent way they looked at the person in front of them, who had been entrusted with the sacred mission of managing their money.

I had always thought Swiss private banking was a unique case, where the client feels indebted to the provider of services. Even when the services are not particularly good. And even when the provider of said services ultimately betrays his client and gives him up to another country's authorities. I was quite disgusted with Switzerland's cowardly attitude during the last years. As I looked at the young wolves sitting around me, I thought their future was not as rosy as they thought.

Etienne and I discussed about it: he tended to agree with me and to hate the arrogance of the financial world. He told me he was coming up against it on a daily basis, as he searched for funding for his project.

Etienne was beginning to trust me, as I he, and he told me a little bit more about his project, on a confidential basis.

He showed me his tie and asked me if l liked it. I told him I loved it and it was the first thing I'd noticed when he arrived, apart from his crab walk...I asked: "Isn't it an Hermès?"

He smiled and proudly turned the tie around so I could see the brand. It had an elegant logo and the name said "EdB, by de Brousse". I looked more closely at the tie and recognized a pattern I'd seen in one of the rooms of the house. Etienne explained:

"I was trying to create a fashion accessory department at de Brousse. But now, since I'm out of the company, I'm doing it on my own and will use de Brousse as my sole supplier. It would have made much more sense to integrate a department into the existing company, but, as things are today, it's impossible. So I'm creating my own company, EdB, which will produce fashion items based on de Brousse wallpapers and fabrics. This tie is an example, but we are going to produce scarves, wallets, handbags, umbrellas...a whole series of lines using the famous and classic de Brousse patterns, in paper or in fabric."

I exclaimed: "Wow! It's a fantastic idea! And the result looks beautiful!"

Etienne ran a hand through his wavy brown hair: "Yes, I think it's a great idea and I'm sure it will be a success. But I have to find some funding and these guys aren't helping" he said, indicating a tableful of fund managers next to us.

We talked about his projects for some time and then got back to the subject that was eating us: the will. He asked me some questions about the research I'd done. He wondered, as I had, why his aunt had not simply given the will to her notary. I bit my lip as I thought about it and said:

"I think she must have been under duress. It looks like the nurse she hired after Caroline's death must have been someone taking orders from the Foundation. At any rate, both the Lombardinis and Giuseppe seemed to think she was suspicious and were wary of her. Maybe she was being threatened."

"But it doesn't make sense! Giuseppe was still there, at least at the beginning, and her secretary also. And she had visitors: not many but a few. And access to the phone: why didn't she call the police?"

I shrugged: "I don't know: maybe they had some kind of hold on her. I can't imagine what. But the fact is she made sure the will was smuggled out and not given openly to a notary."

Etienne sighed: "And now we're never going to find it again…"

I lowered my head:

"Etienne, I'm really sorry. I feel like I opened a door for you and immediately closed it again. It makes me feel terrible."

When I looked up he was smiling at me: It created two adorable dimples on his tanned cheeks.

"It's not your fault Alex: and in a way, I'm thankful, even if we didn't find the will. At least I know that my aunt had changed her mind and didn't die a clueless victim of this horrible man. It makes me feel better, strange as it seems. The only thing I'm really worried about now, is you. They seem out to get you and I fear for your life."

I made a small grimace: " To tell you the truth, so do I. The problem is that I don't have enough evidence to go to the police and tell them someone is trying to kill me. The two attempts could pass off as accidents. Also, even if the police believed me, there is nothing to link the Foundation to those attempts. But I suppose once I go back to New York it will stop."

"Why should it? You have to realize that by now they certainly know that the person who visited their headquarters in Paris was you, Alexandra Tate, owner of the boutique which they had searched twice. They know you're onto them. I don't know how much they think you've found out, but they're certainly not going to let go. Especially if they think you can retrieve the missing picture from your customer in New York."

I nodded: he was right. But what could I do? I replied:

"What I can't understand is their timing: why try to kill me that day with the planter? What made them think I was making progress in my research?"

Etienne chewed a meditative French fry: "You know, there is something else that struck me. I'm pretty sure that car that pushed us off the road on the Salève was not following us, but waiting for us. I thought back to our drive up, and I'm almost sure I saw it parked on the side of the road when we were coming up, very shortly before the accident. And I wonder how they could have known we were going up there."

I raised my eyebrows: "Do you think they're listening in to your conversations at the house?"

Etienne shrugged: "It's quite possible. Anyway, I'm going to have the house swept for any bugging devices."

"Good idea."

We finished our lunch and skipped dessert: I had decided to be virtuous and Etienne didn't want to be drowsy for his afternoon meetings. He had asked me when I was leaving: I told him that I would be going in three days.

As we left the restaurant we kissed three times, in traditional Swiss way. Always a problem because in other countries it leaves you hanging in mid air for the third kiss. It was a friendly kiss, but the way he caressed my arm was slightly more than friendly.

As light as his touch was it still hurt and I repressed a yelp. Etienne left for his appointment and I decided to exit the restaurant through the back exit on the lake side. I crossed the road and found myself in the Jardin Anglais, a pleasant so-called garden by the lake.

Dulce was delighted to have her little paws in the grass and to follow invisible trails. I kept an eye on her, as the Jardin Anglais is the meeting place of all kinds of drug peddlers. They mix with the tourists and a few students who come to get their illegal substances. It is a pity, really, as the place is pleasant. There is a nineteenth century music kiosk, where bands play from time to time.

Virtuous or not, I thought I owed a small ice cream cone to myself. I was, after all, recovering from an attempt on my life, which had left me looking like a leopard. I had caught one or two curious glances at my bruised arms. I located an ice cream vendor and sauntered over to buy a small cone with just one ball. Half virtuous.

I sat on a bench to watch the crowds and Dulce, who had been running like a rabbit since we had arrived in the garden, settled down under my bench. I gave her a drink of water from the small bottle I carried with me. We sat peacefully together, enjoying the warm afternoon.

Suddenly, Dulce, who had been sitting quietly under the bench, jumped forward, barking madly. I just managed to hold on to her leash as she tried to run in a man's direction. I looked at the man and caught my breath: it was the one I'd seen at the house and who had made her bark already. I recognized the peculiar purple color of his hoodie.

He glanced in my direction and turned away immediately, walking off very fast. I caught my breath: that glimpse of the man's face had been enough. I had seen it before. Dulce was trembling with rage and I took her in my arms to calm her down..

"It's him again! Why don't you let me run after him?!"

I tried to concentrate and remember where I had seen him. His face was familiar, I was sure of it. There had never been a man other than Etienne at Clair-Chant, so it wasn't there. In Paris, at the Foundation? I tried to remember the people I'd seen there, but I was pretty sure it wasn't where I'd seen him.

Putting Dulce back on the floor, I gave her the tip of my waffle cone, which she happily crunched. Once she had finished, she sat back on her furry behind, expecting more. I laughed and asked her: "Where did we see this man, Dulce?" She gave a short bark and suddenly it came back to me.

CHAPTER XXI

One thing my friends found amazing, was that I never forgot a customer of the gallery. I could forget other faces, and often did. But never, ever, someone who had been at "Tate". And this was where I'd seen this man.

I remembered him quite well. It had been a few days before the first break-in. He had walked in one morning, and immediately I had been on guard. After five years of running a gallery in the Upper East Side, you know what kind of clientele it attracts. And when you see someone coming in who is radically different from your target customer and who on top of that looks slightly threatening…you pay attention.

The man was of medium height, with very pale skin, sandy hair and greenish eyes. I put his nationality as Russian, or maybe Ukrainian: he had a bit of a look of Putin. He was more powerfully built and taller than the Russian president, though and his mere presence was menacing. He had tried to be as discrete as possible, looking around him and trying to blend in. He was particularly interested by Denise's works and had asked about two of them I'd had in the back room and which had a small tag which said "Not for sale". I told him these two belonged to my personal collection and that I wouldn't part with them. He had looked around a little longer: I had followed discreetly his every move, as he looked exactly like the kind of guy who will filch something the moment you turn your back. He hadn't stayed long and had left without buying anything and without opening his mouth again. But I remembered him very well: there was absolutely not the slightest doubt in my mind that this was the man I'd just seen.

What's more, Dulce's attitude confirmed it: the man had probably been reconnoitering the place before burglarizing it. And after searching and robbing the boutique twice, he'd found out some of the paintings had been bought by my neighbor. And proceeded to burglarize her apartment. Dulce recognized him from there. I asked her to confirm it and she woofed.

"Of course, Alex! I've been telling you ever since I smelled this guy at Etienne's house, but you won't listen, will you?"

All kinds of mixed emotions were going through me: on the one hand I was terrified. This man was really not the kind of enemy I'd want to tackle. On the other hand, my suspicions were now confirmed. It was the Foundation who was behind the incidents in New York and Denise Kübler's death.

The fact that this man was following me was very ominous. If he, or others like him were set on eliminating me, I didn't have a snowball's chance in Hell. I had to do something.

I walked back home, taking care when I crossed the street, and keeping aware of my surroundings. I knew I could rely on Dulce to sniff out any individual with nefarious intentions. But as far as getting run over by a car was concerned, the responsibility of keeping us alive was mine.

After another sleepless night spent turning and tossing, I finally made up my mind. There was only one course left to me and, unpleasant as it was, I had to take it.

In the morning I told Felicia at breakfast that I was going to Paris for the day. I decided to take Dulce with me: I needed the comfort of her small furry presence.

My train left Geneva at a quarter to ten: I reached the station at a quarter past nine and had just enough time to go and buy the smallest cell phone I could find, with a throw away chip. I had plenty of time during the trip to organize my thoughts and decide what I was going to say.

I had decided that my only course of action was to confront Damien. And now I thought I knew how to put some pressure on him. I took out my cell phone and rang Etienne. I told him about the man from the Foundation and asked him to do two things. Then I told him what I intended to do: I heard him choking on the other end of the line. He sputtered and protested but in the end had to admit my solution made sense. He promised to call me back as soon as he had had done what I asked.

My cell phone rang as the train was coming into the Gare de Lyon. I thanked Etienne, hung up and patted Dulce's head, telling her: "Let's go, Dulce: it's show time!"

Three metro stations later I was in front of the Foundation's building. I took out my new cell phone and dialed my home number in New York: everything would be recorded on my answering machine. I took a deep breath and stomped in, stopping in front of the reception desk. The unpleasant receptionist was there and started telling me in vinegary tones: "Madam, I already told you dogs are not admitted here and..."

I interrupted her with a peremptory gesture of my hand and said in the most haughty voice I could muster:

"Call Mr. Damien, now, and tell him I want to see him. Immediately. I'm Mrs. Tate."

She was furious but probably too much in awe of her boss to protest. Without saying another word she took her phone and called Damien's secretary. She waited for a second and then told me he would see me in five minutes. As I waited, pretending to ignore her, she glared at me and Dulce. If looks could kill, Damien wouldn't need his assassins! I almost giggled but managed to keep my cool.

A few minutes later I heard a clatter of heels and saw a woman approaching. She was impeccably groomed, a tall and severe looking woman who asked me politely to follow her. She ignored the fact that I had Dulce with me. We took the elevator and went to Damien's office. He was not there when we arrived and she left me, after asking me if I wanted something to drink. I declined and she took off, telling me Mr. Damien would be there shortly.

I would have bet my last cent Damien had actually been in his office when the receptionist called and his making me wait there was part of his intimidation process. So I used the technique that works so well in those cases. I took out my phone and pretended to make a call. When he arrived, I was listening and talking to an imaginary correspondent. Holding onto Dulce's collar, so she wouldn't growl at him, I smiled politely and signaled that I'd be with him shortly.

Which totally blew his entrance. I could see he was annoyed his plan hadn't worked. He sat down behind his desk. I concluded my imaginary conversation with someone much more important than him and, putting my phone back in my bag, looked up at him with a smile.

Now he was confused, not knowing what to expect. He pretended to look through papers on his desk but was clearly unsettled. I kept silent, forcing him to open the conversation, which he did:

"Now, Mrs...Tate? Is it? This time? What can I do for you? I'm sure you realize I'm a very busy man, so please tell me quickly what justifies your interrupting my schedule."

I gave him a sweet smile.

"How about attempted murder, Mr. Damien? Would that be enough to interrupt your busy schedule?"

He stiffened and there was now a wary expression on his face, as well as doubt. He was dying to throw me out of his office, but I seemed sufficiently self assured to make him want to know more. He crossed his hands in front of him on his desk and replied: "Please explain yourself?"

"Mr. Damien, I want you to listen carefully to what I'm going to tell you and to refrain from interrupting me. If you have any comments, please keep them for the end."

He blushed with anger but nodded. I went on.

"You are evidently going to deny everything I will tell you now and you probably suspect I'm carrying some kind of listening device. I can assure you that I don't, but no matter. All I want from you right now is to listen to what I have to say."

Hum. I could lie too, when I wanted.

He nodded again, impatiently.

"Mr. Damien, in the past week there have been two attempts on my life, from members of your organization. I want you to desist."

He blurted out: "This is outrageous! Ridiculous! How…"

I stopped him with a gesture of my hand.

"Please wait and hear me out. I now know what your people were looking for in my boutique in New York, and why they robbed my neighbor and friend and another one of my clients.

What you are after is the last will of Mrs. Alice de Brousse, whose entire fortune was bequeathed to you in the will that was executed. You know, as I do, that this will probably left her house in one roll of a series of wallpapers, which she gave to her friend Denise Kübler. The wallpaper was used by the artist in a series of pictures, of which I sold a few.

We both know that there is no way we can retrieve the missing picture, which most probably contains the will, as I sold it to an unknown customer who paid in cash.

Apparently my digging through this imbroglio has caused you some annoyance, to the point you've tried to eliminate me. I want you to stop. You have to understand that, for me, this issue is closed. I wanted to know why I was being threatened and what was behind this desperate search for those wallpapers. Now I know and I also know that, much as you threaten me or make my life difficult, the last picture is lost for good.

So I want you to call back your goons and leave me alone. I am going back to New York tomorrow, and I want to resume my peaceful and uneventful life there."

Damien had been on the point of interrupting me several times, but refrained from doing so. Now he was silent for a moment. He leaned forward and replied with a leer:

"Mrs. Tate, as you now call yourself. I would like to point out, first of all, that you entered these premises under false pretenses and a false identity, both of which I could have you arrested for."

I shrugged and raised my eyebrows in a sneer, to show him just how seriously I took his threats. He raised his hand in a pacifying gesture:

"However, I was prepared to overlook this: but now you come with a crazy story and I think this calls for more serious action on my part."

I sighed and gathered my bag, as if preparing to leave. I said:

"I was quite sure you'd take it like that. It doesn't matter. However, you must know one thing: I have proof of what I am saying. Your men are quite clumsy and I have material proof that links the break-in at my boutique to the attack at the house. And there was one witness of our car "accident" who saw quite well the man in the car which pushed us off the road. Of course, with no suspects, his description was a bit useless. But now, I can tell the police much, much more.

But you see, rather than opening this can of worms, I'd rather drop this whole thing and be left in peace. I have no interest as to whether this will is found or not. All I want is my personal well-being and to be left alone. On the other hand, if I see someone following me or if I think my life is in danger, I will not hesitate, of course, to go to the police. You have to understand that the evidence I have leeds directly to this Foundation, and therefore to you. So now, it's your decision"

Damien was furiously thinking. I had gathered my bag and Dulce's leash and half rose to leave. He snapped at me: "Please sit down. We need to talk."

I sat down, allowing myself an inward sigh of relief: the fish was baited. I waited for him to make the next move.

"Mrs. Tate, your story is of course preposterous and I deny any involvement of myself or the Foundation in the incidents – which I'm hearing about for the first time today – which you mention.

However, and on a purely theoretical basis, I would like you to tell me what makes you think that someone belonging to this institution might have been involved in these purported attacks?"

I smiled, amused at his caution. He must know I was wired or something…

"When your man "cased the joint", as I believe you say in the business, at the boutique, he touched two of Denise's paintings, which he subsequently stole. But he also touched one object: he will probably remember which one and why. Yesterday I made sure this object was photographed in situ and removed to a safe place by someone whose word will not be put in doubt. I know there will be at least two or three usable fingerprints. Secondly, this smart dog here (I showed Dulce, who was sitting on her tail and looking indeed very smart!), recognized this man at the house, the other day. I was intrigued by her attitude, as she is, as a rule, a very friendly dog. I asked about him and was told he works for you. And of course, he will have told you that I saw him yesterday in Geneva. What he probably doesn't know, is that he has been filmed several times driving into the property by the neighbor's security camera. Since the house next door is an embassy, their cameras tend to cover a very wide area and they systematically catch the visitors of Clair-Chant."

Damien began to open his mouth but I stopped him:

"And last, but not least, I've secured several objects he touched while he was at the house. I'm sure the fingerprints there will match the ones at the boutique."

Damien snickered: "Even if what you say is true, it would only prove that there is a criminal working at the Foundation. I'm not responsible for my employees actions!"

"The man is on the Foundation's payroll and I'm sure we can find proof that the Foundation paid for his trip to New York and his stay there. I think you are going to find it a bit difficult to justify that. And I'm not sure he will want to endorse the responsibility for these acts. This kind of person tends to rat on their employers sooner or later…But, don't worry: if this goes to a police investigation, I'll make sure you get involved.

The problem, Mr. Damien, is that I have absolutely no trust in the justice system. Whether in the US, in France or in Switzerland, I think it is inefficient, biased or corrupt. I do believe in the police though, but I think their action is greatly hampered by the judicial system.

So I would rather not involve anyone and let things lie. But of course, it all depends on you."

Damien sat back in his chair, thinking. I could see all the little wheels and cogs getting in place as he tried to think himself out of this conundrum. He couldn't be sure all I was telling him was true, but he knew the facts were right. He could not be sure of what clues his man might have left. I had also noticed a small twitch when I'd mentioned the airplane fare and stay in New York. It was probably in the Foundation's books somewhere. He knew that there was probably enough evidence to indict his man and implicate the Foundation.

I didn't think he cared about the press and negative publicity: he'd had plenty of it throughout the years and the Foundation had survived just fine, swindling old ladies along the way. But he realized something I hadn't said aloud: if there was an investigation and evidence of a posterior will surfaced, Mrs. de Brousse's assets could be frozen. Etienne might take it into his head to prove the Foundation had destroyed a will in his favor and the legal battle could go on for years.

On the other hand, if he swore to leave me alone, he could go on with his business and forget about the will. The decision wasn't too easy to take though, for two reasons.

Firstly, I could see that his pride was at stake. There was this chubby woman, the kind of person he would never take into account, who was putting a spoke in his wheels. I could see a murderous glint in his eyes and I was sure he would have liked me dead, if only out of personal satisfaction.

And secondly, he didn't trust me. He was such a twisted rat himself, that he probably imagined I had a hidden agenda. Maybe he thought I knew where to find the will and would blackmail him.

In the end, he must have thought that those were things that could be managed in due time, but that the present threat of revelation was immediate, and needed immediate response.

He directed his gaze at me and I couldn't help shuddering at the intensity of hate I saw in his eyes. His tone belied the look in his eyes: it was smooth as cream and very polite.

"Mrs. Tate, I don't believe a word of this crazy story of yours involving one of my employees. I do believe, however, that your actions of the last few weeks might have…disturbed some person or persons. And that these purported attempts on your life are the consequence of your…interference. I'm sure if you go back to New York and resume your life, without attempting to interfere further in this person or persons' affairs..that you will find that they will leave you alone."

I looked at him for a moment. Dulce, who would usually lie down under my seat if she saw I was settled for some time, was on her guard this time. She was sitting down, but her ears were pricked up and she was attentive to every nuance in our conversation. I ran my hand on her head, over her silky ears, taking comfort and strength from her intelligent presence.

"Alex, be careful: I really don't like this man…"

This was as far as he would go, but it would have to do. I asked him: "Do I have your word for it?"

He smiled crookedly: " Insofar as I don't know the people we are talking about, I don't see what that would change. But I think you can take it for granted, yes."

I rose: "Very well, I will. And please don't forget that I have taken measures if something were to happen to me."

He smiled, a small tight smile which revealed grudging admiration: "I'm sure you have. Good bye Mrs. Tate."

I didn't wait for him to accompany me downstairs and walked down, unhurriedly but determinately. Once in the lobby, I didn't even look at the receptionist and stepped outside, glad to be out of the building and away from it's unpleasant occupants.

CHAPTER XXII

The meeting with Damien had lasted for half an hour: I had time to make the four o'clock TGV back to Geneva. I went to get the subway to return to the Gare de Lyon.

I kept on looking behind me to see if I was being followed and was particularly careful in the subway. I stayed far from the edge and only stepped forward once the train had arrived. But Dulce and I made it safely to the Gare de Lyon and onto the train.

Once I was settled into my seat I looked out at the platform, to see if there was anyone suspicious. This time, everything seemed to be in order and no one seemed to be on our track. I sat back in my seat and relaxed, breathing freely for the first time since I'd left Damian's office.

The TGV left the station and I realized that the tremor I'd been feeling wasn't from the train but from myself! I was shaking all over. Dulce was on her blanket on the seat next to me, looking curiously at me. I patted her head and told her she was a good dog. She snorted.

"I know that!"

I had been so tense during my meeting with Damien, that the relief that suddenly washed over me made me burst into tears. Dulce was alarmed and scrambled over the armrest to sit on my lap and lick my face. I hugged her closely, wiping my tears on her fur. It was a good thing that the train was three quarters empty and no one was looking at me: I must have been a sorry sight.

After a while I calmed down a little, and by the time the conductor came to check the tickets, I had regained my composure and some of my calm.

I called Etienne and gave him a brief summary of my meeting with Damien. He said he would come to pick me up at the station and take me out to dinner.

That sent my heart racing again, but for other reasons. I wobbled my way to the bathroom to see what kind of emergency repair work I could do on my make up before we reached Geneva. In the end I shrugged and swayed back to my seat. There wasn't much I could do.

I was wearing jeans and a light jacket and decided it would have to do. Not that I had any choice, anyway. I gave a call to Felicia to tell her my plans, and ask her to keep her next evening free. It was my last evening in Geneva and I wanted to spend it with my friend.

Etienne was waiting for me in the parking lot of the station. I looked at the car he was driving and asked, as I got in: "You've already bought a new car?"

"No, this one is lent by the garage until the new one arrives. I should have it by next week."

I installed Dulce on the backseat once they had exchanged greetings with Etienne. We drove out of town and went to the small village of Corsier outside of Geneva. There was a pretty lakeside restaurant, which served the traditional "filets de perche". This is fillets of a type of bass, which is fished in lake Leman. They are usually cooked in a lemon butter sauce and served with a salad and fries. It's one of the most typical things you can eat around the area.

There was a beautiful view across the lake and the place wasn't too crowded. We arrived just in time so Dulce could have her meal, which I'd taken along in case we didn't make it home in time. Once she had finished her own meal, she sat down expectantly to see if something would come her way from our dishes.

"Alex, remember I like fish, OK?"

Etienne asked me to tell him about the meeting with Damien. He said:

"It took a lot of guts to go and see this man. I've only met him twice, but he really gives me the creeps!"

"Yeah, he has that effect on me too. But I tried to look at him dispassionately, and above all, to dissect his attitudes and his manipulation techniques. That helps!"

I summed up my conversation with Damien. Etienne was full of questions, which I answered. I had a few for him too:

"Did you really go next door to ask the embassy if you could have their security tapes?

"I did. Of course they said no, but they were quite nice and said if at some point we really needed them or the police asked to see them, they would not object. I told them that knowing they had them safely stored was enough for the moment."

"What about fingerprints?"

"This guy's been working on some electrical repairs and plumbing in the house. I removed the box around the fuses in one of the rooms and I'm pretty sure the only prints that will be found there will be his. No one has touched these fuses in years!"

I whistled: "Wow! Great! Where did you put them?"

"I stored it in a safe deposit box at my bank. What about New York?"

"Um, well, there, I lied. The object the guy touched is still in the boutique. But I doubt very much they'll try to get it back: I think I was quite convincing. Anyway, by the day after tomorrow I'll be back there and I'll take good care to put this sculpture where no one can get at it!"

"I can't believe you remember exactly what objects he looked at and touched. Do you do that for every customer?"

"More or less. Sometimes people come back after a year and I tell them "Oh, yes, I remember you were interested in the landscape by so-and-so..." and they can't believe it. On the other hand, I once met the cashier of my local supermarket, whom I see practically every day, on the subway, and I didn't recognize her."

I shrugged: "I guess it's my seller's memory!" I took a sip of my dry white wine.

"Etienne, I've been thinking about something during the train trip...once I'd stopped sniveling! Damien seemed pretty worried when I talked about the missing will and I wonder if you couldn't try to contest the existing one, based on the knowledge that there was another one made after it.. I mean, OK, I told Damien I'd stay put. But if making this story public could help you get your inheritance back, I wouldn't hesitate."

Damien smiled and put his hand on mine. I felt there was some melting going on in my inner core. He said:

"I wouldn't jeopardize your safety for that: there is too much uncertainty, it is really not worth it. We could never prove the will would have been in my favor, to begin with. Then we would have to prove that the Foundation made it disappear, and that would be almost impossible. Especially since they didn't. The chances would be much too thin to risk money and time on it."

I sighed: "Well, I hope Damien doesn't think so!"

Once we had finished dinner, we took a walk along the lake. Dulce ran ahead of us, occasionally stopping to inhale some mysterious scent. She kept an eye on us, but ran back and forth, letting out a small bark from time to time.

We walked to the end of a small wharf, where tourists and fishermen sometimes tied their boats. The moon was almost full and the water made a tinkling lapping sound at our feet. Etienne put his hand around my face and kissed my mouth. It was a soft, tender kiss, that left me breathless and about as stiff as a rag doll. I felt my stomach doing weird twists and my legs seemed to have turned to marshmallow. I sighed and Etienne smiled. He whispered: "What a pity you are leaving, Alex! You have been so wonderful!"

I felt like telling him that I'd cancel my trip, close down my art gallery and abandon my friends in New York in half a second if he wanted me to. A last shred of reason prevented me from doing so and I kept silent. Dulce, on the other hand, resented very much his getting so close to me and manifested her discontent with some loud barking.

"Get away from her, now! Just because I like you, doesn't mean you can get fresh with Alex!"

Despite my attempts to shush her, she only stopped when we moved apart. Etienne laughed and bent down to scratch her behind the ears, her favorite after belly scratches. He exclaimed: "Your dog is very jealous, Alex!"

He put his arm around my shoulders and we walked back to the car. He dropped me off at Felicia's place and asked me if he could see me the next day. I told him I would be busy visiting a couple of friends I'd neglected to see during all this trip and packing my suitcase, but that I would call him during the day.

Packing my suitcase took me less than an hour the next day, but I did have to see as many of my friends as I could. I ended up spending the whole day having coffee, lunch and more coffees with my old friends. It all kept my mind busy and I didn't think too much about Damien and his creepy crew.

In the end I had talked with Felicia and I had decided to invite her and Etienne to dinner, so they could finally meet. We settled on a place in the Old Town, so that I could get a last whiff of Geneva before leaving.

Felicia and I walked from her place to the main square of the Old Town. We had decided to have a drink at the Clémence, the café on the square where all the tourists and the Genevese congregated.

Geneva is not a very beautiful town: the architecture is drab and apart from the lake side, there are not many handsome buildings. But there is the Old Town, crowned by the Cathedral, and that part of the city is truly worth the visit. After our drinks we strolled up to the Grand-Rue and stopped at one of the cafés there.

I kept a wary eye for any suspicious characters, but, miraculously it seemed as though I was being left alone.

Etienne joined us a bit later. He looked as handsome as ever and Felicia emitted a mini wolf whistle when she saw him coming in. She whispered: "Wow…I understand you, now!"

Dulce escaped from under the table and was up and running towards him before I could react. He caught her leash and brought her back to the table. I made the introductions with him and Felicia and we all sat down.

I hadn't had time to tell Felicia about the latest developments, so we discussed that and many other things that evening. It was a most pleasant evening and we all had a great time. At the end of the evening Etienne offered to take me to the airport the next day.

He drove us back home after dinner. Once he was gone, Felicia and I had a last drink in her sitting-room. We chatted and drank and laughed. She told me she was sure that Etienne liked me, and I said "Yeah,

yeah…" and Dulce barked. Felicia promised to come to New York soon.

The next morning Etienne was there at nine thirty sharp. While we drove up to the airport he asked me about my plans and if I was intending to come back to Geneva any time soon. I asked if he was planning on coming to New York and he said he might, if his project took off.

We promised to stay in touch. When we arrived at the security check, he kissed me again, a light, almost friendly kiss on the mouth. He patted Dulce who was peering at him from her travel bag, and left us.

I walked slowly to the gate, mulling over what I had to admit was a defeat: I was alive, would probably be left in peace by Damien and his hooligans in the future…but neither Denise, Florence or Caroline would be getting justice. And that hurt.

CHAPTER XXIII

The trip back to New York was longer than the other way, but the jet lag is always easier to deal with in that direction. It just makes for a longer day.

I was glad to be home, to breathe my beloved New York air. Dulce, although she had been living in the apartment only for a few days before we left to Switzerland, immediately felt at home. She went directly to her bed and sat watching me as I opened my suitcase.

The day after, I reopened "Tate". The first thing I did was to take a Ziploc bag and put the sculpture in it. At lunch time I put it in a large canvas bag and went to the bank to put it in my safe deposit box.

In the afternoon I called on Mrs. Herz, to find out how she was and if she any news from Mrs. Dettwiler. Mrs. Herz told me she had moved in with her daughter and was as happy as a lark, being a doting grandmother. I was reassured to hear that and decided to call her one morning.

The next days were spent catching up with my friends and coping with the paperwork that had accumulated during my absence.

It was a warm summer in New York like it had been in Switzerland. I took Dulce as often as possible to Central Park, where she made some canine and human friends.

I had a lurking suspicion Dulce believed herself to be a small, furry human being, from her attitude to other dogs. She was friendly with them, but obviously believed they were not of the same race. She was much more enthusiastic meeting her two legged fans and engaged in serious conversations with them.

Most of the time I felt relaxed and happy, thanks in great part to having Dulce around. But from time to time I would think about the events in Switzerland and it left a sour taste in my mouth. It seemed so unfair that Damien and his pseudo-foundation would go unpunished for that at least one murder they were responsible for, and on top of that got to keep what should have been Etienne's inheritance.

I still kept checking warily over my shoulder to see if I was followed. I was very careful when I took out the garbage in the back alley. I triple checked the street before crossing it and, in general, I tried to see if there were any unwanted people around.

After two months, I decided Damien was keeping his word and leaving me in peace. At any rate Dulce had not shown displays of aggressiveness against anyone, and I trusted her instincts very much.

I kept in touch through Skype, emails and Facebook with Sylvie and with Etienne.

Sylvie told me she was trying, unsuccessfully for the moment, to have the inquest into her sister's death re-opened. The police said that if there were no new elements, they could not do anything.

Etienne's project was stalled: it was summertime and he knew nothing would happen until September. He said he would go down to the South of France with some friends and call me from there.

He did call, a few times: he seemed to be having a great time. I wondered with burning jealousy who was sharing his holiday. Sometimes I heard female voices in the background: it was pretty frustrating.

Despite what I had told Damien, I had, of course, tried to locate the fourth painting. I had racked my mind to try to find a clue which would enable me to find the client. But it was looking for a needle in a haystack.

I remembered him well: a sale of 950$ was an event at the gallery. He was a man in his fifties, well-dressed. He had come into the boutique because of another picture by Denise that was hanging in the window. He had hesitated only for a few minutes and then taken the slightly larger one that was hanging on one of the walls.

I had no idea who he was or where he came from. I had never seen him before in the area and did not see him again. Very often, when I was at the supermarket or walking in the Park, I'd look around to see if he would suddenly materialize. But he didn't.

There were so many unanswered questions with this mysterious missing will: it frustrated me to no end. It was now late summer and I didn't know that I was going to get some answers, very soon.

CHAPTER XXIV

There were a few chores I had to take care of, one of them being to get back some paintings I'd had reframed at my friend Gary's shop. I had completely forgotten about them and he called to remind me they had been sitting there since the month of April!

I scolded myself for being so negligent. On the other hand, I had excuses: all this kind of thing had been written in my big black sales books, which had been stolen. I shuddered to think what else I might have forgotten...

Dulce was delighted when I had morning chores to do. She loved walking around in the neighborhood and meeting her many admirers. We walked down the three blocks to Gary's shop. Dulce's tail was up and plumy and she trotted proudly next to me.

Gary welcomed us when we came in and was very happy to meet Dulce. Dulce, as always when she met a friendly person, gave a small bark of approval. Gary went to get my paintings and began wrapping them up.

Suddenly Dulce, who had been sniffing around the shop with many snorts of disgust (she wasn't too enthusiastic about the turpentine and other chemicals), dashed off into the back of the shop. She ran away so fast her leash escaped from my hands. I called after her, but she had disappeared behind the curtain which separated the front from the back of the shop.

"Alex, Alex, come quickly! I recognize a smell from Mrs. D.'s house! Come!"

I ran behind her, trying to catch her, but she was faster than me. I found her in the back shop, barking and wagging her tail in front of a picture that was stacked with others on the floor. I bent down to take her leash and stayed there, mouth open: it was one of the two paintings by Denise Kübler I'd sold to Mrs. Dettwiler.

It all came back to me in a second: of course! Mrs. Dettwiler had bought the pair of paintings but didn't like the fact that they were framed differently. She had said she would have one of the two reframed. She hadn't told me she had gone ahead and brought the picture to Gary's shop and I had no way of knowing it. And the Foundation guy had no idea either.

I had to act, quickly. I called out: "Gary, I think my dog is thirsty, do you mind of I give her a drink?"

I heard his voice, muffled by the curtain: "Of course not, go right ahead!"

There was a small sink: I turned the tap and let the water run. I grabbed a sharp instrument from one of the tables. It took me a few seconds to cut the back of the painting and expose the inside.

And there it was: stuck in the backing of the painting, I could see a written text. I tore it out and rolled it up. I quickly hid the eviscerated painting behind a pile of what seemed to be unclaimed daubs and put the roll in my handbag. I gave Dulce a sip of water and a big kiss on her intelligent head and walked out.

Gary had my package ready and I paid and left, filled with elation. I had it, I had the will!

Clutching my handbag with its precious contents I returned to "Tate": I was walking so fast, Dulce almost had to run behind me.

When I got to the store, I locked both doors, and, my heart beating wildly, I sat down at my desk and carefully unrolled the papers.

It was one of de Brousse's more intricate designs: the wallpaper was flocked, with an upraised design in dark purple on a maroon background. It was one of the latest models, so it was autoadhesive. Denise had only snipped off the edges, so there were good chances that whatever was inside was intact. Or almost. I carefully pulled the shiny paper backing off, revealing four pages of writing paper, the first of which was stuck to the adhesive back of the wallpaper. It was blank, like the top one. There were two pages covered in writing sandwiched in between them.

It wasn't a will. It was two short letters:

"Dear Denise: as my oldest and trusted friend, I beg you to give the letter herewith to my nephew, Etienne. With much love,

Your friend forever,

Alice"

The second letter was addressed to Etienne. I hesitated for one second before reading it: then shrugged and went ahead.

"My dear Etienne,

Do you remember your favorite game with Patricia? You will find a key there. Florence should have explained, but the poor girl is dead, probably killed by Damien or one of his people. I trust your intelligence.

Your loving aunt,

Alice"

I sat back, feeling disappointed and elated at the same time. It wasn't the will, but it was progress. Etienne would certainly know what his aunt had meant. I had to call him immediately.

Etienne was back from his long holidays and hard at work. I caught him in a meeting, but told him to call me asap back, and preferably from a discreet phone. I told him I had some very exciting news.

Less than half an hour later he called me back, from an unknown number.

When I told him what I'd found, he was stunned. He was silent for a long minute and then whispered: "I can't believe you did it, Alex! You're incredible!" Suddenly he let off a whoop which could almost be heard back in New York City. I waited until he'd let off some steam and then asked him:

"Etienne, do you know what your aunt meant?"

"Yes, of course! Patricia was the cook's daughter, with whom I used to play at Clair-Chant. We used to spend literally hours trying to open my aunt's "box of secrets". It's a silver jewelry box inlaid with ivory: one of a set, there's a hairbrush and a mirror that go with it."

I exclaimed: "I know that box! I saw it at Denise Kübler's house!"

Etienne said: "What? I didn't even notice it wasn't there anymore!"

"Your aunt bequeathed it to Denise: probably to keep it out of the Foundation's mitts."

He was worried: "Do you think her husband will object if I ask him to look at it?"

"No, of course not! Edouard Kübler is the nicest man. I think you should go there as soon as possible!"

"I will. I'm calling him right now and I'll go there tomorrow if he agrees."

"Of course he will. But, Etienne? Be careful. Don't let anyone at the house know what you're doing. You never know."

He agreed: "Don't worry. I'm calling from a phone I borrowed and I'll make all my calls from the outside. Although I did have someone come and check for any bugging devices, and it looks as though the house is clean. I'll call you as soon as I have news."

He added as an afterthought: "Give a big kiss from me to Dulce: she is the smartest dog!" I duly delivered the kiss and the message to Dulce, who wagged her tail in delight.

"Thanks!"

I had told Etienne her role in finding the picture and he had been flabbergasted. We both thought she had recognized the smells she associated with Mrs. Dettwiler and her old home. She was a great detective!

"You bet!"

My cell phone rang at 6 in the morning: through the mists of sleep I heard the excited voices of Edouard and Etienne, telling me that they'd found the key in the box. I sat up in my bed and yawned .

"OK, great, you have the key. What key?"

There was a silence on the other end. Finally Etienne said: "We have no idea."

I tried to get my sleepy brain to work: "What do you mean you have no idea? What kind of key is it? Isn't there a name or a number on it? Like a safe deposit key?"

"No: it looks like a safe deposit key, but there's nothing written on it."

I scratched my head: "Hm. Well, you'll have to figure it out. It's probably for a bank. You'll have to make the rounds and ask them if it's one of theirs.

There was a big sigh on the other end:

"This is Geneva, Alex. You know as well as I do how difficult it is to ask this kind of question…if I ask if my aunt or Florence had an account…it just won't work. In the case of my aunt the only people who could ask if she had an account and a safe deposit box would be the

Foundation, as her heirs. And for Florence, it would have to be her sister."

I yawned again and said: "Let me think about it, and I'll call you back."

The first thing I did was to call Sylvie, to ask her if she knew if her sister had rented a safe deposit box somewhere. Sylvie said that no, not as far as she knew. When her sister had died she and her father had shut all of Florence's bank accounts and there was no sign of a safe anywhere. I thanked her and tried to get some more eyeshut.

It's almost impossible to go back to sleep under these conditions, especially when you have an intellectual problem to solve. I tried to shut everything out and to snatch another hour or two of sleep, but there was nothing doing.

At half past seven, just as I was drifting to sleep again, the little lamp bulb lit over my head. I grabbed my cell phone and called Etienne. He answered on the first ring. I told him:

"Take the key and wear your best smile. Make a list of banks and visit them. Tell them you were doing some spring cleaning and you found this key. Since your aunt used to have a safe deposit box in this bank, which was closed, years ago, you were wondering if it was theirs. In which case you could give it back. They will of course tell you immediately whether it is one of theirs."

There was a stunned silence at the other end and then he said: "You're a genius! I love you Alex!"

Music to my ears! He then worried again: "Yes, but what if I find the right one! They'll want the key back!"

I sighed; he wasn't too bright sometimes…

"In that case, they'll want to know in whose name the account was.

You can stall, invent a name and we'll take it from there. If you manage to locate the bank, it's a big step forward. Personally I think the box must have been in Florence Rivière's name: I called Sylvie and she says she isn't aware of any. But she didn't know all the details of her sister's life and Florence might not have told her about it. If you find the right bank, we can ask Sylvie Rivière to inquire. She has every right to do so, as her sister's heir."

"Oh. OK, fine. I'll start tomorrow."

I said: "And, Etienne? Put the key in a safe deposit box. Today."

"Yes of course!"

He then passed me Edouard, who was fascinated by the story and had kept Etienne for lunch in Gruyères. By the time I hung up I was fully awake and my brain was chugging along.

During the next few days I had daily calls from Etienne, who was making the rounds of the numerous banks in Geneva. The story I had cooked up worked quite well, as I had known it would. Banks usually only have two keys for their safe deposit boxes: it happens very often that clients forget to give one of them back when they close their account, or lose them. Sometimes they are mislaid by the bank employees themselves, and as a result the bank can't rent the boxes, because getting new keys made is a complicated legal process. So I knew they would be delighted to get a key back.

He told me he had no problem at all getting them to check if the key was theirs, but after 52 banks he still had nothing.

It took him two more weeks to give up: he'd extended his search to the suburbs and to the towns outside of Geneva, as far as Lausanne. But the key didn't match anything.

One morning he called me and said:

"Alex, I'm stumped. Maybe I'm too stupid. My aunt said to use my intelligence: I've exhausted it. I need you to come here and help me solve this. I'm booking you a seat for next week, with Dulce of course. Will you come?"

I was flabbergasted. And flattered. And of course I accepted.

It was only a matter of organizing to have my "girls" replace me for a week at the gallery. They were both available, which was great as they'd cover all the opening hours.

CHAPTER XXV

Geneva in the summer becomes animated and alive: there are tourists, flowers, events. Now it was October, and it was back to sullen Geneva. The lake was a dull grey and the sky was leaden. It looked as though the sun would never come out again. As a matter of fact, it almost never comes out some winters…

The only nice thing was the autumn colors, as there are a lot of trees in Geneva and the countryside around it. Etienne came to pick me up at the airport. We had decided I'd stay at the hotel, as it might be dangerous for Felicia if I stayed with her, and to show my face at Clair-Chant was out of question. The "burqa team" as Etienne dubbed them was still in residence: the least one could say was that they took great care of their asset!

We had discussed the fact that Damien might consider a breach of our tacit agreement the fact that I was back in the area. So I was to keep as low a profile as possible.

Etienne did come to pick me up at the airport though, in his brand new Jaguar. His reunion with Dulce was touching: more so in fact than his reunion with me.

I'd been fantasizing during the whole flight about a torrid embrace in the arrivals hall, complete with a bouquet of red roses. All I got was an enthusiastic hug and peck on the cheek, while Dulce copped all the attention.

It was shared enthusiasm, as she rolled on her back, jumped up and down, did a small dance and barked so lustily we got irritated glances from the other travelers.

"Yipeeyaaaay! Etienne! I'm so happy to see you! How are you! I missed you! Let me kiss you!"

When Dulce finally calmed down, we walked to the car.

The first thing I did was to give Etienne the letter from his aunt which literally brought tears to his eyes. He said: "This is more important than anything else to me, because it proves to me that my aunt's feelings towards me hadn't changed. It really means a lot."

I put a hand around his shoulders (a difficult operation, since he was a whole foot taller than me!) and squeezed hard. He winced and smiled.

He drove me down to the Hôtel Métropole, which we had chosen because of its central location. Etienne had made the reservation in his name. If Damien got wind that I was back in Geneva, he'd be looking for my name in the hotels, but certainly not for Etienne's. We retrieved the key from the reception and I settled myself and Dulce in the room.

Etienne had left me the famous key to ponder on, which I considered an exceptional mark of trust on his part.

After I'd taken a two hour nap (my foolproof remedy against jet-lag), I called Sylvie and arranged to have lunch with her somewhere close to her place.

We met a bit later at a new restaurant in the area: although new was not the exact word. There'd been a restaurant in that place forever, only it was a different one every two or three years. In its latest incarnation it was a Vietnamese restaurant. It had the advantage of having a pleasant terrace slightly recessed from the road, so it was quite calm.

My heart sank when I saw Sylvie arrive: she was as gorgeous as ever. Her curly natural blonde hair was loose on her shoulders and she wore a strict navy suit with a crisp white shirt which made her look even prettier. In fact, with her fresh complexion and beautiful blue eyes, she looked like an ad for cosmetics.

I stole a glance at my reflection in the restaurant's window: it was still the same me, as plump as ever. Definitely not model material there. Or maybe as the "before" in a "before and after" campaign.

Sylvie listened to me with passionate interest when I told her about the latest developments. She repeated that she wasn't aware of her sister renting a safe deposit box, but that she wouldn't necessarily have been.

I waited until we had been talking for a while until I took out of my bag a copy of the letter Alice de Brousse had left for her nephew. I said to Sylvie: "I have something here you should see."

For the second time that day, I saw someone crying after reading that letter. Dulce, with her unerring instinct, went close to her and pushed her leg with her small nose. Sylvie laughed through her tears and took her on her lap. No need for a tissue, Dulce took care of cleaning her face. I thought it rather sweet that she submitted to my little dog's thorough licking without grimacing or looking disgusted.

"Why are you crying? Can I do something? Let me kiss you, OK?"

After a while she let Dulce down and went to refresh her face in the ladies' room. When she came back she had regained her composure and was smiling her luminous smile again. She ordered a coffee. I asked her if she was feeling better and she replied: "Much better, thanks to you, Alex. Strangely enough, I feel relieved. I should be angry, because my sister was murdered and this letter from Mrs. de Brousse proves it in my mind beyond any doubt. But in a way, I feel lighter…I can't explain it."

"Perhaps you feel that way precisely because you have no doubts now. I think that there is no worse thing than incertitude."

Sylvie nodded: "I think you're right. It's like a huge weight has been lifted from my chest. And now I'm prepared to go all the way to see justice is done."

"Yes, but don't forget that his letter proves nothing: it only shows that Mrs. de Brousse had serious doubts about Florence's death. Which is certainly why she wasn't allowed to see the police."

Sylvie thanked the waitress for her coffee and said thoughtfully: "You know, I've been thinking about this. I wonder who this doctor was who forbid the police from seeing her. I'm pretty sure my sister said something about a new doctor, but I can't be certain."

I thought about it for a while: maybe this was something that could be checked by looking through her bills. I'd have to ask Etienne to have a look.

When I left Sylvie, she seemed transformed. If I had thought she was pretty before, now she positively glowed. I sighed and patted Dulce, who gave me a tiny reassuring lick.

"You're the one that I love, the center of my life!"

Felicia had organized to invite a few friends for my first evening in Geneva, so I decided another nap would be necessary before the evening. Exceptionally I took Dulce in bed with me, getting comfort from her small warm and furry body. I felt her breathing softly and from time to time she let out a muffled woof: she was certainly dreaming of chasing another dog.

Etienne was invited also, so I did my best to look good. Although, after having seen Sylvie that afternoon, I felt slightly depressed. Still, I put a little bit of make-up, to make my eyes look bigger and shinier, to make my round face look slightly thinner, and in general, to try to improve what could be.

Francis was going to be there that evening, as well as three or four of our mutual friends. I went to Felicia's house a bit ahead of the other guests, to help her set the table and lay out the food.

Soon we were all sitting around the table: Etienne had been introduced to our friends and we were all discussing. It was a friendly gathering. Everyone seemed to appreciate Etienne and he appeared to enjoy our friends very much.

After dinner we went to sit in the living room. This created three groups, each of which was busy with its own discussion. Etienne and I decided to show the key to Francis, Felicia and a couple of friends who worked in banks. They all had different theories as to what the key could be.

I had looked at it carefully and had to admit I couldn't imagine from where it came. It did look like a bank key, the traditional keys. Usually though these have a number on them, and this one didn't. It certainly wasn't from a station locker, which was our next idea. The lockers at the train station have very specific keys, which also have a number on them.

By eleven we had exhausted all the possibilities we could imagine and we were beginning to despair we'd ever find to what this key belonged.

Marlene was a friend we'd known forever: she was a nice girl, but not very smart. She had been talking to another friend while we were looking at the key. Being a polite girl, she decided to change groups and come to talk to us.

She sat down next to me and listened to our conversation, in her usual vacant way. Someone passed me the key and she said to me: "I didn't know you were a member of Florida! I've never seen you there!"

I looked at her blankly, feeling sucked into the abyss of her vacuity: what did she mean? It was Felicia who came to the rescue, saying patiently: "Marlene, Alex lives in New York: she is not a member of your gym club."

And then it dawned on me: Marlene had been looking at the key when she made her brilliant – as usual – remark. My throat went dry as I asked her, as nicely as possible: "Marlene, is this the key to a locker at the Florida Gym Club?"

By now, everyone was silent and looking at her. She looked around at our expectant faces and giggled: "Yeeeees, of course! They have these adorable lockers which look like old-fashioned safe deposit boxes. Not for the clothes, you know, but for jewelry, watches, etc. The customers complained that they had their stuff stolen, because the clothes lockers have holes in them and somehow thieves managed to open them or pull valuables out through the holes. So they brought in those boxes a couple of years ago! Isn't it sweet?"

She beamed at us. I didn't know whether I wanted to strangle her or kiss her. I stole a glance at Etienne: he wasn't acquainted with Marlene yet, so he was totally flabbergasted. He looked at me and I shrugged discreetly.

Everyone was talking animatedly now: thanks to our hapless friend, the puzzle was, partly at last, solved. Felicia went to look on her PC: there were eight Florida Clubs in Geneva. The question was how to find the right one.

Sylvie would certainly know which club her sister patronized. I said I would call her the next day to find out.

Etienne was deliriously happy and kept hugging me when he left, kissing me on both cheeks again and again. Much as I appreciated these displays of joy, they only showed a friendly and grateful attitude on his part. There was no way I could interpret them as a sign of being madly in love with me.

Once they had all left, we sat talking quietly with Felicia. She had to admit that Etienne wasn't showing the signs of infatuation and that he was nice with me in a brotherly kind of way.

I sighed and said: "I'll get over it." Dulce, who had been a remarkably well educated guest at the dinner party, came and snuggled next to me on the couch. I dug my fingers in her fur and gave her a nice doggy massage. In the end she rolled on her back and fell asleep. I giggled: there is nothing funnier than a doxie sleeping on its back, totally relaxed.

Felicia and I went on chatting for a while: we didn't realize how late it was getting. I looked at my watch and told her what time it was and she moaned: "Oh damn...I'll never have time to go to the Post office!". I told her I'd be free in the morning and if I could do some errands for her, feeling guilty to have kept her up so late during a week day. She thanked me and said no, but then added as an afterthought, gave me a couple of envelopes: "If you could just drop these in a mailbox it would be great! There isn't a single one on my way to work!"

She gave them to me and I noticed one of them was still open. I told her not to worry, that I would close it, and stuffed them in my bag. We called a taxi to take me back to the hotel.

CHAPTER XXVI

The next day I called Sylvie as soon as I woke up: which wasn't very early, since I was jet-lagged and tired. I knew Etienne must be up since dawn and chomping at the bit to get going, but I thought a two hours more wait wouldn't kill him.

Sylvie replied immediately: yes, her sister had a membership at the Florida Club. Since it was a chain, she didn't always go to the same one, but she thought she usually went to the one in the center of town.

I asked if she'd ever been there and she said yes, she'd been invited once by her sister. I was wondering how we could find out which locker she'd been using: the only way, in my opinion, was to go with Sylvie and explain the situation. We decided to meet there after she finished work. She had a commitment for lunch she couldn't break, so the earliest she could make it was at six, at the gym.

Next I called Etienne to tell him to be there. His cell phone didn't answer, but he called me five minutes later from the house. He took down the address of the gym and asked me if I wanted to meet for lunch. I hesitated and then said no. He seemed slightly taken aback by my refusal and said huffily: "Fine, then I'll see you at six at the gym."

I had decided to take the day for myself, to go shopping downtown and meet for lunch a cousin I hadn't managed to see during the summer. I put Dulce on her leash and we walked down, taking our time. The weather was chilly and the sky its usual unappetizing grey. But at least the colors in the windows were bright. Shopping in Geneva had always stopped at the windows for me. Even when I had lived there and earned an impressive salary, I thought the prices were exorbitant. Now, coming from New York where I earned US dollars which were worth pitifully little, I couldn't afford to even think of buying!

On the other hand, the fashion was nothing to write home about. And nowadays, you see the same brands everywhere. But it was a way to get reacquainted with the city, strolling through the "Rues Basses", which are Geneva's shopping district.

Here Dulce was a total hit, and I was stopped by people who wanted to pat her or talk to her every five minutes. She took it all with dignity and duly greeted everyone.

Lunch with my cousin was nice but uneventful: we caught up on each other and on the rest of the family. It was a bit stilted, as I had mostly lost touch with the others and sometimes had trouble remembering who was who, who was married, divorced and sometimes dead. The fact was that I wasn't giving him my full attention, wondering what we'd find that afternoon.

At one point during the meal I thought I glimpsed the familiar silhouette of the Foundation's goon, but quickly dismissed the idea: there was no way they could know I was here.

It started raining during the time we were in the restaurant, and I decided to go to the hotel to get changed. It wasn't very far from the Brasserie Lipp where we'd had lunch.

I had been wearing a skirt and heels in the morning, but now it was decidedly too chilly. I changed into comfortable jeans and a parka and flat, waterproof boots: the rain was pelting down now. After one last look in the mirror, I went out to meet Etienne and Sylvie.

I've always hated umbrellas and I hadn't taken one, as I was wearing a waterproof parka with a hood. Of course, it limited my vision to quite a large extent. It was pouring so hard that I was carrying little Dulce in my arms: she would have been drenched if I'd let her walk.

I didn't see it coming. I had gone out of the hotel in the direction of the gym, which wasn't very far. There was one intersection to cross, though. I had just crossed the first section, when I felt myself catapulted forward by someone behind me. He pushed me in front, almost landing on the traffic in the road I was about to cross. I heard tires screeching behind me and a crash and turned around to see a car careening back down on the road from the pavement on which I'd been standing.

The hero who had saved my life was a tough old gentleman, who was now hurling insults at the reckless driver. I was still speechless and he explained: "I'm sorry, I hope I didn't hurt you, but this car was heading right onto you: he actually drove onto the pavement and if I hadn't pushed you he would have hit you!"

I regained my breath and whizzed: "Sorry? What are you sorry about? You saved my life! I don't know how to thank you!"

He patted my back and turned around to leave in the other direction, smiling and saying: "My pleasure! Take care now!" and left.

I crossed the road in a daze: Dulce still clutched to my chest. What I feared had happened: somehow Damien had learned I was back, and he was after me. I gulped and tried to get the shivering under control. Suddenly everyone around me looked like an enemy and I felt trapped.

It was a two minute walk to the building where the gym club was located. Etienne was waiting for me, stamping his feet and looking eager to get on with it. When he saw my face though, he noticed how pale I was and asked if anything was wrong.

I told him about my near encounter with a large car, which I supposed belonged to the Foundation and he whistled: "We have to end this fast. We can't have you in danger anymore."

He took me in his arms in a bear hug, to stop the shaking. I dug my nose in the crook of his neck, breathing his light cologne and feeling, despite my incipient fear, in Heaven. We went to sit down at a small café from where we could see the entrance of the building and wait for Sylvie.

We both scanned the street for Sylvie but also for anyone who could be from the Foundation. I asked Etienne if he had talked to anyone about my arrival and he said, of course not. We discussed the key and the will, to try to get our minds off the killers.

Etienne and I were deep in speculation about the contents of the box the key opened. His eyes were shining and he was looking at me with…passion? Then suddenly, he stiffened and his eyes widened, as if in shock.

I heard a silvery voice behind me saying "Alex?" Sylvie was there. I rose and turned around to kiss her and introduce her to Etienne. My heart felt heavy as a stone as I looked at Etienne, his face transformed by what was, without any doubt, love at first sight!

Sylvie must have been aware of it, as she blushed prettily: it was the first time I saw this energetic young woman seem embarrassed. Etienne was totally lost for speech and I felt like extending a finger to push up his jaw. I wondered if he would start drooling.

The young woman sat down, crossing her impeccable legs encased in long boots. Etienne gulped audibly when she took off her strawberry pink raincoat and revealed a form fitting white sweater underneath. She bent down to say hello to Dulce, who gave her a friendly woof. I asked her if she wanted a drink and ordered coffee for the three of us.

I looked into my handbag to see if I had some change, but Etienne absentmindedly took out a bill to pay. I felt some paper under my fingers and realized with dismay I had forgotten to mail Felicia's letters.

By the time the waitress brought the coffees Etienne had regained speech: more or less. It was mainly incoherent babble and it took only a smile from Sylvie to make him sound almost senile. I got them talking about the key and how we were going to proceed to ask to open the box, and that seemed to get him back to something closer to his normal self.

I had asked Sylvie to bring her sister's death certificate. She had a copy of it at her office, so she was able to bring it. I prodded Etienne, who was reduced to a quivering jelly, and told him we'd better get going. He shook himself and said vaguely: "Yes, of course, let's go!"

We walked the short distance across to the building where the gym was located. It was in fact part of a very large building complex, where Geneva's oldest department store is located. There were two entrances to the building, one to the store itself and one to the rest of the building, which housed several floors of offices and the gym, on the last floor.

I was quite miffed with Etienne, whose eyes seemed literally glued to Sylvie: so much so, that I was almost tempted to leave them right there and go back home. But, knowing Etienne, I was sure he would come against some problem which he wouldn't be able to solve alone. So, with a big sigh, I got into the elevator with them.

The gym was pretty full at this hour of the day: a lot of people came after work and jumped, pedaled or ran like hamsters for an hour or so. I remembered that when I'd lived in Geneva, I had taken out a trial membership for one month. One thing I was pretty sure of, though, was that they hadn't had the safe boxes then. Or the glamorous clientele they seemed to have acquired in the meantime. There were several people behind the reception desk. Sylvie went up to them and explained our problem. The not too bright but splendidly fit girl behind the desk declared the problem too intense for her, and went to get someone higher in the hierarchy of the gym.

In due time a muscle bound Apollo appeared, and took a look at Sylvie's ID and Florence's death certificate. Glancing at the girl who had answered us he shrugged, expressing in one brief movement his opinion of her brains, and typed something on his computer. He printed out a sheet which he gave Sylvie, saying:

"There you are: your sister's subscription is until the end of December, she had paid in advance for the whole year. You can ask for a refund if you want, under the circumstances. She had box number 1378. It's right there, on your right." He asked: "is there anything else I can do for you guys?" and, looking at me he added: "Would you like to become a member here? I'm sure it would do you a world of good!"

I blushed furiously and stomped off towards the row of safe deposit boxes, glaring in his direction. Etienne and Sylvie followed me and we arrived in front of the rows of identical boxes. It looked to me as though the gym had bought old bank safes: the similarity was striking. Except, the locks took only one key, whereas bank boxes need two, the client's and the banks. We found, with beating hearts, the right box and Etienne put gingerly the key in the lock.

I watched the key turn and heard a low growl coming from Dulce. Her nose was pointing in the reception's direction: just as Etienne opened the door of the locker and reached out to take its contents, I glimpsed two men coming in and stopping at the reception.

"It's HIM, Alex! It's the enemy!"

And I recognized one of them: the guy whom I'd first seen in New York, the Foundation's henchman. He'd seen us.

In one gesture I whipped the two envelopes that were in the box out and into my handbag and pushed Etienne and Sylvie in front of me, saying "Run! There's another exit straight ahead!" They looked at me, startled, and did what I told them.

Two seconds later we shot out of the other exit of the gym, which opened directly into the department store. We ran down a flight of stairs and found ourselves in the cooking department. I looked back and saw the two men at the top of the stairs. Etienne grabbed Dulce under his arm and we all ran down the escalators, pushing our way past unhurried shoppers.

I shouted to Sylvie: "Leave in another direction: they don't know who you are and they won't chase you! No need to put yourself in danger!"

Etienne turned to her and shouted: "She's right, Sylvie! Stay here in the store, you're safe!"

Without another word, Sylvie got off the escalator and we went on running down. There was one more flight of stairs left and then we were on the ground floor. I thought for just one second and pulled Etienne in the direction of the other entrance of the store. We had entered from the lake side and the other exit was on the Rue du Marché: a pedestrian street with a tramway line along it.

It was totally dark by then and still raining. We ran across the street and hared up some stairs, in the direction of the Old Town. I glanced back and saw the two men in hot pursuit: one of them slipped and fell on the railway line. We went on running up the stairs, then more stairs. I was exhausted and stopped for a second: it was Etienne's turn to pull me, saying: "If they find us they'll get the will and destroy it! Hurry!"

I signaled to him to wait for one second and took out the two envelopes we'd retrieved from the gym. I got one of Felicia's envelopes from my handbag, the one that had been left open and rammed the two letters into it, tore the adhesive strip and closed it. We took off again as we heard heavy footsteps running up behind us.

I skidded to a halt in front of the mailbox I knew I'd find at the top of the rue de la Pelisserie and slipped the letters into it. Etienne's eyes widened, but he didn't say anything: he took the opportunity to let Dulce down, to the little dog's delight. She hadn't appreciated being carried for such a long time and being shaken on the way.

"Well, about time, too! I can run just as fast as you do! Let me down!"

We shot off to the left, on the Grand-Rue. It was almost totally deserted, the paved street in the old town, bordered left and right by buildings dating back to the 16th century. It was slippery and I was glad I was unhampered by heels and wearing flat boots.

Our steps echoed in the empty street and soon we heard the ominous sound of two pairs of feet catching up on us. I gasped: "We have to try to go down the hidden passage: maybe they don't know it!"

Etienne said: "Yes, come on!"

We turned left past the canons and down the rue du Puits Saint Pierre, and right past the Hôtel des Armures where Bill Clinton had eaten his fondue. We pelted down the street leading to the Cathedral, across the large square in front of the majestic church and up the small street de l'Evêché. There was an opening in that street, which led to a well-hidden passage. The passage in turn opened onto the square of the Madeleine church.

We slipped into the passage and stopped, hearts beating, breasts heaving. I knew I couldn't run anymore: my bulk was exhausting me. We heard footsteps in the rue de l'Evêché above us. They didn't stop at the opening and went on in the direction of the Bourg de Four.

Etienne and I stayed there, panting, for a few seconds. Dulce was at our feet, totally silent. I told Etienne we should go back up and meander through the little streets and then go back down from where we came. Etienne shook his head: "No: let's go down through here. Once we're on the rue de la Fontaine, we can get back to your hotel. I don't think it's a good idea to go to Clair-Chant right now: the hotel is probably the safest place.

I shrugged, too exhausted to protest. We stepped down into the dark passageway and came out in the rue de la Fontaine. It was mercifully quiet, now: it looked like we'd lost our followers. The walk to the hotel took us five minutes.

We went directly up to my room. The elevator was empty, as was the carpeted corridor on my floor. I let Dulce run along, as running on soft, carpeted surfaces is one of her favorites. She zoomed down the corridor, making as much noise as a herd of big dogs. When she arrived at the end, she did a crazy about turn, almost rolling over, and ran to the door of my room.

I slid in the card key and we went in, Dulce rushing past us to get to her food bowl. But instead of going into the bathroom, where the door was open and she had her stuff, she rushed into the room.

She stopped in front of the wooden wardrobe, changing in one second from a happy bouncy dog to a mini pointer, fur raised and barking.

Etienne and I looked at each other: something was very wrong. I opened gingerly the door: there was nothing awry at first sight, my clothes seemed to be as I had left them. But Dulce climbed into the wardrobe, snuffling and growling at the same time. I tried to see what was upsetting her, but didn't notice anything out of place. Dulce pushed her way into the wardrobe: she was totally inside it now, and getting more frantic by the second. Her nose was pointing in the direction of one of the panels of the wardrobe.

"There's this man's smell here, Alex! Come and see!"

I ran my hands on the wood and detected something that shouldn't have been there: a small black plastic bag, stuck with tape to the panel.

Pulling carefully so as not to tear it open, I unstuck it and took it out. It wasn't very big, weighing probably about half a kilo, and seemed to contain some kind of powder. Etienne took it from my hands and we lay it down on the desk.

Dulce followed us suspiciously, obviously disliking very much the smells emanating from the package. I patted her and thanked her profusely, while Etienne punched a small hole in the package. Our hearts sank as a white powder trickled out of it: it didn't need genius to see what had happened.

Damien had found out I was staying at the Metropole and managed to plant some drugs in my room. The police would probably be there soon.

I said: "We've got to flush it down the toilet, immediately!"

Etienne nodded and went towards the bathroom, holding the plastic bag.

It all happened so fast, I didn't have time to think and I'm sure it was the same thing for Etienne.

CHAPTER XXVII

As he stepped into the bathroom, I was following him and so was Dulce. But again, instead of going to the bathroom, she ran towards the door and skidded to a stop. If she had looked dangerous before, now she was a tiny ferocious beast, fur raised, teeth bared, emitting a low, menacing growl.

"It's the enemy again, Alex! Be careful"

I heard the click of a card key and simultaneously the door handle moving. Etienne turned around and came to the door of the bathroom, while the room door opened. Dulce jumped at the person who was coming in and I stepped back and grabbed the first heavy object I could find. It was a flower arrangement, which featured some orchids in a shallow stone container and a large stone. It was probably supposed to give the impression of a zen garden. At any rate, the stone was handy and I took it firmly in my hand.

In the meantime, Dulce was weaving herself in the intruder's legs, tripping him up, while Etienne lunged at him, socking him in the jaw. The man turned around to face this attack and I jumped on him from behind, hitting him on the head as hard as I could with the stone and trying to grab his gun. A shot went off, making a small plopping sound. I let go of the gun, startled.

He staggered into the room holding his head and then I saw the other man behind him. The guy I'd first seen in New York, the Russian, looking more dangerous than ever, a gun in his hand. In the meantime that first man was falling down, shot by his own gun. His head jerked bizarrely and he lay down, blood trickling from his skull.

The Russian slammed the door behind him and pointed his gun, signaling us to move further inside the room. Dulce was going berserk, barking furiously and trying to bite him. He tried to kick her, but she was too nimble for him and attacked from the other side.

"I'll get you, you just wait! I'm going to get a bite off your leg!"

He said in a cold voice, pointing his gun at her, now: "Dog shut up or I shoot."

I bent down and swept her up in my arms, holding her protectively against my chest, as Etienne moved in front of both of us. The Russian surveyed the scene in the room, looking at his fallen partner. He stepped back and glanced into the bathroom, where the black plastic bag was still in evidence.

A slow and very ugly smile appeared on his face. He said: "This perfect." He waved his gun at us: "Now you come with me and no trouble. Otherwise I shoot you. I don't care if people see."

As he pushed us towards the door, I grabbed my handbag, peering at him to see his reaction. He shrugged and let me take it and made us go outside, without another look at the man lying on the carpet. I had to ask: "Is he dead?"

The Russian glanced at the man: "Probably, yes. He doesn't breathe."

A shiver ran through me as I thought I'd killed a man. Etienne put his hand on my shoulder and squeezed it, without a word. We stepped out into the deserted corridor and went towards the elevator. Despite the fact that the hotel was pretty full, we didn't meet anyone on the way.

By the time we got out of the elevator, the Russian had a scarf in his hand, hiding the gun. We walked through the lobby, nobody paying us any attention. I wanted to shout, to run, to escape: but I realized that he would not hesitate for one second to shoot us and to shoot anyone who would get in his way.

So we walked meekly out before him and got into a black limousine that was parked in front of the hotel. He tipped the concierge and told us to get into the car, Etienne in front and me in the back. As soon as we were in the car, he locked the doors with the central system. I had thought it would be a good time to try to run, or to signal the concierge that we were in trouble. But the windows were black, the kind that you can't see inside, and we were locked in.

I wondered if Etienne would try something during the drive. After all, the man couldn't drive and shoot at the same time. But as soon as he had the doors shut, the Russian took out a pair of handcuffs and locked Etienne to the strap on his right, in a very uncomfortable position. The man glanced at me through the rear window and said in this voice I was beginning to hate like no other sound: "You stay put. The doors are locked and I shoot your friend if you try something. You understand?"

I nodded and sat back, holding Dulce as close to me as I could: she was trembling with rage, agitated and angry, knowing something was terribly wrong. But she stayed close to me and had given up trying to make an evening snack out of the goon.

Neither Etienne or I bothered with asking him who he was or what he wanted. We all knew perfectly what the situation was.

He drove us, to my great amazement, to the villa Clair-Chant. The gravel crunched under the wheels of the black limousine: it was still raining and very dark. Apart from the small spotlights on the side of the driveway which marked it out, there was no light at all coming from the house.

The Russian parked in front of the door and came out to get Etienne first, putting on the handcuffs again so his two hands were tied together. Then he came to the back and made me come out. This time Etienne asked:

"What the hell are you doing?"

The man simply shrugged and pushed us into the house. Arriving in the large entrance hall, he made us turn left, to where the kitchens and the ancillary rooms were located. Just before the kitchen there was a door opening on the right. He opened it and turned on the light. I saw with dismay a long flight of stairs going down. Etienne whispered: " The cellars…"

We trundled in single line down the narrow stairs, and found ourselves in a large, airy cellar. We crossed it and walked into another one and another one until we were in what I thought must be the last room. There was one wall stacked with wine bottles on the right and several shelves in the middle, which contained all kinds of preserves and foodstuffs.

The left hand wall had only one row of shelves, also stocked with wine bottles. He took out one bottle and Etienne sighed: "Damn it: the cold room."

I looked at him and he shook his head: "This is worse than I thought."

The Russian had apparently pressed on a button or activated some mechanism, as the shelf moved forward to reveal a solid wooden door behind it. The man took out a key from his pocket and opened the door. He made us go into the room the door opened into.

It was another cellar: but whereas the first ones felt relatively warm, this one was much colder and definitely humid. I understood why when I saw the floor. It was wood and I could hear the lapping of water underneath it.

The room was not totally empty: there were piles of wine crates against the wall and in the middle of the room, and some building materials in another corner, some sand and a couple of paint buckets. But that was all. Having prodded us inside the room, the Russian went out without a word, locking the door behind him. We heard the shelve sliding back into place, and then there was silence.

I let Dulce down on the floor and Etienne went to get a few crates to sit on. My first thought was to take out my cell phone and call for help. But there was no signal. Which was probably the reason why the man hadn't bothered to take it away from me. Etienne took his out of his pocket, but it also showed no signal.

He put his head in his hands:

"Damn it! What do we do now!"

Dulce, seeing he was upset, came and gave his hands a friendly lick. He smiled and patted her, getting more licks on the way. He said: "Where did you send the papers?"

I shushed him immediately. Who knew who could hear us? Then I leaned over and whispered, so low that no system in the world could hear my words:

"To the Geneva Tax authorities. It's with some additional papers they asked Felicia to send."

He gasped and laughed and whispered in my ear:

"What if they throw them away?"

I said, aloud this time: "Well, it was a risk, but what else was there to do?"

He admitted that there hadn't been much choice. One thing seemed to preoccupy him:

"I don't understand how these people knew in which hotel you were. You're there under my name, it's difficult to understand how they found you."

He was going to get an answer to that question sooner than he thought.

About an hour later Dulce jumped up and started barking: a few seconds later the door opened. It was the Russian, and he wasn't alone: Anny was with him. Etienne drew in his breath and watched as she walked in, perfectly composed.

He sputtered: "Anny! What are you doing here? Do you know who these people are?"

Anny looked back at him, her small eyes in their deep sockets showing hate and contempt:

"They're the people who are looking after me. Not like you who wanted to take everything from me!"

Etienne exclaimed: "What do you mean, Anny, take everything from you? Aren't you happy as you are? Don't you have everything you need?"

"Yes, I do. But not thanks to you. I'm not as stupid as you think, you know. They explained to me that the will I signed as a witness, is what you are trying to find. And I'm not going to allow that!"

Etienne frowned: "But why, Anny, why? It was my aunt's last will, why don't you want it to be executed? I don't understand!"

Anny smirked: "You see, I told you I'm not so stupid: right now I have a job and I'll have one as long as I want. Because it said so on the will. The one that was executed. But they explained to me that if I was a witness to another will, I cannot be a beneficiary. So Mrs. Alice wanted to cut me out and you want to cut me out with this will."

Her face had closed in an expression of incredibly mulish stupidity. It was no use arguing with her. The Russian signaled to her and she addressed me, brusquely: "I have to search you."

I winced but submitted to the search, while the two men supposedly looked the other way. She then turned my bag upside down and examined the contents: the goon looked on, increasingly annoyed. All I had in my bag were a comb, my purse and my cell phone. The man then gave Anny his gun, which she held firmly while he searched Etienne. He let out a few curses when they didn't find anything on us. Anny then went out with the Russian, without another look at Etienne.

Once more he sat down and put his face in his hands, unbelieving. I sat next to him and put a consoling arm around his shoulder. He was muttering: "I can't believe this! Anny! She's been with us since she was a child!"

I said, running my hand through his hair: "Well, at least this solves some mysteries. You probably talked in front of her without paying any attention. Anny for you was family, someone who you would never associate with betrayal. And someone too stupid to even think of betrayal. I have to say, it was genius on Damien's part to think of corrupting Anny. He must have found out about the will, probably through Florence, and reflected that the only people your aunt could use as witnesses would be Anny and the gardener.

And you know Anny: if you ask her a straight question, she answers. You and I never thought of asking her straightforwardly if she'd witnessed the signature of a will. At first, because you had no idea such a will existed, and afterwards because we didn't need to, since we knew it for certain from Giuseppe.

She must have been the one who told Damien about our dinner date on the Salève, back in the summer. And I'm sure she heard you when you told me you'd made a reservation in your name for me at the Hôtel Métrople."

Etienne nodded: "You're right, of course. In fact, she must have told them about our every gesture. Damn the woman! Doesn't she realize she could get us killed?"

I laughed: "I'm pretty sure she doesn't!"

My laughter didn't last for long: our situation was still as dire as ever. I looked at the time: it was eight, Dulce's meal time. I sighed: would we be fed?

Strangely enough, we were, and quite soon. About half an hour later, the Russian came down and brought us a hamper in which there was bread, some cheese and some ham, a few apples and a bottle of water.

We tried to ask him what he intended to do with us, but he never said a word. He came down again a bit later and brought an empty bucket and some toilet paper: which I looked at, wincing. We exchanged glances with Etienne and sighed. The man came down for the third and last time with an armful of blankets, which he threw on the floor.

Once he had left, we got organized, splitting the food between us and Dulce. She was given a large helping of ham, which she found quite nice. Thankfully I had her small traveling bowl with me and she got her little corner organized, with a folded blanket and her water bowl. She tucked herself in, looking quite snug.

Etienne and I looked at her with envy. We would certainly be less comfortable than her. The humidity and the cold were beginning to have their effects on our bladders: I looked with distaste at the bucket. Etienne had an idea: he built two walls in a corner with some empty crates, to create some privacy. We took some sand from the pile on the corner and threw it in the bucket, and it became almost civilized. Dulce had chosen a far corner as her private toilet.

Those details taken care of, we had to get organized for the night. In the end, we decided to build a sort of small cabin, with walls made of crates piled two high on three sides, to keep in a little bit of heat.

If we wanted to keep warm enough, there was no choice but to sleep on two blankets, close to each other. We piled on the other two blankets and squeezed Dulce between us.

Etienne went to turn off the light, which consisted in one bare bulb hanging from the ceiling.

CHAPTER XXVIII

Thanks in large part to Dulce, who produced as much heat as the two of us together, the night wasn't too cold. In other circumstances, I would have been in Heaven, in the arms of this handsome man. As it was, I had given up any hope of seducing him, now that he had met Sylvie. Besides, contrary to what movies and books try to make you believe, this kind of life threatening situation isn't exactly conductive to flirting or otherwise amorous behavior.

It was a slight change in the darkness which woke me up: the floor was made of boards which weren't perfectly joined and the water reflected the light of the day. By the light of my mobile I watched Etienne who was sleeping holding Dulce tightly in his arms. She had woken up as soon as she felt me moving and she was looking at me. But, polite and thoughtful dog as she was, she remained put, not wanting to disturb Etienne.

"Is this man going to sleep forever? Come on, get up and let's do something about getting out of here!"

She sighed and put her muzzle down, wondering when she could get up. Finally, Etienne stirred and woke up: he wiped his eyes and yawned, allowing Dulce to move away from him. She shook herself and came to me, wagging her tail. I went to turn on the light, asking Etienne how he'd slept. He scratched his head and mumbled:

"Actually, better than I'd thought. Thanks to this mini heater, here!"

Dulce, understanding he was talking about her, woofed proudly. He laughed and scratched her behind the ears, which turned into an extensive belly rub.

We did what we could in terms of morning ablutions, missing sorely our toothbrushes. An apple would have to replace them. It was early, a little past seven. We discussed our options. Etienne said:

"I wonder how far they're prepared to go to get the will back? Do you think they would kill us?"

"I haven't the slightest doubt about it, do you?"

"No, not really. They've already left a trail of bodies."

We sat despondently, thinking of the alternatives: there wasn't much we could do except wait. The envelope must be on its way to the Tax authorities. A lot depended on what was in the papers and what the person who eventually opened the envelope would do with them.

Etienne shrugged: "I guess if we don't tell them where the will is, their alternative is to kill me, as the probable heir."

I dismissed his argument: "It's not that easy to kill people and why would they do it if they're not certain you're the heir?"

He sighed and ran a hand through his hair. I whipped out my comb and said: "Anyway, there's nothing we can do but wait and see. And in the meantime, you could use this…"

He laughed and combed his hair. We sat there for another four hours, having eaten our breakfast apples and passing the time speculating on our - bleak - future.

Dulce heard him coming back before us and rushed to the door, barking. I ran to grab her and whipped her out of the way just in time. The door opened and the Russian came in, followed by Damien.

He looked as impressive as always, tall, very dark, with black piercing eyes. He didn't waste time on niceties or polite conversation but said brusquely:

"Where is it?"

Etienne began saying : "I don't know what you're talking about"- which I had told him was a stupid line to take - when the Russian walked up to him and smacked him in the jaw. Etienne staggered back and Damien said in a flat voice:

"Mr. de Brousse, don't play this silly game with me. Give it to me now. Or do I have to ask Boris to search you both again?"

I was getting fed up, so I told him: "Don't be silly: he's already searched us and you know very well we don't have it anymore."

Damien looked daggers at me and barked: "Do you take me for an idiot? My men were behind you from the moment you got the papers. They saw them in your hands. Where are they?"

I faced him, planting my eyes into his, not wavering for a second and replied:

"I got rid of them".

Damien came very close to me: I could feel his breath on my face and his eyes were boring into mine. He said, very distinctly:

"Where. Are. They."

I remained silent.

I had expected it, but it still took me by surprise: a violent slap across the face, which sent me reeling back. Dulce was barking like mad and wriggling in my arms to try to jump at Damien. Etienne bounded forward, but the man named Boris held him in a painful grip. Damien looked down at me and said:

"Very well. I'll give you some time to think about it. And to think about something else: right now, the Swiss police is looking for you in connection with a fallout between drug dealers. If you give me this will, I could arrange things. Otherwise, you'll just be two more victims in a drug war. I have all the time in the world, and I think you'll begin to find this place very uncomfortable after a while."

He turned around and left, followed by Boris.

We stayed up, side by side, as we watched the door close. Etienne and I then examined cautiously our mutal jaws. Boris had hit him very hard and there was already a bruise on his face. I had been luckier, as Damien had hit me flat handed: my cheek and jaw were red, but probably wouldn't change colors. I applied some fresh water on Etienne's face and we sat down to think about our predicament.

CHAPTER XXIX

I looked at him:

"We have to escape. We can't stick around to wait for Damien to come back and kill us."

He thought for one moment: "Maybe we can overpower them when they come in next time. We could organize a trap with the boxes…"

His voice trailed off: his idea didn't make much sense.

My attention kept going back to the floor. Could this be a way out? I asked Etienne if we could somehow dislodge one or two floor planks. He said: "No need for that, there is a hatch."

I gasped: "Whaaaaaat? There is a trapdoor and you didn't mention it before? Where is it?"

He got up and started pushing around some of the wine crates that were in the middle of the floor, until a trapdoor, about three by three, appeared. I exclaimed: "But we can go out through here!" He shook his head: "No, I don't think so. Look."

The hatch opened directly into the lake: the water came flush up to it. Etienne explained: they used this as a well, to cool things down in the summer. At the beginning of the 20th century, a child had drowned there and since then the room had been closed, it's door hidden by the shelves. Everyone knew of its existence, but since now, if you wanted to cool your water or your wine you simply put in the fridge, the cooling well wasn't necessary anymore.

He added: "The child drowned because the opening is pretty narrow and if you fall in and don't come up, and there is no light to guide you,

you drown. You would either have to find your way back to the opening or to swim to the lake and that's a long stretch."

I peered down and asked: "How long?"

Etienne looked at me, startled: "You aren't thinking…"

I shrugged: "Can you swim?"

He blustered: "Yes, I can. But it's a huge risk. You'd have to swim underwater for quite a long way".

"Just how long, Etienne? It can't be that much. The house isn't built on the water, so I suppose this is a sort of outcrop of the house. It can't be that long. In fact…"I looked at the room. The trap was located approximately in the centre. "In fact, I would think it would be from here to this wall, which must be the outer wall."

Etienne looked across: "I…I suppose so. I have never really thought about it. But, if you're right, it's still a good 20 feet to swim, underwater, in the dark. And you easily lose your sense of direction. If you go slightly off course, you could end up swimming into the bank, or going further under the house…"

He clearly wasn't too happy about this option, but I thought we had no other choice. Jumping Boris wasn't high up on the list of things I wanted to do before I died. Besides, Anny, among her more unappealing features, seemed extremely muscular.

Etienne looked at me dubiously: "Do you think you can do it?"

I felt slighted: "I may not be a top model, but I do, occasionally, exercise. And I am a very good swimmer."

He sighed. I added: "The only thing…"

Etienne perked up, hoping for a reprieve. I went on:

"Dulce? I have to carry her and swim at the same time. And it's a long time for her to stay without breathing."

Etienne looked dubious. He said: "I could carry her."

I replied impatiently: "That's not the point, Etienne. The point is how long can a little dog like her stay without breathing?"

I had made my decision and I knew that Etienne realized it. He protested weakly: "Do you know how cold the water is in this season?

He was shivering just at the idea. I told him: "Would you rather be a little bit cold or totally cold, as in "dead"?"

Etienne sighed: "OK, let's do it then."

The first thing we did was to pile up all the crates in front of the door. That would certainly stop them for some time. Then I started worrying like crazy about Dulce and her trip underwater. For myself I wasn't worried in the least: twenty feet underwater was nothing. I supposed the light would be visible and I couldn't go very wrong.

I wasn't too sure about Etienne but he had said he could swim. But Dulce? Could a small doxie hold her breath for the one or two minutes it would take to cross? And was it better to hold her against me or to let her swim beside me?

She was watching me closely, as if trying to guess what I was planning. I caressed her soft head and whispered: "Dulce, you're not going to like it, but I'm afraid we have to do it. What do you prefer? That I hold you or you swim by yourself?"

"Are you crazy? I can't swim! We do this, lady, you hold me tight!"

She nodded sideways and gave a short woof. I told her: "You want me to hold you?" She barked more energetically. I shrugged: "Fine. As you want!"

Etienne was looking at me and said: "It's better if I hold her: I'm stronger."

I didn't want to hurt his feelings, but Dulce's well-being and maybe survival was at stake, so I asked: "Etienne, just how good a swimmer are you?"

There was a silence and I pressed on: "Can you swim underwater? Have you ever done it?"

After a while her replied, reluctantly: "I'm not the world's best swimmer and I hate putting my head in the water. But that's not the problem, basically. My problem is I can't open my eyes in the water." He coughed: "I don't know why. It's stupid."

I squeezed his hand: "Of course it's not stupid. But we have to find a solution."

In the end, we were ready. And a strange picture we must have made. I was first, holding Dulce wrapped in a blanket. I had taken off my boots and put them inside my parka. Etienne was behind me, my handbag slung across his shoulder. Dulce's leash was tied to her harness and the other end was tied to the strap of my handbag.

It would ensure Etienne followed me. We lowered ourselves slowly into the freezing cold water. Etienne went blue and I started shaking. It was awful. Dulce was still wrapped in the blanket and hadn't felt the cold yet. I gave Etienne some last advice and we took one huge collective breath.

It was the longest minute in my life. As soon as I was underwater I could see the light in front of me: swimming in the right direction wasn't going to be a problem.

But swimming with a squirming little dog clutched to me on one hand, and a man who pulled me in all directions on the other hand, was excruciating. I wished Etienne would just let me pull him along. It took much longer than it should have and I was terrified Dulce would drown. She wasn't wriggling anymore and I tried to gather as much strength as I could to swim and to pull Etienne struggling weight behind me.

We finally made it out from under the building, emerging suddenly in the cold lake water in front of the house. I saw with relief that Dulce's eyes were open and she was spitting and coughing. So was Etienne.

It was only then that I realized why I hadn't seen that part of the building before. It wasn't connected to the main building, but jutted out as a small separate wing some ten meters from the main house, on the lake bank. It was totally covered in vegetation and was almost invisible if you didn't know it was there.

We swam to the side further from the house and clambered onto the bank. We were hidden from the house and reasonably safe for a little while. But it was awfully cold and poor Dulce was shivering. So was I, but I was too preoccupied with the dog to worry about myself.

Etienne was squeezing the water out of his clothes and getting his shoes back on. He said: "We have to get away. Let's go to the garage, there might be a car there we can take."

We snuck up to the garage, being careful not to be visible from the house. There were two cars there, the black limousine in which we'd been abducted the day before, and Anny's little red car. Etienne smiled when he saw it: "She always leaves the keys in the keybox, near the door."

I eyed the little red car with distaste: "I'd rather take the big one." Etienne went to check the key box: "Well, I'm afraid the Boris guy hasn't yet gotten the habits of the household. The key isn't here."

I looked out towards the house: "Etienne, if we take the car out now, they'll see or hear us."

He looked at his watch: "It's almost six now: it will be dark in less than half an hour. We could wait."

Something else worried me: "At what time does Anny leave work?"

"Usually not before seven thirty, since she cooks dinner and sometimes serves it. But I'm not sure...since I'm not dining...in the dining-room..."

He snorted derisively: "Maybe she'll stay to cook us a gourmet dinner for tonight."

I thought back to the tray she had brought us for lunch: soup and grilled chicken and rice. Maybe.

"I think it's worth taking the risk. Besides, it's quite warm in here and our clothes are beginning to dry. And there are plenty of places to hide in case anyone comes this way."

Etienne nodded: "We'll hear them: the gravel is awfully noisy."

We found some blankets in the back of the garage. They smelled of petrol, but they were clean and helped us get dryer and warm. Dulce got first service and was thoroughly rubbed until she was dry.

By the time night fell without any other incident, we were almost dry. We had decided to roll out the car until the curve in the driveway, where it wouldn't be visible and the noise of the main road would muffle the engine's noise. We pushed it silently on the grass on the border of the driveway. We kept on looking over our backs, terrified to see a face appearing at one of the windows and all hell breaking loose.

But nothing happened, and we made it to the bend without any problem. Etienne got into the driver's seat and I got in on the other side. He turned on the engine, but not the lights yet and drove slowly to the gate. He had the remote control to the gate on his keychain, which was still in his pocket.

The gate opened silently, and seconds later we were driving away, in the direction of Lausanne.

We both yelled with joy and thought about our next destination. I turned on the radio: Damien's assertion that the police was looking for us worried me.

CHAPTER XXX

At seven there were news, and they were not good for us. The brief report said that after the body of a man and a substantial quantity of cocaine had been found in a Geneva hotel, the police was looking for two people, a French citizen residing in Switzerland and a woman, a Swiss citizen residing in the United States, to help them with their inquiries.

I exclaimed: "We have to go to the police and set this straight! It's ridiculous!"

Etienne shook his head: "We can't do that! How are we going to prove we were framed? The police have a bag full of cocaine and covered in both our prints, and a dead body. The guy was certainly a known criminal and we killed him. And ran. So OK, we didn't run of our own volition: but how do we prove it?"

I chewed my lip: "Mm. You're right. The only way we could prove all this would be if we had the will. We have to wait until we get it back."

Etienne put the blinker on and turned off, leaving the Route du Lac. He said: "I'm going to go through the vineyards. You never know."

As we meandered through the roads on our way east, we tried to figure out how long we had to keep off everyone's radars. We thought that by now the envelope must have arrived. I had to talk to Felicia to tell her to get the contents back.

Our phones hadn't liked their sojourn in the water. I looked disconsolately at my dear iPhone, wondering if it would ever work again. However, surprisingly, the cheap phone I'd bought before my trip to Paris, seemed to have fared better. The screen did strange things, but it looked as though it was working.

I called Felicia, who was absolutely mad with worry. Sylvie had called, panicked because we had disappeared. Then she had watched the news and immediately understood that it was us they were talking about.

I had to tell her I would call her later to explain, and then explained about the letter. She sputtered: "What did you do??? You sent it with my tax papers?"

I sighed: "There was no other solution. Can you please call them tomorrow morning and tell them you put these papers in the envelope by mistake and could they send them back to you? Or rather, ask them to keep them and tell them you'll come to pick them up. It's safer."

There was a big, martyred sigh on the other end of the line, and Felicia said she would do it. I told her as soon as she had them to give me a call. She asked where we were and I told I had no idea but would tell her, eventually.

I hung up and told Etienne: "I'd better call Sylvie: she's worried sick!"

He looked as though he'd been stung by a bee at the mention of Sylvie's name. I rather thought he'd forgotten about her in the last few hours. He said: "Sylvie!"

It was pronounced with such passion, I couldn't help laughing. I said: "Don't worry, you'll see her again!"

We were weaving through the tortuous roads of the Genevese hinterland, through vineyards, fields, orchards and picturesque villages. I asked Etienne: "Where are we going?"

He shrugged: "I have no idea!"

I glanced at him: his hands were clutched on the wheel and he looked worried. I thought for a moment and said:

"We should try to find a hotel for the night and plan our next move."

"And how are we going to get a room, if the police is looking for us?"

While we were talking, I was rummaging through the glove compartment of the Mini. Like the rest of the car it was spotlessly clean and organized. I found the car's papers and a very good surprise: Anny's driving license. I waved it under Etienne's nose. "This is how! I'll take the room in her name!"

Etienne looked doubtful: "But they will ask for some ID other than this! Do you think a driving license is enough?"

I smiled: "Don't worry."

Etienne frowned but didn't say anything. After a while he asked: "And where do you suggest we go?"

I had thought about it and replied: "Let's go to Montreux. It's where I was born and I lived there a few years. At least I know it well and I think that's essential under the circumstances."

Etienne stole a look at me: "But won't someone recognize you?"

I shrugged: "It's been years: I don't think so. And so what if they do? The police hasn't given my name, so only people close to me, like Felicia, would associate me with the person the police is looking for."

"I guess you're right. Then let's go to Montreux. I think we should stop for dinner somewhere, though. I'm starving."

By then we were almost dry: Etienne had turned on the heat at maximum volume when we got into the car, and the warm dry air had done a good job. The only part of me that still felt unpleasantly humid was the one I was sitting on, but that could not be helped.

We drove on until we found a restaurant in the deeps of the region of Aubonne. It had a convenient courtyard surrounded by tall walls, which served as a parking lot. We tucked the car in a dark corner and emerged from it. We were stiff and full of all kinds of aches, because of the stress, the humidity and the cold cellar. Dulce, on the other hand, was her usual sprightly self and was glad to jump out of the car and take care of urgent business in a small patch of grass.

The restaurant is known the world over for its cuisine and despite the fact that it was a working day, was quite full. There were two rooms, the more formal one where most people dressed up, and the "salle" which served both as restaurant for tourists and visitors, and as the village auberge. There the dress code was casual and we were able to sit down and order without anyone giving us a second glance.

I ordered chicken, not because it is my favorite, but because it is Dulce's favorite. I thought the little dog deserved a treat, especially since she was nowhere near getting her own, carefully selected doggie food. She also got some rice and I gave her some carrots from my salad. On the whole, a perfectly acceptable meal for her.

Our ordeal had opened our appetite and we were glad to sit in a warm, friendly place, surrounded by normal people. Etienne wondered when they would discover our escape.

"I should think they would have done so by now: Anny would have noticed her car was gone at around seven. That was almost two hours ago."

Etienne laughed: "Well, at least its' a consolation that we stole her beloved Mini! The bitch…"

"I think you are a bit hard on her, Etienne. After all the girl is half-witted. She must have been very easy to manipulate."

"Half-witted she may be: but even she must have known these people are dangerous!"

"It's hard to tell."

"When I think that I trusted her as if she were a member of the family! I can't get over it!"

There was a fireplace in the big room and I had my back to it. During most of the meal I surreptitiously raised my bottom to let the heat dry the seat of my pants. Thankfully, there was no one sitting behind me!

Etienne ordered coffee and dessert and I declined. He was relaxing in front of his cup of coffee and seemed on the point of falling asleep. So I took the wheel leaving from Aubonne.

We decided that taking the highway we would be safe from our pursuers: it was a forty minute drive to Montreux. There was little traffic at that hour and we made it in less time than that. A few kilometers before the Montreux exit, I saw a gas station and stopped there. The gas tank was still almost full, but the station had a convenience store which was open all night. We were able to buy toothbrushes, toothpaste and a few essentials, and they even had dog food.

I had decided to go to the hotel Helvétie, which was in the center of town and was very discreet. It was a three star hotel which had the advantage of having some parking spaces nearby, where we could hide the car.

Etienne started worrying about IDs and passports and I told him to stay next to me and take care of Dulce and I would take care of the registration.

The nice receptionist told me she had a few rooms left: I asked her for a double with two beds and she gave me a rate. I agreed and took the room, and when she asked for my passport, I pretended to look in my handbag and exclaimed:

"Oh, of course! I left it at home. Darling, I don't suppose you have yours, do you?" He looked at me, bewildered, as I took out Anny's driving license and said to the girl: "I'm sorry, we had no intention of spending the night at a hotel, but my husband drank too much at some friend's house and I'm such a bad driver I daren't go back to our house in the night. So we don't have our papers but I do have my driving license, is that enough?"

She nodded with a smile: "Yes, no problem. Please fill out the form. Can you give me a credit card please?"

That was another problem. I called out to Etienne: "Darling, I don't suppose you have a credit card with you? Do you have cash?" He stumbled over, looking drunk, and gave me a wad of notes. I carefully picked out the price of the room and paid it in advance, saying: "I'll pay now: if we manage, we'll try to leave very early tomorrow. We both have to be at work in Geneva before eight!"

The nice receptionist winced and handed me the card key. We took the elevator to our nice room on the fourth floor, which had a view of the lake.

It had been two exhausting days, and after taking each in turn long luxurious warm baths, we dropped into bed, without even having the courage of thinking of our near future. Dulce slept on a blanket over some pillows and looked the happiest dog on earth.

It was the second night I was spending next to Etienne: he had undressed down to his boxer shorts and was a scrumptious vision. I had decided to sleep in the burnous provided by the hotel, which was three sizes too big and left nothing much of my anatomy in sight. But, looking at myself in the mirror, I thought I looked rather sexy, wrapped in the thick white robe, with my freshly washed hair.

Despite this, nothing was further from my mind than hanky panky with Etienne. Stress does that, I guess…we were exhausted and anxious. The minute our heads hit our pillows, we were asleep. The only noise in the room was Dulce's soft snoring.

CHAPTER XXXI

The next morning, we ordered breakfast in the room and sat around the small table in front of the minuscule balcony, watching the marvelous view. Montreux is certainly one of the nicest towns around the lake. It has always been a favorite of foreign visitors. Its era of splendor was in the late 19th century to the early twentieth century, when people from around the world flocked to stay in its grandiose palace hotels. The Hôtel Helvétie was one such hotel, though a minor one, built in 1865. It still kept most of its architectural elements intact and had an old fashioned charm of its own.

The rain of the previous night had cleared the atmosphere, and for the first time since I had arrived in Switzerland there was a bright sun and blue skies. The view from our room was spectacular: the other side of the lake, the French side, with towering mountains rising mistily above the shimmering grey blue lake. On the left hand side the lake opened onto the valley of the Rhône, bordered on both sides by tall mountains, whose summits were already covered in snow.

As we munched our crisp croissants, a boat of the CGN, the lake's main boat operator, glided across the lake. It was a lovely and picturesque sight, as the CGN operates mainly historical steamboats, meticulously preserved and maintained.

My iPhone rang and I heard Felicia's voice on the other end:

"I've called the Tax offices: they haven't received the envelope yet."

"Whaaaat? But it left two days ago!"

"Yes, well, I'm afraid Switzerland has changed a lot since you lived here, darling. Letters can take up to three, sometimes four days to go from one point to another."

"Oh, no!"

"Oh, yes. Patience, Alex, patience. Where are you now?"

"We're holed up in a hotel in Montreux, waiting for the damn envelope to surface."

Felicia laughed: "Well, there are worse things than to be spending time in a nice hotel with a gorgeous man!"

I snorted: "Umph. No comment."

She laughed again and told me she'd call me the next morning.

I was wondering if it was a good idea to use my phone: if the police was really looking for me, they could easily locate it. On the other hand, in order to do that they'd need to contact the police in New York to find out my number. My mobile phone number was unlisted. In order to buy the other phone, though, I had given my ID and therefore it could be tracked. I threw away the chip and kept the phone.

Etienne was looking at me inquiringly: I told him the envelope hadn't arrived at the Tax offices yet. He said he wasn't surprised, that the quality of postal services was getting worse and worse.

We could only wait and Etienne suggested we go shopping. I asked him if he had any money and he said he still had a lot of cash. I was intrigued. He said he'd prepared a lot of bills to pay the next day and that was why he had so much cash with him. He said sheepishly:

"In fact, I was supposed to pay them the morning we got abducted, but I forgot..."

"Like I forgot to mail Felicia's letters the same day...which saved the will"

We burst out laughing.

There was a young man at the reception desk that morning: we told him we wanted to stay one more night, since we were enjoying the hotel so much, and paid another night in advance.

The hotel Helvétie is the most centrally located in Montreux. Stepping out of the hotel we found all the shops we needed. We bought some clothes and shoes and a blanket for Dulce. Shopping with Etienne made me feel like "Pretty Woman". Well, he could have been a Richard Gere, movie star material, but I had to admit I was no Julia Roberts.

Still, it was fun: I got a pair of jeans and a couple of sweaters and a new and warmer jacket. We both bought warm boots. We had lunch at the Montreux Palace, one of the most beautiful hotels in Switzerland.

The Montreux-Palace is located at the western tip of Montreux and we were able to stroll back by the lake side. There were always people walking along the lake, tourists and residents alike. In the latest years Montreux had become a premium location for wealthy retirees from various spots of the world. They bought luxurious apartments at inflated prices, overlooking the lake and with breathtaking views of the mountains. They whiled their days promenading by the lake, or having tea at the famous Zurcher tearoom, where we ended up after our long stroll.

Once we sat there and ordered some tea, I looked around me and smiled: nothing changed here. There had been some renovations and changes in the decor along the years, but, basically, Zurcher kept the same ambience it had had for the last 130 years.

It was still a mixture of local old ladies and their pooches, employees stopping for a sandwich or a pastry, and an odd assortment of foreigners, tourists and residents.

Our hotel was just across the street and we returned there to take a nap before going out again. It was two, and we still had a long afternoon of idleness ahead of us.

We turned on the TV to watch the news. There was no mention of our story, which had quickly dropped off the first page. We had bought a whole bunch of newspapers and looked through all of them.

The problem with Swiss press is that most of it is now owned by one press group, Tamedia. Which means that apart from a few cosmetic differences, the majority of newspapers are very similar and publish the same news.

There was only a small paragraph on the second page of two newspapers mentioning the body found at the Hotel Métropole, saying that the police was still looking for two persons in connection thereto.

Etienne's Blackberry had been in clinical death since its bath in the lake. All efforts of revival had failed and he'd finally given up on it. Besides, turning it on would not have been a good idea anyway, as it would be easy to track and, contrary to mine, it would be easy for the Swiss police to find the number.

We were therefore extremely surprised when the phone, which had been lying on Etienne's bedside table, suddenly gave out what sounded ominously like a death rattle. It shook and beeped and whizzed and finally started ringing almost normally.

Etienne approached it prudently and looked at the number on the screen. He blanched: "It's from Clair-Chant"

I quickly thought: if it was the police, they knew where we were anyway and they'd be knocking at the door very soon. If I was Boris or Damien, we should answer, to see where we stood. I nodded to Etienne to answer. He picked up the phone and turned on the loudspeaker:

"Yes?"

"Ah, Etienne. I'm glad to hear you, I was becoming worried:"

It was Damien's repulsive voice. I shuddered and so did Etienne, who asked in a pale voice:

"What do you want, Damien?"

Damien chuckled, a horrible noise: "Oh, come on now, Etienne. Have you got it with you?"

"No. It's somewhere you can't find it. And so are we. So get lost, Damien!"

Damien made a "tsk, tsk" noise and went on:

"This may be. But what good is the will going to be to you, if you're in prison? I think we should discuss. I may be able to get you and your lady friend out of the sticky situation you find yourselves in. Against the will, of course. You can go back to your previous lives, I destroy the will…and God's in his Heaven".

I found it particularly revolting that this man should choose to quote the poet Browning. Etienne looked at me, a question in his eyes. I made a rude gesture, indicating to him to tell Damien to go to hell.

Etienne duly relayed our feelings to Damien, who emitted a screeching sound, which he probably thought was a laugh. He rattled: "Well, call me when you change your mind!" and hung up.

We looked at each other and sat down simultaneously on one of the beds, our mood back to a dark blue. The only good thing was Damien couldn't find us. But the police could, now. Etienne meditatively turned off his Blackberry and ran a hand through his chestnut hair. He asked:

"What do we do now, Alex? We can't stay here…"

I shook my head: "No, you're right. Let's go."

"Do we check out?"

"No. We can always come back here later: anyway, we won't take the car, it's too visible. I suggest we hare it to the lakeside and try to get a boat across to France. Once we are there, we're out of reach of the Swiss police, at least for a short while. Etienne sighed: "Passports?"

I waved him aside and grabbed some papers on the small desk. There were several tourist brochures and in one of them I found the timetable for the boat that crossed over to Saint-Gingolph. I looked at my watch: we were too late for the two thirty boat, but these boats are slow. If we hurried, we could catch it at the stop near the Château de Chillon.

We stuffed all our belongings in the large handbag I'd bought and rushed to the elevator. Thankfully the receptionist was busy and didn't even glance at us. We ran to the garage and jumped into the car. We had ten minutes left to get to the Château de Chillon.

It is only a couple of miles from where we were, but there was a lot of traffic. We made it just in time, dumping the car in the parking lot near the jetty. We ran to the boat and were the last passengers to get on, Dulce clearing the gangway in one, neat jump.

We slouched on the benches inside the boat, trying to catch our breath. It was a short trip across to Saint-Gingolph: less than an hour. It gave us time to think about our next move. We decided to find a way to get to Evian and spend the night there, waiting for Felicia's phone call.

Saint-Gingolph is a village which is half in Switzerland, half in France. There is just one narrow street in the village and the border cuts it in two.

To cross it, I hid Dulce in the bag and wore the big sunglasses I'd bought earlier. I hooked my arm on Etienne's and we strolled past, smiling at the French douanier who didn't give us a second look. We went on walking along the village's single street, until I found a small store which was able to give us directions for Evian. He said we could either take a taxi, or wait a couple of hours for the bus.

We ordered a taxi, and half an hour later he dropped us off in the center of Evian.

Etienne must have been missing life in his manor house, as he insisted we stay at the Royal Evian. It took a lot of patience to explain to him that it was highly impractical, because we didn't have a car and the hotel was a ten minutes drive from the center of town. In the end we chose the Savoy hotel, which was located next to the casino and conveniently close to the jetty where the boat to Switzerland stopped.

It turned out to be a nice choice, a comfortable, well-appointed hotel. They, like the Helvétie in Montreux, fulfilled my main demand: they accepted dogs. Dulce was settled on her blanket, got her chow, and we went out.

We were right next to the Casino, so we decided to have dinner there and to visit the casino. We had a small flutter and won enough to pay for our dinner. Then we decided to pick up Dulce and to stroll along the lake, looking across to the lost paradise, Switzerland.

At that point, we both wondered when, if ever, we'd be able to go back. I could imagine myself going to Lyon to catch a flight back to New York and Etienne having to return to live in France, if we couldn't prove our innocence.

Although innocence was a debatable word: I had, after all, killed a man. Even if it was in self-defense. It was a bit depressing. For once, it was Etienne who comforted me, putting his arm around my shoulder and holding me close. We sat on a bench, watching the lights on the other side of the lake, and he said:

"It's strange: I've never felt closer to anyone than you."

My heart fluttered, but my brain kicked it and said to me: "Don't get your hopes up, girl: he doesn't think of you that way." We stayed there for a while and slowly walked back to the hotel, Dulce trotting ahead of us, her tail proudly plumed.

"I like this life! Getting to know new places, lots of walks, interesting food!"

Another night, another hotel... we had rested enough the previous night and that day, and we were getting anxious. We were both restless and had trouble getting to sleep. We were up early and went down to the dining room to have breakfast. It was mainly to keep us busy and to wile away the hours until Felicia's call.

It was useless for her to call the Tax office too early: the mail wouldn't have arrived and would not have been distributed.

Finally, at eleven, the call came. Felicia said, in her usual calm voice: "They've received the envelopes and I can go and get them at lunchtime. I'll call you back then."

I looked at Etienne across the table: "It's there. She'll have it by one!"

We didn't admit it to each other, but we both had jitters. We still had no idea of what the will contained, although we both strongly believed that it was in Etienne's favor.

I asked him: "What will you do if it isn't?"

Etienne sipped his coffee thoughtfully: "I'm not sure. But I don't think it's useful to speculate about it, do you?"

"You're right Etienne."

"The thing is, once we have the will, is it going to be enough to exonerate us from what happened at the Hôtel Métropole"?

I had been thinking the same thing: if the will was in favor of Etienne, could we prove that Damien had made several attempts on our lives, abducted and threatened us to get it back? And that in the course of his intimidation campaign he'd framed us at the hotel? And even if we could prove all of this, there still remained the dead man in my room. I had done this, no one else.

We went for a walk to get some newspapers. They had Swiss papers and we tried to find something about the hotel Métropole, but there was nothing. Strangely enough, we did find an article in a local French newspaper.

It told the story in greater detail than we'd read in the Swiss press. It said that an anonymous call had sent the hotel manager to look into the room. He had found the body and immediately called the police. The police had identified the body as an Albanian citizen who was a known criminal with a rap sheet as long as my arm. The occupant of the room, who had been identified as a French citizen living in Geneva, and his companion, had still not been found.

Etienne was reading over my shoulder: "Nothing new, huh?" I shook my head.

My iPhone rang and I jumped on it. Felicia's voice on the other end sounded a bit exasperated: "You owe me one! It took me almost two hours to get these bloody envelopes!"

"You have them? In your hands?"

Felicia sighed: "Yes. I'm back at work. What do you want me to do with them?" I looked at Etienne, saying: "Could you open them and fax the contents to us?" I gave her the fax number of the hotel and added: "And then store them in the safe deposit box in your office. They couldn't be safer anywhere."

"I'll do that immediately. Take care."

We went up to the reception, telling them we were expecting a fax. It took another five minutes and the receptionist came back with a wad of sheets.

My heart was beating wildly and Etienne was suddenly very pale. He took the papers and we went up to our room. Once we were there, sitting on the two small armchairs around the table, he handed me the papers. His hands were shaking and he said: "Please read them. I can't."

CHAPTER XXXII

I took the papers from his hands and began reading. The first page was the will. It was extremely succinct and named only two beneficiaries: Etienne de Brousse received the bulk of Alice de Brousse's estate. Her shares in the company, all her real estate, all her chattel and all her bank accounts and cash, except for a sum of one million Swiss francs, which was to go to Miss Florence Rivière, her secretary, in reward for services rendered. There were no other bequests, but a line asking Etienne to take care of what she called "her people" in the manner she would have done herself. The will was written and signed in a firm hand by Alice de Brousse, and witnessed by Giuseppe di Natale and Ana Maria Da Silva Dos Santos.

Etienne's relief as I read the will, was almost palpable. I looked up to see him beaming.

I smiled at him: "Well, that's one thing solved! Let's see what the letter says." Etienne moved closer to me and we read the letter together. It was several pages, written in a firm and elegant handwriting, like the will.

"My dear Etienne,

I hope that this letter will help you understand my attitude of the last few months, and that you will forgive me.

I have acted very stupidly and what I am about to tell you here may explain my attitude, but certainly not excuse it.

Two years ago, I was exhausted and slightly depressed. Jean's death ten years ago had been a shock, and even more so when I realized in what shape he had left the company.

Jean was a wonderful husband and a great person. I loved him as much as a wife can love a husband, but I was not blind to his faults. The main one, was that he had been called to a position he just could not cope with. When your grandfather died, much too young, he entrusted the management of the de Brousse company to Jean: he didn't have much choice, as your father, my dear Etienne, wanted to study medicine.

De Brousse at the time Jean took it over, was a large, thriving company. Your grandfather had encouraged innovation and the company had patented several new techniques. Unfortunately, Jean was not like his father: he was a terrible manager, had no idea of diplomacy and as a result came too often into conflict with the unions. Apart from that, he had no imagination and could not grasp the ideas that were presented to him by the creative committee his father had founded.

Despite this, the company somehow survived: probably due to the impeccable quality of the products, which is one thing Jean was good at keeping. But it was slowly sinking: wallpaper was out of fashion and the price of de Brousse textiles was much too high. When Jean died, ten years ago, I discovered a company on the brink of bankruptcy.

You were still too young and inexperienced to take over, so I had to step into my husband's shoes.

If there is one thing I am proud of, is that I brought back de Brousse to its former glory. It wasn't easy: but some of my ideas were extremely effective. For example, managing to get our wallpapers used in the most popular TV shows on decoration: which made our sales jump. Or having world known designers create couches and armchairs upholstered in our textiles.

When I left the company in your hands, two years ago, it was thriving: I had increased the turnover by more than six hundred percent in eight years. The workforce had been pacified and was loyal and content with its working conditions. The creative department was coming out with new ideas. You took over a bright, gleaming and sharp instrument.

But these eight, intensive years had exhausted me: I had been taken up in a whirlwind of decisions and actions. Once you took over - very competently - I was suddenly at a loss. For the first time I realized what losing Jean meant on a personal level. I had been so busy with the company, that I hadn't felt his loss that much.

Now I was alone and, to tell you the truth, I think I was a bit depressed. Again, I'm not trying to find excuses: but I want to explain how it all happened.

I met Damien at a charity event in favor of his Foundation. What I am telling you is with the benefit of hindsight, of course. I can't be objective, as I now realize what a foul crook he is.

Damien has a special gift: he has an almost hypnotic power of persuasion. In fact, although I don't believe in this kind of thing, I wonder if he does not actually use hypnotism. In any case, he does know how to manipulate people and has an uncanny ability to find their weak spot.

My friend Yvonne, who introduced us, was gushing about him. He concentrated all the evening on me, flattering me, cosseting and caring about me. Now I realize he had found a juicy prospect. Then I was flattered that this charismatic man was concentrating all his attention on me, making all the other women in the room green with envy.

He used every ruse in the book to wheedle himself into my life. Again, I have no excuse: I should have known better. But he was good, very good. He managed to keep a slight distance from me, and the other women who contribute to the Foundation. It made him seem lofty and noble and made us want to be nearer him. It was competition between several women and he very cunningly used this.

Etienne, I was totally taken in. In a few, short months, he managed to cut me off from most of my friends. The one person who saw through him was Caroline. You didn't know Caroline very well, as you did not have the opportunity to come to Geneva very often in the last years. She was a wonderful character: a strong woman with little or no education, but generous to a fault and with an intelligence of her own. She was never taken in by Damien and she tried to warn me about him.

When she died, I believed the police's version and did not question it. Now I know that Damien was behind this so-called accident: he admitted as much some time ago.

I was devastated by her death and did not care much who replaced her to take care of me. Damien brought in a woman, Eliane Reverdin. I was too distracted, too sad, to realize that he had simply planted a spy next to me. Little by little, he managed to isolate me. In the end, the only people around me who remained who were not his instruments were very few. There was my poor Anny, who as you know is almost retarded. Giuseppe, my dear friend and gardener, who kept to his duties in the garden. And Florence Rivière, my secretary.

Damien was coming to the house at least twice a week to visit me. These days I was having some tough times with my chemotherapy. I was feeling sorry for myself, lonely and he seemed, at the time, like the only person who cared for me. He gave me a new goal in life, with his Foundation's work.

It was exhilarating to think that thanks to my money, temples, mosques and churches were being built, to allow people all over the world to worship as they wished.

Damien managed to present all this in a way that made us, the donors, feel as if we were doing extraordinary things. He showed us short movies where children and elderly people thanked us, in tears. He showed us the buildings being planned and built.

In the meantime, he was monitoring me and insinuating that I had been abandoned by my family. That is, by you. Deep down I knew perfectly well that I had only to make one phone call and you'd be there within hours, if I felt I needed you. But Damien used the fact that I was feeling sorry for myself to make you look selfish and too involved in the management of the company to care about an elderly and ailing aunt.

Through subtle and less subtle hints, manipulation and pressure, he managed to persuade me to make a will in favor of the Foundation. He said that of course, you would remain at the head of the company, since you were doing an excellent job. He was smart enough not to advise me to disinherit you completely and said, of his own initiative, that I should leave the usufruct of Clair-Chant to you, plus a small stipend, in case you ever needed it.

No skin off his nose: what he was advising me to leave you, plus the small bequests to people like Anny or Florence, was a tiny percentage of my fortune. And I, like the foolish, weak old lady I'd become, signed this will.

Damien then thought he just had to sit back and wait until I died. We both knew it wouldn't be long. I've refused some of the therapies that were proposed to me by the doctors. I want to keep my mind sharp and to live at home for as long as possible. Even if it means living a few months less.

What Damien had not counted on, was that I'd wake up. It happened very suddenly, one day I was looking with him through some papers of the Foundation. I can't explain why precisely that day, at that moment, things I'd be seeing for the last months, suddenly jumped at me from the papers. All I can tell you is that it felt as if something had snapped.

One minute I was the bleating, worshiping victim of Damien. The next, Alice de Brousse, the businesswoman, was back.

Damien was doing his usual "maintenance work": stroking and persuading the benefactors, of which he made me believe I was the most important one. I suppose he held the same speech with all the other gullible women he'd entrapped. He was showing me the latest place of worship to be built "almost entirely with the money I had contributed".

It was a tiny Protestant temple somewhere in Mexico. Apparently, there was a small minority of Mexicans who, for some reason, had been Protestants since 200 years. Their community was dirt poor and they could not afford to rebuild their temple, which had been flattened by an earthquake.

The FLC had stepped in. They cleared the ground where the old temple had stood and had built a brand new one. Damien was showing me glossy photographs of it, with the usual beaming children and emotional scenes. I asked him how much the building had cost.

Damien mentioned a number, which sent me reeling. He misinterpreted my reaction, and with his usual kind and understanding smile added that yes, it was extremely cheap. But then, he said, costs were very low in Mexico, and that was why this temple had cost so little.

That was the moment when I snapped and I opened my eyes. I did not say anything, but looked through the papers he had handed me. As usual, he allowed his benefactors to look through the accounts, claiming he wanted us to know everything. I usually glanced at them without much interest, trusting him entirely. This time I looked more closely, noting the names of the contractors which had been used.

Once Damien was gone, I asked Florence to look up these companies on the internet. There wasn't much information on them, but she promised to do some more research at home.

Florence is a very smart girl, Etienne, and I hope you will keep her near you after my death. She has helped me very much in my quest for truth these last few weeks. She is another person who was never taken in by Damien. I think he realized when he met her that he could not coerce, intimidate or seduce her and he decided to leave her alone. Florence was shocked to see how much that man influenced me: she almost quit when I decided to leave all my assets to the Foundation, but chose to stay on and fight.

You can imagine how happy she was when she realized I had come out of Damien's influence.

Her research on the companies produced some interesting results. We discovered that all the contractors used by the Foundation, were owned by the same holding group. It wasn't difficult to guess that they all belonged to Damien and Florence told me that we might prove it, with some serious and professional research. I asked her to retain the company de Brousse works with when they need information.

She gave orders from her place and paid in cash from the amounts I always have in the safe box here. We had understood that we were surrounded by people from the Foundation who would report any unusual activities on our part to Damien.

We soon understood how Damien works: it is pretty simple, in fact. He rakes in money from his various benefactors. Large amounts. The Foundation does, indeed, build places of worship. But the building costs are hugely overpriced: the contractors bill just about anything they want, bringing the costs to ten, sometimes twelve times what they should be.

Of course, the benefactors have no idea. He carefully selects his victims: I met some of the other people who have contributed to the FLC. Usually they are elderly and sometimes almost senile. They have no idea of building costs outside of their country...or even inside.

There is also the fact that the FLC is a Panama foundation: even if some benefactor complained about the way the money is being used, I'm not sure to what extent he or she could do anything about it.

Florence is investigating. She believes there may be a chink in Damien's carefully built armor. She is looking into the Association loi 1901, which governs non-profit organizations.

I cannot tell you how distraught I was to have fallen a victim of such a crook. Again, I want to apologize to you, especially in view of what followed.

Apparently Florence was not discreet enough in her inquiries, or maybe the repellent Eliane overheard one of our conversations. Suddenly Damien appeared at Clair-Chant, and he was a changed man. Gone was the smooth and seductive operator, the big hearted humanitarian. He showed his real nature.

He came one afternoon and told me, in no uncertain terms, that I was not to change my will. When I told him that I was not scared of him, he said that it was a big mistake on my part. He said he could understand that an old, sick woman with a few months to live might not be scared. But that I had a nephew that I seemed to love and that he was in Paris, vulnerable.

He then added, with the coldest look in his eyes, that he was sure I didn't want you to end up as Caroline had. It chilled me to the bone when I understood that he had her killed. Damien ordered me to tell Florence to stop her inquiries, or she would be the victim of a regrettable accident too. He said she would be followed from now on. If he saw her going near the police, a notary or anywhere whereshe could do harm, she and you would be eliminated. He said he would monitor every visit to the house and every telephone conversation.

I was so scared for both of you after this conversation, that I did what he told me. Florence could not understand my attitude. She suspected that something had happened to scare me, but I begged her not to ask more questions. This is when I cut off all contact with you: I wanted to show Damien there was no risk on that side.

After a couple of days of moping, my common sense took over. I didn't want this man to win. And I wanted you to get what was due to you. So I decided to make a new will, and to hide it from the FLC. If this will surfaced after my death, Damien would be thwarted and there was nothing he could do about it, especially if this letter was attached to it.

I asked Giuseppe and Anny to witness it. Giuseppe is the most loyal man I know and he is very discreet. Anny is too stupid to understand what she is doing.

I have told Florence of my plans and she is elated. In compensation for her loyalty and the help she has given me in this matter, I am leaving her one million francs. She knows it, as she has the will in her hands. Florence's only defect is that she is a bit rapacious: but because of this, I am quite sure she will do everything in her power to see to it that my last will is executed. I will give her this sealed letter to hide with the will.

She has been informed that she cannot deposit it with the courts or with a notary and that it has to stay hidden until after my death. I know she is smart enough to have found a place no one will think of. She will give me the key to this hiding place tomorrow and I will in turn put this key in the silver box you played with so often when you were small.

Thinking of you, Etienne, the chestnut haired, blue-eyed cheerful boy you were, spending whole afternoons trying to solve the riddle of this box, brings tears to my eyes. I know I was never very sentimental. Maybe I did not show you enough how much I loved you. There should have been more hugs, more kisses. But you have to know that you were, for Jean and for me, the child we never had.

Florence is to tell you that the key is in the place you loved to play when you were small. She does not know about the box, for her own protection. As I do not know where she has chosen to hide the will. The day after my death, she will contact you and give you my message.

I beg you to forgive me for these last months. I know that you love me as much as I love you and that you must be feeling hurt and surprised by my attitude. I hope you have now understood that it was for your own safety. I thought dozens of times of sending Florence to the police with my story. But I never did because I knew that somehow, Damien would be able to get to you.

Please take care of my people as I would have. In the first will I made, there were several small bequests: I wish you would respect them. Take care of the company and infuse some new life in it, and carry on the de Brousse tradition of quality and innovation. And, finally, find yourself a loving, warm and caring young woman to marry.

Your loving aunt,

Alice."

CHAPTER XXXIII

It was a long letter and a lot to assimilate for Etienne. When I looked at him, there were tears running down his face. I squeezed his hand and said nothing, waiting for him to regain his composure.

After a while I said:

"Your aunt seems to have been a remarkable woman, Etienne."

That turned on the taps. I am always embarrassed to see a grown man crying, and there Etienne was sobbing like a child. I went to get him some tissues from the bathroom and Dulce ran to his side, with a worried whimper.

"What's wrong with him, Alex? Why is he crying? Is he hurt?"

He stuttered between sobs: "What have I done, Alex! I should have been there for her! I left her alone when she most needed me."

I had to put a stop to this nonsense, so I snapped: "don't be an idiot, Etienne. Your aunt was a very sensible woman and she did what she felt was her duty. She kept you away for a good reason. Anyway, how were you supposed to know she was in trouble?"

He shrugged and bent his head. He read again some passages from the letter and commented on them:

"You know, Alex, when she says there should have been more hugs and kisses: it's funny, but I never felt that way. Tante Alice wasn't a very effusive kind of person. As far as kisses and hugs went, the most I would get from her was a peck on the cheek. Yet despite this, I knew that she loved me. I guess that's why I felt so hurt when she shut me out."

I thought he was heading of another session of weeping, so I quickly got on another subject:

"Well, at least we have most of the answers now. And we know why Florence was killed. She was a very brave woman."

"I suppose that after her death aunt Alice didn't have the time or the means to make another will. She didn't know what the key opened and Florence was not there anymore to tell me what it was about: so she jotted down these two notes and placed them in the wallpaper she gave to Denise."

"Which Denise, being the absent-minded artist she was, did not even notice. And she cut right through the wallpaper without even seeing there was something written on it."

Etienne said: "What I don't understand is how Damien learned about the will?"

I shrugged: "Don't forget that Anny witnessed it. That girl is so feeble minded that if he asked her about it she certainly replied. Without having any idea of what it meant."

Etienne chewed his lip: "Mmm...yes. It sounds possible. If that Eliane woman noticed something unusual...such as Anny and Giuseppe being summoned together into my aunt's office, together with Florence...and if she told Damien...he could have put two and two together."

"Right: he certainly suspected there was another will, despite his threats to you and Florence. But he couldn't be certain, until he asked Anny. And maybe even then: Anny certainly had no idea what she was signing and she would answer "yes" to anything he asked her if she thought it pleased him. Let's say he could be reasonably certain."

"I think Florence got killed because she was asked about it and refused to answer."

Etienne nodded: "Most probably".

I sighed and got up. I walked to the window and looked at the peaceful view of the lake. It was so calm, so harmonious out there, it made it hard to believe this story of violence and greed.

In a gesture that we shared with Etienne, I ran a hand through my hair. It fell back on my brow and I blew it away. Dulce was sitting close to Etienne, ready to intervene if he showed signs of wanting to burst out into tears again, but keeping an eye on me. I asked the intelligent canine: "What do we do now? This hasn't solved our problem."

That was the moment my iPhone chose to ring. It was Felicia's number, so I answered. Her voice sounded strange:

"Alex? It's me, Felicia."

"Felicia? You sound strange? Where are you?"

"I'm at work. But there is someone here I think you should talk to."

She got off the phone and a second later I heard a male voice saying:

"Mrs. Tate? This is Commandant Renaud, of the Geneva police. We have been looking for you. Can you please tell me your exact location?"

It was useless trying to lie. It would take him all of two minutes to locate me. I answered:

"In Evian."

"Is Etienne de Brousse with you?"

I looked at Etienne, who nodded.

"Yes."

There was a silence at the other end and he said: "Mrs. Tate, I think you and I and Mr. de Brousse need to have a long conversation. Can you give the phone number of the place you're staying and I will call you in half an hour?"

I hesitated, then gave him the phone number and that of our room.

The next half hour was spent waiting with some trepidation. We expected our door to burst open any minute by French gendarmes. But nothing like that happened, and fifty minutes later the phone rang. We then had a very long conversation with Commandant Renaud.

CHAPTER XXXIV

Later in the day Etienne's phone rang. It was the mellifluous and insufferable voice of Damien. He asked:

"Well, Etienne? Have you thought about my proposal?"

Etienne sighed: "Yes, we have."

There was a chuckle at the other end – if you could call a chuckle something that sounded like a nail against a blackboard. He said: "I suppose you have realized by now that you and your lady friend are in very deep trouble?"

"Yes." Etienne's voice was flat. "It looks like all the Swiss police is on our tracks."

"Well, I can solve that for you. Do you have the will?"

"Yes. We had mailed it and now we have got it back."

"I thought as much. We shall meet then, and you can give it to me."

"In exchange for what? How the hell do you think you can make this murder accusation go away?"

"How about the gun, with nice fresh prints…those of your friend Boris? He needs to leave the country anyway, things are getting too hot for him. He has agreed, for a small compensation, to take responsibility for the shot. He will then leave the country immediately to go back to the lovely place he calls home."

Etienne was silent for a moment. He looked at me and I nodded. He answered:

"Fine. Let's do that then. How do you propose we proceed?"

"Where are you?"

"We're in Montreux, but we could come up to Geneva"

"No, stay right where you are. We'll meet there, tomorrow."

"Where and when?"

"I'll call you."

Damien hung up and we looked at each other. We had a long twenty four hours ahead of us.

We had decided to tell Damien we were in Montreux, so as to meet him in Switzerland. We hadn't expected he'd want to meet us there, but it didn't matter. It was just a matter of getting back. We checked out and went to the jetty, to board the boat to Lausanne. Dulce seemed to have gotten her sea legs and to become a real maritime dog. She stood on the deck, ears in the wind. It took thirty-five minutes to get to Lausanne. The Lausanne metro took us to the railway station and we arrived at the Hôtel Helvétie at seven. They were not surprised to see their vanishing guests and gave us the same room.

We had enough time to go and retrieve the red Mini, which we had abandoned on the parking lot in front of the Château de Chillon. It was another lovely evening and we decided to walk there. The lakeside on the Vaud part of the lake is much more friendly than on the Geneva side. After Geneva and up to Lausanne, the shore is taken up by private mansions and a few assorted restaurants, tennis and marine clubs. It is impossible to walk along the lake.

Whereas the coast from Villeneuve, at the end of the lake, almost all the way to Lausanne, is one, long promenade. We strolled along with Dulce, who absolutely adored this walk. She ran back and forth, barked at the occasional dog and wagged her tail when someone bent down to pat and admire her.

It took us half an hour to get to the famous castle, and as we went past it, it gave me an idea. I discussed it with Etienne and he agreed.

We found the car where we had left it, in the parking lot. There was just an additional piece of paper on it: I sighed. The vaudois gendarmes were anything if not efficient. I tore up the parking ticket and we got into the car.

I convinced Etienne to have dinner in the small town of Villeneuve. It is a pretty medieval town, with a paved main street. It also has some excellent fish restaurants, which serve the ubiquitous "filets de perche". I discovered Dulce was a great fan of fish: not quite as much as chicken, but almost.

When we walked back to the car, I had the impression that I caught a glimpse of the redoubtable Boris. I dismissed the thought and we went quietly back to the hotel.

The next morning there was a knock on the door of our room and a courier brought us the papers we had asked Felicia to send us: the will and the letter.

We waited for Damien's phone call, which came at ten. Etienne answered and turned the loudspeaker on. Damien's voice filled the room:

"Good morning Etienne. We will meet at four this afternoon, at this place."

He proceeded to give us an address: I knew where it was, an isolated road in the heights of Montreux. I said:

"No way, Damien. We are not going to meet you in an isolated place. You will meet us at the Château de Chillon, in room number 14. This is final."

There was a long silence at the other end. I looked at Etienne: my heart was beating fast. He was very pale. Finally Damien replied:

"Fine. Be there at four, with the will."

Etienne hung up and we stood there for one minute. He said: "Let's roll!"

At a quarter to four we took our tickets at the entrance booth of the castle, politely refusing the audio tour. It had been a long time since I hadn't gone to the Château de Chillon and there had been some renovation work done in the meantime.

But the castle was still one of the most impressive ones in Europe. It is a magnificent structure built on a rock off the lake shore of the lake Leman. It has been splendidly preserved and remains one of the most visited monuments in Switzerland. I had chosen it as a meeting place because there were always a lot of tourists there and we hoped it would prevent Damien from trying something.

We walked around, reconnoitering the site and trying to see if there were any of Damien's men around. Dulce was happily snuffling around in the paved courtyard. We did not see anything, so we went to the large banquet hall where I'd told Damien to meet us.

At four o'clock he walked in, accompanied by Boris.

We had been very stupid to think that the fact there were people around would stop or hamper him. He simply walked up to us and showed us discreetly the gun he was carrying. It had a long muzzle, which I thought must be a silencer.

So much for our best laid plans. I sighed and Etienne looked somber. Damien pushed us in front of him, towards the lower floor. No one paid any attention to us, despite the fact that Dulce was constantly growling at the two men. I had to keep her leash tightly in my hand to prevent her from rushing to take a bite out of their legs.

"Let me go, Alex! Please let me take a bite off these people's legs!"

He made us go down to the lower floor, where the prisons had been.

There was the famous room where Bonnivard had been kept prisoner and that had inspired Lord Byron's "The prisoner of Chillon". But that wasn't where he was taking us. Apparently Damien knew the castle very well and he pushed us towards a closed door. It was a small room which was being renovated and which was not supposed to be accessed by the public.

There were a only couple of pieces of furniture covered by plastic sheets in the room. We turned around to look at Damien who addressed me: "Give me the will."

I shook my head: "Not until you give us the gun"

Damien gave one of his weird, crooked smiles. He took a package out of his pocket and said:

"Here it is."

I shook my head, mulishly:

"How do we know Boris' prints are still on it? You will have wiped it clean!"

Damien smiled again. He said, giving the package to his henchman:

"Boris, here, has no problem in leaving some good, solid prints. Haven't you Boris?"

The Russian took off the plastic wrapping around the gun and put his large hand firmly on the gun, all the while smiling his hideous smile.

Damien went on:"Good. Now we have a nice scenario. Our friend Boris, after killing his associate at the Hôtel Métropole in Geneva, caught up with you. But you were armed and managed to overpower and kill him…"

While he was saying that, Boris was listening and grinning at us with infinite contempt: I don't think he understood what was going to happen. To be honest, nor did we: it took us two seconds to realize and Damien was already shooting him.

There were only the sound of small "plops" and Boris slumped on the floor, two neat holes in the region of the heart starting to bleed. Damien was looking at us with a glint in his eyes that betrayed his ruthlessness as he added:

"However in a last spasm, the bad guy shot you…"

He had stepped over to Boris and was bending down to retrieve the gun from his hand, while keeping an eye on us. He wasn't fast enough though to avoid Dulce, who came barreling at him and bit his hand with gusto.

She had pulled so hard on her leash it had escaped my hand and had finally been able to take a chunk out of this man she hated and who made us sound frightened.

"Finally! Now I'll get you, you horrible person!"

I yelled at her to come back while we ran out of the room. Damien had already recovered the use of his hand and shot in our direction. We whisked around the corner as a bullet lodged itself in the door of the room. We ran down some stairs, and then up, Damien in hot pursuit behind us. I realized we were now on the walkway, on the shore side. We galloped ahead, the wooden planks shaking under our footsteps and then down again. We crossed the last paved courtyard and shot through the entrance booth. There was no help there and we ran in desperation towards the car, hearing Damien's footsteps not very far behind us.

We skidded to a halt in front of the car and crashed in, Dulce leaping on my lap. Damien had stopped behind us and was calmly shooting. The rear window shattered as Etienne turned on the engine. The little car shot off into the traffic, narrowly missing an oncoming bus and two cars. I turned around, clutching Dulce on my knees, to see Damien getting into his car, a powerful Jaguar.

I yelled at Etienne: "Turn right, here! Where the hell is the police? They were supposed to be there!"

Etienne took the street I had indicated, which went up sharply from the main road. I hoped Damien would miss us and go straight ahead. Etienne was pushing the little car to its limits, zooming along the narrow road, going straight. I still didn't see Damien's car behind us. We sped on and Etienne asked, while negotiating the narrow road: "Where do we go?"

"We have to try to get to the police station in Montreux! Straight ahead and then turn left at the next junction."

Except when we got there we saw Damien's powerful car bearing down on us. We had no option but to turn right, in the direction of Glion and Caux and the mountains. We went past the lovely neighborhood of Les Planches, the old city of Montreux, and found ourselves on the road to the mountain, with its hairpin curves.

Damien was very close behind us. I grabbed my phone and called the number Commandant Renaud had given us, shouting: "Where the hell are you? This man is going to kill us!"

He answered in a tight voice: "It went too fast for us but we're behind you. Hold on."

I had trouble keeping Dulce on my lap as the curves got more dangerous: Etienne was hanging on for dear life and driving like a Formula One champion. But the small car was no match for the Jaguar and he crashed into us, almost getting us off the road. A few seconds later he rammed into us again, making the Mini bound ahead. We went through Glion, at a dangerous speed.

Suddenly Etienne gave the wheel a violent turn to the right and we drove into a tiny path that led into the forest. He had managed it so well that the Jaguar zoomed past us and had to spin around in a u-turn to get back on our tracks.

We were already out of the car and running along the path, the Mini crashed into the trees and blocking the Jaguar's way. We belted up the small path, hearing the Jaguar screeching to a halt and the noise of the door closing. Damien was again behind us and he was shooting in our direction. His shots were coming nowhere near us, fortunately.

We were running as fast as we could, and I was totally out of breath, envying Dulce, who sprang ahead at full speed, turning around from time to time.

"Come on, Alex! Move your fat butt! I told you should go on a diet!"

Etienne stopped suddenly, pulling me and Dulce down into the high bushes that bordered the path. He grabbed a large tree limb and gave me another one.

Without a word we got ready and when Damien came careening up the path, Etienne shot out of his hiding place, hitting him with the heavy branch. I walloped him with mine and Dulce angrily planted her small sharp teeth in his ankle. We all struggled ferociously until all of a sudden we heard some voices and Damien was plucked from our grasp.

Etienne and I flopped down on the autumn leaves, exhausted, as a police officer gently tried to pry Dulce's teeth away from Damien's leg.

"No, no, and no. I've got him, I'm keeping him!"

Commandant Renaud was there, giving orders and asking that we be helped back to the road. We were checked for wounds and when they were sure we were in more or less good shape, we were taken down to the police cars waiting nearby.

On the way we passed the Mini, which was now a total wreck and the Jaguar, with marks on its side. Renaud walked by our side, excusing himself for the snafu. He explained:

"Despite the phone, we didn't hear anything, at all. We didn't know if you'd met him or not. The man we had in the courtyard saw you go into the banquet hall and then he never saw you come out again. The first inkling we had that something was wrong was when we saw you run out of the castle with Damien behind you. By the time we got back to our cars, you had both driven off. We caught up with Damien when he was trying to push you off the road and we were just behind him when he got out of his car to catch you."

To be fair to them, it had seemed like hours: but in reality, when I looked at my watch, I was amazed to see that between the moment we had met Damien at the castle, at four o'clock sharp, and now, less than quarter of an hour had passed.

We were both a bit wobbly on our legs and Renaud offered to take us up to Caux, to rest a bit and have a hot drink before we went back to Geneva. As we sat there sipping a hot chocolate and looking at the breathtaking view, we couldn't believe our ordeal was finally over.

Dulce was being congratulated for her stellar role and offered a job in the police, which she politely declined, while chewing a small piece of chicken someone had found for her.

"Nope: thank you , but no thank you. Alex needs me: as you can see, she has a tendency to get into all kinds of scrapes! But thanks for the chicken, anyway!"

I walked to the window and looked outside at the glorious mountains, the peaceful lake. There were a few stray clouds and the light was going through a whole array of pastel colors. The scenery outside looked exactly like a painting by my favorite Swiss artist, Ferdinand

Hodler. It breathed calm and harmony: Switzerland as I knew it.

We were driven back to Geneva and allowed one day of rest, before meeting again with Renaud to give our final statements.

On the way back I called Felicia to tell her that everything was fine: that we were all in one piece and cleared of any suspicion. There was a big sigh on the other side and she said: "Could you please call Sylvie, then? She has been calling me almost every hour for the last two days...I think it's Etienne she's worried about."

I handed over my phone to Etienne, sighing: "Here, call your Dulcinea: she's worried about you."

His face was suddenly transformed by a half-witted smile and he dialed the number. The rest of the conversation was on kindergarten level and I refused to listen anymore, disgusted. I turned my attention to Renaud, who was explaining their inquest.

CHAPTER XXXV

Two days later, Etienne and I met at the police station to give our statements. Once that was done, we were taken back to Renaud's office.

He stood up and shook our hands, offered us some coffee and asked us how we were feeling after our ordeal. Etienne mumbled that he was OK: I said that I was fine, and asked if Damien had talked. That got a chuckle out of Renaud who said:

"He's talking. He's talking so much it's hard to shut him up!"

I frowned: "That's strange?"

Renaud smiled and replied: "Not really. The man has got an oversized ego and now that he's been finally caught, he wants everyone to know just how smart he was all these years."

He settled back in his chair and leafed through a report on his desk.

"I won't go into too many details, especially since he's giving us new information all the time. But I'll tell you the part of his story which has to do with you, as he told it to us.

Mrs. de Brousse was one of the women he was preying on. He was extremely satisfied he'd hooked her, as her fortune is considerable. In fact, I think she was his largest catch since he started the Foundation. Everything was going swimmingly for him, she'd made a will in favor of the FLC and he knew she had very little time to live.

But one day one of his IT people called, telling him there had been repeated visits on the construction companies websites. The IP label gave the visitor's name, Florence Rivière. Damien understood that Mrs. de Brousse was on to him. He feared one thing, that she would make a new will. So he rushed to Geneva to prevent her from doing so. He knew she loved very much her nephew, who was also her legal heir, and he threatened to kill both you and her secretary if she looked as though she was changing her will.

He said they kept an eye on the household and especially on Florence Rivière. Eliane, the nurse he had placed in the household, called to tell him there had been a suspicious meeting in Mrs. de Brousse's office. Damien came back to Geneva and went to see Anny, who had been one of the people at that meeting. He had sized her up and decided she would be a very good subject for hypnotism. He said she was stupid, greedy and incredibly gullible: the perfect tool.

She told him she had been asked to sign a document and Damien was pretty sure it was a new will. But he couldn't be sure. He decided to try to get more information and sent Boris to interrogate Florence Rivière. She was a strong girl and did not let herself be intimidated. She laughed at Boris and told him that, yes, there was a new will, and that they would never find it where Mrs. de Brousse had hidden it.

Boris went to grab her and hit her with his gun: he knocked her out and panicked. He turned her face down in the water letting her drown."

I remarked: "She was a very brave woman, Sylvie."

Renaud nodded and went on: "Damien was now sure that there was another will. He also had to make sure Florence's death was declared an accident. He had a corrupt doctor friend of his prescribe some strong depressant drugs to Mrs. de Brousse, which Eliane administered. With the result than when Alice de Brousse's usual doctor came to see her after Florence's death, he found her in such a bad state that he forbid her from seeing anyone and from talking to us. I'm sure that, despite the threat on you, Mr. de Brousse, she would have denounced Damien at that time.

271

Things accelerated after that: Mrs. de Brousse took a turn for the worse, maybe in part because of what she had been made to absorb. She had one last, impromptu visit by some old friends, the Küblers. Eliane had the afternoon off and was therefore not able to prevent the visit. But as she returned to the house, she caught sight of them just as they were getting in their car, putting rolls of wallpaper in the trunk.

Shortly after that Mrs. de Brousse fainted and was hospitalized. She died in a few days, without having regained consciousness.

Damien was in a pickle: he was sure there was another will out there. He had realized how smart the old lady was and he couldn't imagine where she had hidden the will. The only solution was to search the house. The will in its favor provided for the Foundation to bear the cost of maintenance of the house. Therefore Damien was justified in sending his people to clean and maintain the house on a daily basis.

But as soon as he made it to Geneva, Eliane informed him of the Kübler's visit. He realized that the will might well have been hidden in the wallpapers and began tracking them.

They began by burglarizing Denise Kübler's workshop, killing the poor lady in the process. The papers they found contained nothing but they had her ledgers, which said she had left some paintings with you, in New York. One of their men was sent over to try to buy all the paintings: but when they realized that there were two of them you wouldn't part with, they decided they had to break in and take them all. They broke into your gallery twice, getting the list of the people you'd sold paintings to and then tried to frighten you into telling them where the other one was."

I said, indignantly:

"That was particularly stupid of Damien, as it is what made me come to Europe. No one likes being threatened, especially to turn over an object one doesn't have!"

Renaud went on:

"They also went on searching Clair-Chant. By that time, as you told me, you had become suspicious and wanted to get answers about the incidents, and especially about Denise Kübler's death, and decided to come over. And when you realized that everything led back to the Foundation, you decided to go over to Paris. Damien tells me to convey his admiration: when you showed up, both at Clair-Chant and at the Foundation, you were taken at face value. It took them some time to realize you were the owner of the art gallery on New York. In fact, it was your dog who betrayed you."

Dulce, intelligent canine that she was, barked and wagged her tail, hearing herself mentionned.

"What did I do?"

"The crew at Clair-Chant had reported your visit and mentioned her. He didn't click immediately when you went to visit him the first time. But after you had left he put two and two together. He decided to put a tail on you.

As soon as he felt you were becoming too curious, he tried to get rid of you. He says he was quite impressed when you came to see him the second time in Paris: it took guts. He decided to take your word and left you alone. But he kept an eye on Clair-chant, and as soon as Anny told him you were back, he knew you must have found something.

He planned to plant some drugs in your hotel room to get rid of you for good. When his man was killed when they came to abduct you, he was delighted: it gave him some leverage."

I wailed: "Oh no! How can I live with that!"

Renaud raised a pacifying hand:

"Miss Tate, you did not kill him. As I told you, the bullet hit his leg: what killed him was hitting his head on the desk when he fell down. It was an accident."

I shook my head: "It's still my fault. If I hadn't hit him on the head he wouldn't have fallen!"

Etienne leaned towards me and took my hand: "Alex, it was an accident. Don't beat yourself!"

I sniffed. Renaud said:

"We didn't suspect you for long, you know. If you had come in immediately..." He stopped himself: "Of course, you weren't able to."

I snorted and Etienne smiled.

"We traced your steps and went to see your friend Felicia, who was extremely helpful. Of course, it facilitated things that she had just received the will and Mrs. de Brousse's letter, which supported her assertions. I'm really sorry we bungled at the Château de Chillon..."

I shrugged: "It was partly my fault, I suppose. I thought if I kept my phone open so you could overhear our conversation, it would be OK. I didn't count on Damien taking us down to the cellar where there is no signal."

Etienne laughed: "Organizing the meeting at the Château de Chillon was not your best idea, Alex! The walls are a feet thick and the rock..."

I sighed: "Yup. But still, we got him. And Boris. Why did he have to kill Boris, by the way?"

Renaud answered: "Boris knew a lot about his business and he took care of the nastiest jobs for him. He was becoming dangerous and Damien took the opportunity to get rid of him."

I piped in: "I don't understand why he didn't kill us before Boris. That was extremely stupid. I think."

"It was another display of hubris, and a way of scaring you even more before he killed you. Ms. Tate, this guy really hates you. He wasn't content with killing you: he wanted you to die scared. And he wanted to take Boris off guard."

"He did that indeed."

"He had it all planned out. Fallout between drug dealers...Boris had some in his pockets...Damien took the will, destroyed it, and resumed his life."

He shuffled though the papers on his desk and asked:

"Do you have any more questions I can answer?"

I leaned forward on my chair:

"Yes: what about his operation. Are we any nearer to find out about it?"

"He's been talking and we have also retrieved a lot of useful information from the firm Alice de Brousse had asked Miss Rivière to contact.

She was totally right in her analysis: Damien siphoned between 80 to 90 percent of the funds the Foundation received. He did it mostly by overbilling building costs through his various building and consulting companies. He has assets all over the world: houses, accounts, stocks...And Mrs. de Brousse was also right when she talked about the chink in his armor. I think that once he finishes with the accusations of murder and the long list of other accusations, he is going to face the benefactors of the Foundation, under French law."

We all smiled. I had another question:

"I know it seems trivial, but why the heck do the women working for him wear veils? It's so weird..."

Renaud looked at me appreciatively: "And that is an interesting question. We're only beginning to get answers on that: but it appears that Damien was even using the little money he actually put into building places of worship, to his advantage. He used the construction of several mosques to convince the local imams to provide him with cheap, unquestioning labor. Likewise for your friend Boris and some others, who were provided by grateful Russian orthodox priests. In other instances he used the parish members to build their own churches, or temples or whatever. It ended up costing him very little. And it was smart. For example, the team of women who worked at Clair-Chant for the last months, obey their imam without question. I don't know what story he sells them, but they are like small robots."

"Talking about robots", I said, "does Damien really use hypnotism?"

Renaud nodded: "Yes, without doubt. It works very well with simple people, like Anny, or with people who are at a moment of their life when they are weak. Physically or emotionally. Like Alice de Brousse. But she was basically a strong person, and at some point she came back to her senses and she snapped out of it. Damien would not even have tried this with Miss Rivière: she was much too strong willed for him." He turned to me: "As for you, Miss Tate, even the idea is ludicrous!"

He rose, signaling the end of the interview:

"Of course this isn't totally over. But Miss Tate, you are free to return to New York whenever you want. And Mr. de Brousse, I think you'll be quite busy with the matter of the will."

CHAPTER XXXVI

It had been raining when we went in. We came out to find a beautiful autumn sunshine. Everything looked new and clean. The air was fresh and smelled of leaves. Etienne drove us back to my hotel, very close to Clair-Chant. I hadn't wanted to go back to the Métropole.

I had taken a room at the luxurious resort La Réserve, at the exit of Geneva, by the lake. It has an excellent Chinese restaurant where Etienne took us. I left Dulce in the room while we went for dinner: she was better off taking a nap than being tempted by delicious smells. She had her own lunch and curled up on her blankets with a satisfied sigh.

Once we were settled in the restaurant, Etienne asked me when I wanted to leave: I said that I couldn't stay much longer, as having someone replacing me at the gallery was costing me an arm and a leg. Besides, there was nothing left for me to do in Geneva.

Etienne was toying with his spring rolls. He raised his eyes and looked at me:

"Alex; I owe you so much, I don't know how to repay you. Really. Please ask me anything you want, anything at all, and I'll give it to you."

I laughed: "You don't owe me anything Etienne, really. I've regained my peace of mind and that's enough for me!"

He was silent for a moment, and then looked at me with a troubled expression: "Alex, I think I was falling in love with you...in fact...I was on the point of telling you so...but..."

My heart beat faster: Etienne, in love with *me*?

"But?"

He sighed and ran a hand through his hair:

"I think you are wonderful, Alex: you're fun, smart, pretty…it's just…"

It was my turn to sigh: "You saw Sylvie and thought how much lovelier she was…"

Etienne seemed embarrassed: "No, absolutely not…I mean, I like Sylvie…in fact…I think I love her…but it's got nothing to do with that. It's just that you are perfect, wonderful…if only you weren't so…bossy."

I stared at him, openmouthed. Bossy? Moi? I couldn't believe my ears and I was about to snap at him, saying that my "bossiness" was what had saved his hide more than once…that without that he would probably be dead in the cellar of his mansion…but I held myself in check and waited for him to continue.

"I know I'm not a genius, Alex, but you make me feel…inadequate. It's not only that you are a little…how shall I say it…overbearing? But you are just too much for me. Smarter, faster…I can't keep up."

He smiled sheepishly: "Of course, I really hope we can stay friends…and in fact more than that…"

I was flummoxed: what did he mean by "more than friends"? Since he'd just ruled out a romantic relationship between us, what did he want to do? Adopt me?

He beamed at me:

"You've been telling me that you want to change the style of your gallery, but don't really know how? Well, I have a proposal: why don't you transform it into an interior decoration shop and become the exclusive agent for de Brousse in the United States? Right now we have a few resalers, but they are not very active. And I mean to conquer the American market."

He looked at me interrogatively: I was very tempted. The new line of products he was planning would be a hit in the US: they combined French flair and quality, with original design. Etienne insisted:

"I have great marketing ideas and we can fund them, now. Please say yes, Alex?"

I speared a siu mai and chewed it meditatively:

"I need to think about it, Etienne, but thank very much in any case."

"Take your time; the offer stands. I know you need some time to get over this whole episode - hell, we all do - but think about it and we'll talk when you're back in New York."

"Let's do that." I looked at my watch: Sylvie was meant to join us for coffee. Just as I raised my eyes, there she was, walking in, looking prettier than ever. She wore a very short cashmere apricot sleeveless dress, that showed her flawless tan and long athletic legs to their best advantage.

She weaved her way to our table, and I couldn't help noticing the admiring looks that followed her, not least of which Etienne's. Sylvie sat next to Etienne and slipped her hand into his. I asked: "What about you two? What are your plans?"

It had become "you two" in a very short time. Watching them, I thought they were made for each other. I didn't have even a twinge of regret. Yes, Etienne was a cute guy. He was also a very nice person, with a good education and now, a great fortune. But after spending these hectic days with him, I had to admit that he was beginning to get slightly on my nerves. As a friend he was sweet: but I could never have shared my life with him.

He needed someone like Sylvie: a fresh young spirit, full of life, who would carry him without bossing him. She admired him and that was something he sorely needed. All in all, I thought she was the wife his aunt would have wanted for him.

Sylvie answered with a small shrug:

"I don't know, yet. I think we have to get to know each other…"

The next morning Etienne took us to the airport. There were heartbreaking farewells between him and Dulce. He let her lick his face so much that I strongly hesitated to kiss him goodbye. He hugged and kissed the little dog, whispering things in her ear. Finally we left, waving our respective paws at him. Dulce was looking forward to eating her Mighty Dog again. I was glad to go home.

Bye Etienne! I love you! Come and see us soon! I'll miss you!

It was good to be back in New York: strangely enough, my crazy city seemed very quiet after my wild adventures in Switzerland.

As I walked into "Tate" the next day, I was already planning how I was going to convert it into the first de Brousse outlet in New York.

When I called Etienne to tell him, he whooped with joy and then told me his news: he and Sylvie had set a date for their wedding, next summer, and wanted me to be their bridesmaid. And they had adopted a long haired doxie.

Made in the USA
San Bernardino, CA
28 January 2013